SUNBURN

LUCY REYNOLDS

BLACK SWAN
DIGITAL

First published in 2025
Concept created by Black Swan Digital. Developed by Mark Coleman.

PROLOGUE

VILLA LIMACCIA. TEN YEARS AGO

Leo had always been afraid of the dark. Not in the way little kids were, not because of monsters or shadows, but because darkness had too many places to hide the truth. And tonight, the darkness was everywhere.

He ran as fast as he could. The path was slick with salt spray and old moss, a half-worn trail that twisted along the cliff edge like a serpent. His breath sawed through the night, sharp and frantic. The torchlight behind him bounced, casting jerky, grotesque shadows along the stone walls. He didn't look back. Looking back meant slowing down. And he couldn't afford to slow down.

"Leo!" someone called behind him, too sweet, too close.

A girl's voice. Not mocking. Not quite. But not concerned either.

His name shouldn't have sounded like that.

He cut left into the undergrowth, branches slapping his arms and tearing his shirt. Somewhere far below, the sea roared like it was laughing. Villa Limaccia loomed behind him, its shuttered windows dark, its secrets older than anyone remembered. They thought it was funny, this place. Thought it was all part of the tradition.

Truth or dare. Confession night. A stupid game they played every year, like children dressed up as wolves.

But this time, it had turned. They'd made him the target. The outsider. The sacrifice.

He could still hear them laughing. Drunk on wine and power and the invincibility of youth.

A foot caught on a root. Leo went down hard, palms scraping across gravel, knees jarring into stone. He hissed, held his breath, and crawled into a thicket beside the trail. The recorder was still in his jacket pocket. He pressed it into his chest as if it could protect him. As if it mattered.

"If anything happens to me..."

He hadn't finished the message. He'd wanted to wait. To get it all, get the voices. Get their words. Prove what they said.

The footsteps were getting closer now.

He held his breath and lay flat, heart hammering. A figure passed on the trail above him. Then another. Then a third. All laughing, whispering.

"He'll come back," one said. "He always comes back."

They were used to being followed. Worshipped. Forgiven.

Leo stayed still for a long time after they passed, until his breath stopped rattling like loose glass in his chest. Then he got up, moving carefully, slowly. Toward the chapel.

It was the only place he could go.

The ruined chapel had always frightened him. Even in daylight, with its scorched altar and the hollow where a bell used to hang. The roof was half-collapsed. Ivy curled in through the windows like fingers.

But there was quiet here.

He ducked through the side entrance, brushing through gauzy cobwebs. Moonlight fell through a hole in the ceiling, casting a circle on the floor like a spotlight. Leo stepped into it, shaking.

He pulled out the recorder and clicked it on.

"My name is Leo Marinetti," he whispered. "I invited my friends to Villa Limaccia for the summer. I thought it was a joke. I thought they wanted me in their group. But..."

A noise. He stopped. A creak of stone behind him. A footstep.

"Leo," a voice said. Closer now. No longer sweet.

He turned slowly. Three of them stood in the chapel doorway. Silhouetted by the broken arch, their shapes were indistinct. They were little more than shadows against a wall of silver mist. Their faces hidden beneath the hoods of drenched jackets, their hands still, gloved or bare, he couldn't tell. The tallest tilted their head, like an animal scenting blood. One of them stepped forward, the movement too smooth, too calm.

Leo backed away, recorder still in hand.

"I told you," the tallest figure said, voice cool and almost unfamiliar in the echo of the chapel. "You weren't supposed to record anything. That wasn't part of the game."

"You said truth," Leo said. "I told you the truth. And I found out yours."

A laugh. Soft. Chilling.

"You told *your* truth," the second said. "Not ours."

"Give it here," the third ordered, stepping forward. Boots scraped stone. Their breath fogged in the cold air.

Leo took another step back. Then another. He felt the edge behind him.

"Don't," he said. "Please. Just... just let me go. I won't tell anyone."

"You already told," came the reply. Calm. Even.

Then everything happened too fast. One lunged. Leo turned to run. A hand grabbed his shoulder. Another knocked the recorder from his grip. It hit the stone floor with a click, spun once, and fell silent. Leo screamed.

Or maybe he didn't. Maybe the sound never made it out. Maybe the wind stole it, swallowed it, carried it out to sea.

Then came the fall. Then came the silence. And in the chapel, half-lit by the moon, the recorder kept rolling. A gust of wind stirred the ivy. The bell tower, long empty, groaned. The silence deepened.

"If you find this... Please. Tell someone."

Outside, the sea slammed itself again and again against the base of the cliffs. Far above it, Villa Limaccia stood like a sentry, dark windows gleaming, stone walls slick with old secrets. In its bones, it remembered. In its silence, it waited.

Somewhere in the villa, a candle guttered out. Somewhere else, a door creaked open by no hand. The game had ended. But it had only just begun.

1

A REUNION

Present Day. Villa Limaccia

The sea shimmered, silver and endless, as the sun stretched itself over the curve of the Amalfi Coast. From the clifftop terrace of Villa Limaccia, the water looked painted on. Calm and perfect. Cicadas chattered in the olive trees. A lemon tree's scent drifted in the breeze, sweet but sharp, like something forgotten.

Camille stood barefoot on the terracotta tiles, coffee cooling in her hand, a thousand kilometers from her usual life. Her white linen dress fluttered around her knees in the morning breeze, brushing against her skin like a whisper. The moment should have felt idyllic, like one of those travel ads come to life. But the quiet here wasn't peaceful. It was expectant.

She hadn't wanted to come.

When the invitation had arrived, printed on perfect, creamy cardstock, in an anonymous font, with no return address, she'd felt the first prickle of unease.

You're invited, it read. *Villa Limaccia. June 3–10. For the memories.*

No sender. No explanation.

It had been nearly a decade since she had seen most of the

others. Camille had only really stayed close to Soren. They'd had a fling for a while, but it was too hard. The past sat between them like a fat toad. But they'd stayed friends.

When she'd called him to check, he'd been surprised.

"Oh," he'd said. "You got your own invite this time. Interesting."

Of course, the previous time, she'd gone as his plus one. The girl he was trying to seduce with his cool friends and fancy villa. And it had worked. She'd gone. She'd fallen for him. And even after they split, the villa seemed to tie them together. The villa, or what had happened there that summer. Ten years before.

Soren had laughed her worries about the invitation off, brushing it away like dust from a jacket.

"It's probably Rowan," he'd said. "Or Mara. They always were dramatic. Look, I'll go if you go."

So, she'd agreed to go. For old time's sake. Maybe it was a good idea to get everything out in the open. It was so long ago. And it had all just been a terrible accident, hadn't it?

They'd all arrived the day before, disoriented by the sharp heat and the eerie quiet. No staff had been waiting at the front gate, only a note pinned to the front door: *Alba will attend you shortly.*

Alba had appeared an hour later. A thin, olive-skinned woman, with salt-and-pepper hair twisted into a knot. She'd carried herself like someone who had worked here long before these guests had ever heard of Villa Limaccia. She said little, just showed them to their rooms, handed out keys, and disappeared into the kitchen. Her politeness felt studied, like a language remembered more than spoken.

Matteo, the groundskeeper, had barely spoken at all. He'd

nodded at them as he unloaded cases from their cars, then vanished behind the villa into the groves.

That night, they'd found the table laid out for dinner. The wine was already decanted, long white tapers flickered in the breeze, and soft music played from discretely hidden speakers. Each place setting had been marked with a folded note.

Camille had opened hers slowly. A single sentence, printed in block capitals:

LET'S DRINK TO THE PAST. TO THE MEMORIES WE BURIED. TO THE TRUTH WE NEVER TOLD.

The message was the same for each of them. No one admitted to writing them, but then, that wasn't unusual. In this group, there had always been secrets, games, little tricks to try and unnerve each other or out-do each other.

The mood had shifted as they all read them. Just slightly. But it was enough for Camille to notice. A dent in the studied politeness they'd all been showing since they'd arrived.

Now, she looked round at all of their faces, studying their expressions, looking for some kind of tell. Some tic that would tell her who had invited them all back here. Who wanted to make them drink to old memories and hidden truths.

Rowan sat stiffly at the table, untouched wine sweating in her glass. The strange cryptic note had unnerved her. Just as she assumed it had most of them.

She stared past Jasper, who was laughing at something Mara had said, and her expression flickered. A small sneer of resentment and bitterness crept to the surface for him.

She and Jasper had been engaged the last time they came here. They had still married, despite everything that had happened. Or maybe because of it. And now? Now she was considering ending it.

Jasper had become a different man since the last book advance ran out. Restless. Careless. Too willing to use charm in place of apology. But it wasn't just her feelings for Jasper she was keeping from the others.

In the side pocket of her travel bag, hidden beneath a scarf, was a second note. One she'd found on her pillow when she'd arrived. Like the one on her place setting, it was printed in a plain font. It simply said:

It's time to share what you know. No one leaves until we know the truth.

Rowan hadn't told anyone what she'd seen ten years ago. Not even Jasper. So who could know what she'd done? What *they'd* done.

She reached for her wine and took a long, slow sip. The sun dipped lower behind the cliffs. Shadows lengthened in the dining room. The heat outside ticked against the windows. Oppressive, rather than comforting. The villa seemed to be listening to their conversations, and maybe even to their thoughts.

2

A NIGHT TO REMEMBER

Evening settled slowly over Villa Limaccia, the golden light melting into amber, then bronze. The sea below still shimmered, but now with a subtler sheen, as if the day had been softened by drink. The air was thick with salt and lemon and the musky perfume of crushed rosemary from the path beneath the olive trees.

Candles flickered in cut-glass lanterns strung above the long limestone terrace. Their flames danced with the breeze, casting fractured shadows across the table and the guests seated around it. Somewhere behind them, the sun slipped toward the horizon, a burning orange wound in the sky.

Camille sat between Charlotte and Jasper, the heat clinging to her skin in a light sheen of sweat, her wine glass already fogging in her hand. Ten guests in total, all carefully arranged like pieces on a board. They were former friends. At times, some had been lovers, others rivals. Now, they were all little more than strangers pretending to belong.

Selena's laugh rang out across the terrace, bright and loud. She was leaning toward Max now, her hand on his arm, her smile wide and glossy. Max was drinking heavily, the way he always did in heat, his shirt unbuttoned too far, sunglasses still perched in his greying hair despite the sun being long gone.

"You haven't changed at all," Selena purred, tracing a finger down the condensation on her glass.

"You either," Max replied, letting his gaze linger. "Though you've learned how to fake modesty better than any of us."

Laughter again. Too loud. Too practiced.

On Camille's other side, Jasper rose from the table. "Back in a minute," he muttered. Renata caught his eye as he passed, then followed him moments later with a soft laugh and an untouched glass of wine. Their voices disappeared into the shadows beyond the lanterns.

Camille watched them go, a sour taste in her throat.

These people had known each other since university, their bonds steeped in ancient wine and long-forgotten transgressions. Even when they fought, even when they lied, there was something that drew them back into each other's orbit. Shared guilt, maybe. Shared memory. Or just a refusal to let go of the version of themselves that had once mattered.

Camille hadn't gone to Oxford. She hadn't been part of the champagne-soaked debates, or the infamous confession nights that came after. She had been Soren's plus one. A stranger among a carefully curated set of insiders.

Down the table, Rowan was quiet. She rarely joined the laughter, but tonight she was especially still, her body angled slightly away from Jasper's empty seat. She twirled the stem of her glass between her fingers but didn't drink.

Mara sat opposite her, playing hostess with the grace of someone used to being watched. She refilled glasses with practiced ease and commented on the view as if she owned it. Everything about her gleamed. Not just her teeth, but her skin, her eyes, her love of control.

Noel had taken the seat at the head of the table, posture

straight and tense, as if holding court. His voice was louder than necessary, his jokes a touch too sharp. But even he was quieter and more reserved than she'd recalled. Camille noticed the way Renata flinched slightly when he'd raised his voice earlier, and how he hadn't once spoken directly to Charlotte all night.

Charlotte sat beside him, speaking little but watching everything, her dark eyes tracking every movement, every subtle shift in tone. Her hand stayed near her glass, but she rarely sipped. She nodded when spoken to, smiled when expected, and said almost nothing.

Soren seemed a little happier now they were all back together, as though something he'd been dreading had turned out to be just fine, actually.

And Alba, ever silent and composed, slipped in and out like a wraith, clearing plates and replacing them with olives and cheese and figs, her face always unreadable.

Camille felt like she was on the outside of a painting. All of this was artifice. Beautiful, curated, and brittle, but totally false. She sipped her wine and let the conversation blur around her. Laughter rose, hollow and echoing. Someone turned up the music, a soft and strange piano piece she didn't recognize.

Across from her, Mara tilted her glass toward Rowan. "You've been quiet tonight. Is it the wine or the company?"

Rowan looked up slowly. "Neither. Just listening."

"Dangerous habit in a place like this," Max said, draining the last of his glass. "Places like this hold a lot of secrets."

A ripple passed through the group. Small, but discernable. Camille caught Rowan's eye. For a second, something raw flickered behind her composure, as though she'd remembered a flash of something buried.

And then, looking out the window, she saw him. Matteo. The grounds man was standing at the edge of the olive grove. Just far enough away to be mistaken for shadow. He was smoking, the red tip of his cigarette blinking like a firefly.

Camille rose, murmured an excuse, and slipped away from the table. Her sandals whispered against the stone as she crossed to him.

"Long day," she said, smiling.

He didn't answer right away. Just nodded once, eyes on the sea.

The silence between them stretched, but it wasn't uncomfortable. Matteo's presence, though quiet, felt solid. Ancient, even. Like the stone walls of the villa, he seemed to have absorbed time.

"This place," she said after a moment, "feels... different now. Older, I guess."

Matteo took a drag of his cigarette. The smoke curled around his jaw.

"It carries time heavily," he said. "It has seen a lot over the years."

Camille turned to look at him, but his gaze was fixed somewhere beyond her, somewhere down the cliff path where the wind moved through the trees like whispers.

"But does it forgive what it's seen?" she asked.

He flicked the ash into the rosemary and didn't reply. Behind them, another burst of laughter rose from the terrace. Glasses clinked. Someone called for more wine. Camille stood with him a little longer, until the sky turned plum and the first stars began to push through the veil of heat.

"You remember Leo, don't you?" she asked.

Matteo's eyes finally met hers. Something flickered there. Pain. Caution.

"I remember everyone," he said quietly.

A chill passed through her, sudden and sharp, despite the

heat. He dropped the butt of his cigarette and ground it into the gravel path, bending to pick up the stub.

"You should go back to your friends," he said, and turned to walk back into the trees.

Camille stood alone, her arms prickling. Then she too turned, and went back toward the party, and the past that had followed them all here.

The heat hadn't broken. If anything, as the sun had dipped below the horizon, the warmth had intensified, clinging to their skin and coiling around their spines. Somewhere down the hill, cicadas buzzed in the olive groves. The air was heavy with the scent of lemon blossoms and candle wax, of sweat and salt and secrets.

The terrace glowed in the warm yellow light from the lamps surrounding the pool, the table, the ancient pergola under which they all now sat. With every movement, long shadows stretched across the table reaching for something unseen.

The group, heads spinning from wine and sun, had begun to unravel just slightly. Their shirts were unbuttoned further, voices rising with each refill, old barbs bubbling closer to the surface. Mara stood up, the stem of her glass held delicately between two fingers.

"A toast," she said, flashing a brilliant smile that didn't quite reach her eyes. "To us. To old friends, and new beginnings."

Camille hesitated with her glass, watching the others raise theirs. Some did so eagerly, some by reflex. She wasn't sure which she was yet.

"To us," the group chorused.

The clinking of glasses followed, bright and brittle. But as Noel leaned across to tap Rowan's glass, he knocked his own over. The wine spilled in a dark, blooming stain across the white linen tablecloth. It bled quickly, soaking the note left from dinner. Camille watched as the ink began to blur, the words *truth* and *buried* bleeding into each other.

"Oh, for fuck's sake," Noel muttered, grabbing a napkin.

"It's just wine," Mara said lightly, though her gaze lingered a fraction too long on the ruined note.

Camille stared at the note. The wine had turned the words into something ghostly, like they were being erased. Or rewritten.

Around her, the table had splintered into conversation again, but a tension hummed beneath the surface, the kind that comes when people realize the air has changed. That something has shifted, and it can't be undone.

Max laughed and poured more wine into Noel's glass. "There, crisis averted. Let's play something. A game. Like we used to."

Mara jumped on the idea before anyone could decline. "Yes! Let's do it. Everyone stay where you are."

"I think I'll..." Camille began, half-standing.

Mara's voice cut across hers, firm and decisive. "Just one round, Camille. You'll enjoy it. You need to loosen up a bit. We all do."

There was no bite in her tone, but Camille felt the sting all the same. She smiled faintly, and gave a nod of concession.

"Let's play Secrets or Lies," Mara announced. "Everyone writes a secret, either real or made up, and then folds it, and pops it in the bowl. Alba will draw them out, won't you Alba? And then we'll all try to guess who wrote it and if it's true."

Camille looked around. Selena was beaming at the idea. Jasper had just walked back in, but already had his pen ready. Renata looked like she wanted to vanish. Rowan, unreadable, barely reacted.

Alba stepped forward to pass out slips of paper as if she'd anticipated the game. She offered Camille one with a slight bow. Her fingers were cold to the touch.

The paper was smooth edged. As if freshly cut. Camille unfolded it and stared at the blank space. The candle beside her flickered, throwing faint light across the page.

As the group scrawled, Camille's hand hovered. What would she even write? She didn't want to know these people's secrets, and she didn't want them to know hers. There was a strange power play going on in this group, made worse, perhaps, by them all being here. The comments and glances between them were all twisted and well-worn. And, even after all these years, she was still somehow on the outside.

Her mind flashed with the image of the wine blotting the words on the note. She scribbled something vague: *Sometimes I think I married a man I don't know*. And then she folded it quickly, and dropped it into the bowl.

The game began, and the laughter grew more forced as each of the so-called secrets got bolder. Until one slip was opened which just read:

I watched someone die and said nothing.

It drew a long silence before Max cracked a joke that no one laughed at. Camille felt her heart thud harder. Was that one true? Or one of the made-up ones? Or was it one designed to put an end to this mockery of a party game.

She watched the group more closely now. Renata chewed her lip and wouldn't meet anyone's eyes. Charlotte's hands were folded tightly in her lap. Jasper had that half-smile he wore when something uncomfortable delighted him.

When her turn came, the slip read: *I'm not who they think I am.*

Jasper smirked. "Well, that could be true for any of us."

Charlotte laughed, mirthlessly, but said nothing. Let the

silence stretch. He was right, Camille thought. By the time the last paper was drawn, Mara was radiant. Her idea had been a triumph. With each new secret, the group had become more divided, more fractious. And that's just how she loved it. And throughout, there she'd been, holding court, her eyes bright.

"I think that's enough," Rowan said flatly, pushing back from the table.

Mara raised a brow. "Come on, we're just getting started."

"I'm tired," Rowan said, voice clipped.

Camille stood too. "Me as well. I think the sun's caught up with me."

She slipped away before anyone could protest, the weight of their glances following her like heat. Inside, the air felt heavier, thick with the ghost of perfume and wine and a much older scent, like dried flowers and paper.

Her footsteps were soft on the tiled floor. The villa groaned faintly as she passed. Was that just a settling sound? Sometimes, the whole place seemed to breathe on its own.

~

Her room was dim, the shutters casting long stripes across the bed. A soft breeze stirred the curtains. On the dresser sat something that hadn't been there before. An old photo album. Camille paused. She hadn't brought it. Her pulse quickened. She crossed the room slowly and opened it.

Inside: photographs. Dozens of them. Glossy prints curled slightly at the corners, tucked neatly into plastic sleeves. They were all from around ten years ago. The same people. Same faces. But younger. Wilder. Caught in the golden haze of university life. There was Leo, smiling, arms around Mara and Rowan, just as Camille remembered him.

The book held page after page of parties, games, trips. Most were labeled in small, looping script. *Trinity Ball. Magdalen quad. Countless Confession Nights.* The last few pages were different. Blurry. Grainy shots taken in the dark. One of them was of a chapel Camille didn't recognize.

And the final image was of the villa. The same terrace. The same table. But all somehow fresher, neater, more maintained. Less damaged, she thought. The people around it were largely the same. Younger, of course, and with smiles that seemed, for most of them at least, genuine. One face had been scratched out in ink. Deep gouges in the page where someone had tried to remove him completely.

But who was he? A slight frame, small shoulder, timid posture. She felt she recognized him, but she couldn't bring his face to mind.

Camille closed the album, her fingers trembling, just as shadow passed across the door in the hallway beyond her room. She froze. Her heart pounded. She stepped to the doorway, but the corridor was empty. The only sound the soft hiss of cicadas, the clink of a bottle somewhere in the distance. But she knew she hadn't imagined it. Someone had been standing there. Watching her.

She walked back inside and closed the door quietly. The room felt smaller now, like it was closing in on her. Outside, the wind picked up and carried with it the faintest whisper of something old. Something forgotten. And on the desk behind her, the photo album fell open again, to the page with Leo's smile, frozen in time, arms draped around his friends.

3

ALL THE UNSPOKEN THINGS

The sun had already climbed high by mid-morning, spilling golden light into the villa's inner courtyard. It filtered through the thick canopy of citrus trees, dappling the stone in warm, swaying patterns. Oranges hung low on the branches, their waxy skins glistening, and a few had dropped and cracked on the ground, releasing their sharp perfume into the heat.

In the center of the courtyard, a Roman fountain burbled softly, its carved cherubs weather-worn and moss-tipped. The water sparkled under the sun, throwing fractured light onto the surrounding limestone walls. Beyond the fountain, a rectangular lap pool shimmered like polished glass. Rowan cut through it with graceful, mechanical strokes, gliding back and forth, back and forth in purposeful, almost punishing movements.

Camille watched from the arched walkway for a moment, unnoticed. Rowan had been out there for nearly half an hour, her body sleek and relentless in the water. From this distance, her face was unreadable beneath the rippling surface, but her jaw had been set when she emerged earlier that morning, towel slung around her neck like armor. She hadn't spoken to anyone at breakfast. Jasper hadn't either.

Camille could guess why.

She remembered the way Rowan had left the terrace the night before, tight-lipped and pale. There was something simmering beneath the surface of that woman, something too restrained. Rowan carried herself like a glass vase filled to the brim. One more jolt and she would spill.

The courtyard was otherwise quiet. The villa's thick stone kept the heat at bay for now, but already the air buzzed with promise of another sweltering day. Alba had appeared only briefly to clear away breakfast, her footsteps near-silent, her eyes giving nothing. Her movements were precise, as if every task was performed in accordance with a long-forgotten ritual.

Camille turned back to her book as Jasper arrived. He stretched his arms up above his head, leaning first left then right, stopping as Rowan pulled herself from the pool, water sluicing from her shoulders. He paused to admire her before crossing the courtyard, a towel thrown over one shoulder, and his shirt creased as though he'd slept in it.

"You look like an Olympian," he said lightly, reaching for a coffee cup from the tray Alba had left.

Rowan didn't respond at first. She wrapped a towel around herself and twisted her wet hair into a knot, eyes narrowed against the sun.

"I thought you hated mornings," she said.

"I do. But nostalgia has a cruel way of rearranging your rhythms."

He smiled. Rowan didn't.

Jasper dropped onto one of the cushioned stone benches and stretched out. "Being back here... it's like the clock's been wound backwards, don't you think? Same heat, same wine, same ghosts."

Rowan turned to him slowly, a drop of water trailing down her neck. "Don't say that."

"What?"

"'Same ghosts.'"

Jasper raised a brow. "It's just a phrase."

"No," she said sharply, her voice slicing through the quiet. "You said, 'back where the sinning began.' last night. You thought it was funny. But it's not."

He held up a hand, lazy in his defensiveness. "Alright. Sorry. I didn't know we were policing metaphors now."

"It's not a metaphor for me," she snapped.

For a moment, the only sound was the fountain. Then Jasper leaned forward, elbows on knees.

"Come on, Ro. We all have our own way of coping. I joke. You swim until your shoulders give out. Mara plays hostess. Max drinks. It's just how it works."

Rowan shook her head. "You're still trying to make it normal. All of this. But it isn't. We shouldn't be here."

"You came."

"I had no choice."

Jasper flinched, ever so slightly. "None of us had to say yes."

She stared at him. "You think that? Really? After everything that happened here?"

He looked away. "It's been ten years."

"That doesn't matter." Rowan's voice cracked slightly, but she masked it with a sharp inhale. She turned her face away, letting the sunlight dry her skin.

He studied her. "Are you afraid someone's going to bring it up?"

"No. That's already happened."

Jasper froze. "What do you mean?"

She hesitated. "I got something. When I arrived here. A note."

"And you didn't think to tell me?"

Rowan glanced at him. "Would it have changed anything?"

Jasper didn't answer. He looked suddenly smaller in the light, his usual swagger dimmed. Across the courtyard, Alba emerged again, this time with fresh water and lemon slices in a cut-glass jug. She set it down with the same elegance, the same unsettling stillness she always bore. Her eyes flicked to the two of them, lingered for a moment on Rowan, and then moved to the pool.

"Even the water remembers," she murmured, her voice soft like crushed petals.

Rowan looked up sharply. "What did you say?"

But Alba was already gone, slipping back through the archway like a shadow.

Jasper laughed once, uneasily. "Jesus. That woman gives me the creeps."

Rowan wrapped her towel tighter and sat, suddenly feeling exhausted.

In the distance, the sound of laughter carried. It was Mara's unmistakable peal of delight. Noel's heavier baritone joined it. They were somewhere near the front of the villa, probably heading for the garden terrace.

"They're acting like it's just a great big reunion," Rowan said. "Like it's just another holiday. But it's not. This is all wrong."

Jasper rubbed his jaw. "Do you think someone's playing with us?" His voice trailed, not wanting to say it.

"I think someone brought us all together here for more than old time's sake. And if they did, they're playing a very dangerous game."

She stood up again, unable to sit still. The sun caught her skin, and Camille, peering over the top of her book, saw for the first time the tightness around her eyes, the hollowness beneath the mask of control.

"Why didn't you tell me?" Jasper asked, quieter now. "About the letter?"

"Because you always laugh things off," she said without turning. "Because you tell jokes instead of really asking why all the hair's standing up on the back of your neck. Because you'll never face the truth head on."

With that, Rowan walked away, towel slipping from her shoulders, bare feet padding on the warm stone. Jasper stayed behind, finishing his coffee with a grimace. He watched her go, then looked toward the water.

The surface had stilled. But there, at the bottom of the pool, something shimmered. A glint of sunlight or a reflection of something dropped, bouncing up just for a second, like a shadow trying to surface and then it was gone.

Rowan barely made it two steps past the courtyard before she heard the unmistakable tap of Mara's heels against the ancient stone. It was a clipped, confident rhythm that made Rowan's skin crawl before she even turned.

"Rowan," Mara called brightly. "Got a second?"

She stopped but didn't turn. The sunlight felt harsher here, and the faint citrus scent in the air was beginning to sour. Mara caught up, her tone falsely casual.

"It's been years since we've had a real conversation. Maybe we could..."

"No," Rowan said, her voice flat.

Mara blinked. "No?"

"I don't want a performance. Or a speech. Or one of your therapy sessions. What do you want?"

Mara opened her mouth, then closed it again. Her polished

mask faltered for just a second. "I'm trying to reconnect. That's all."

"Reconnect with who?" Rowan said, finally turning. Her eyes were cold. "The woman who watched the worst happen to her closest friends and just smiled through it? The one who played guardian of the secrets while we all fell apart?"

A flash of something sharp passed through Mara's gaze, but she recovered quickly.

"You don't know everything that happened. None of us do."

"I know enough."

Rowan walked away without another word, her footsteps clipped, purposeful, echoing down the corridor.

Mara stood for a moment, lips parted, then reached into her pocket and took out a small silver compact. She checked her reflection. Her smile was already back in place, but her hands still trembled.

~

Outside, in the lower orchard near the villa's gravel path, Noel crouched by the stone wall, head in his hands. The hangover had arrived with a vengeance. It hit now in hot, acidic, relentless waves of nausea and regret. He squinted against the glare and made his way toward the nearest figure he could find: Matteo.

The groundskeeper stood among the olive trees, shirt sleeves rolled, his weathered hands deftly wrapping twine around a cracked branch. He didn't look up.

"You got anything stronger than aspirin?" Noel asked, voice like gravel.

Matteo finally turned. His expression was unreadable, the lines of his face carved deep by sun and silence.

"You all act like gods," he said, in slow, deliberate Italian accented-English. "But in the morning, you bleat like sheep."

Noel blinked, caught between confusion and insult. "What did you just say?"

Matteo's eyes bored into him for a long, uncomfortable moment, then he turned back to the tree and said nothing more. Noel stood there for a beat, mouth slightly open, as if about to respond. But he didn't. He thought better of it and stumbled away, muttering under his breath.

Rowan's room was cool when she entered, the shutters drawn halfway. The fan whirred gently above, stirring the heavy air. She tossed her towel over the end of the bed and moved to the desk, reaching for her water bottle. She stopped.

Her laptop was open. She hadn't left it that way. And it wasn't just open, it had been turned on. The screen glowed faintly in the shadows. A single file had been created and left open on the screen. She hadn't made it.

CONFESSIONS.docx

Her chest tightened. She stepped closer, heart beginning to pound, and touched the trackpad. The document was blank apart from the leading title it had been given. The page was utterly, chillingly blank.

Rowan stared. The cursor blinked, patient and waiting. Her own reflection hovered faintly in the screen, warped by the light. With trembling hands, she closed the lid slowly before turning and looking around the room.

Someone had been in here. Someone had left this document on her screen, taunting her. She sat down, pulse thudding in her ears. She didn't know who was doing this. But she knew exactly why.

The invitation had been cryptic: *Villa Limaccia. One week. For the memories we buried.* It hadn't named a sender. Just the date and the destination. Each of them had received it at different times, in different ways. Jasper's had arrived slipped into a review copy of his last travel memoir. Max's had been tucked inside the collar of a dry-cleaned shirt. Noel's was handed to him by a courier who refused to say who had sent it. Rowan's was slid beneath her door in a sleek, unmarked envelope the same day she found the threatening note.

None of them had asked who was behind it. Not out loud, anyway. The truth was, none of them were sure. And it could have been any of them.

Ten years ago, a young man had died. A friend. One of them. And ever since, they'd all lived as though it had been an accident. A tragic misstep. A freak occurrence under the veil of youth and too much wine. But each of them knew better. And some of them knew only too well what had happened. Between them all, they probably knew the whole truth, but each had kept their part secret for all this time.

And now someone wanted them to talk.

Rowan stared at the laptop as if it might blink first. Last night had already frayed something in her. The wine. The game. The note left on each place setting: *Let's drink to the past. To the memories we buried. To the truth we never told.* Then the game of Secrets or Lies, played with forced smiles and heavy silences. And now this.

She got up and paced the room. Her reflection flickered in the tall mirror near the wardrobe. Her face looked unfamiliar. Her skin was drawn, pale, her eyes too wide.

There had been a time when she was at the heart of this group. The careful, rational one. The one people came to for clarity. But in the months before Leo died, she'd become something else, entirely quieter, colder even. She had known what was happening and done nothing to stop it. Her silence had become a shield. And now, someone was chipping away at it, the way Leo had.

She moved to the window and unlatched the shutters. Outside, the sea blazed under the noon sun, light bouncing off the waves in violent glitter. Somewhere below, voices echoed. The shrill sound of laughter carrying up again. Mara's or Selena's. They were too distant to be sure.

A knock at the door made her spin around, heartbeat surging. She crossed the room quietly, put her hand on the knob, then paused.

"Hello?"

"Rowan?" It was Jasper.

She exhaled. "What?"

"Lunch is out. Alba says she won't serve it cold."

"I'm not hungry."

A pause.

"You okay?"

She hesitated, then said, "I'm fine."

"Right."

She listened to his footsteps retreat, fading down the hall. She looked back at the desk. The laptop remained shut, but the weight of that blank document pressed against her like a scream.

CONFESSIONS.

Not a threat. Not a demand. But an invitation to share. And Rowan had no idea who had sent it. Though part of her feared she already knew.

4

THE WOMAN IN WHITE

By afternoon, the sky had turned the color of tarnished silver. Storm clouds gathered over the horizon, slow and swollen, trailing veils of shadow across the sea. The air had grown heavy with the scent of salt and something sweet turning sour in the heat.

Camille wandered the perimeter garden alone, her sandals crunching through overgrown gravel. The once-manicured hedges had grown wild, arching into each other like lovers who hadn't been touched in years. White blossoms spilled from neglected trellises, clinging to the arms of broken statues that leaned askew in their beds of moss and dirt.

It was the kind of garden that once belonged to beauty but had long since handed itself over to memory.

She passed sun-bleached urns filled with dry soil, the occasional twisted vine reaching out like a hand. At the far end of the path, a marble statue of a woman in flowing robes stood partially toppled, her stone face half-buried in ivy. Her outstretched hand pointed nowhere.

Camille paused to look at her.

"Beautiful, isn't it?"

The voice made Camille start. She turned to see Charlotte seated on a low stone bench beneath a fig tree, legs crossed, sunglasses perched high on her nose.

Camille hadn't expected to find anyone out here. Charlotte looked almost ethereal in the dappled shade. Her pale skin seemed almost luminous, and her dark hair was tied into a messy knot that exposed the curve of her neck. A light linen dress, barely wrinkled, clung to her slender frame in the breeze.

"I didn't see you there," Camille said.

Charlotte gave a faint smile. "You weren't meant to. That's the trick of this place. It hides people very well."

Camille stepped closer. "Is that what you're doing? Hiding?"

Charlotte uncrossed her legs, brushing a fig leaf from her skirt.

"Something like that."

Her voice was low, deliberate, with an edge that made Camille unsure whether to sit or walk away. But she sat.

They were silent for a moment. A gust of wind lifted Camille's hair, and she tucked it behind her ear. The silence between them didn't feel empty, but charged like the static in the air just before lightning strikes.

"I've never really thought I fit in with all of you," Camille said finally. "Especially out here."

Charlotte turned slightly. Without the sunglasses, her gaze was unsettlingly direct. Her irises were a shade of amber that didn't seem real, almost like stained glass held up to sun.

"None of us really fit," she said. "That's the thing about groups like this. They hold together because of the wrong things."

Camille tilted her head. "Like what?"

"Secrets," Charlotte said. "Power. Loyalty in the wrong places. And fear, most of all."

"Fear of what?"

"Being on the outside, perhaps," Charlotte said softly. "Or reality."

Camille blinked, not quite knowing how to respond. Charlotte had a way of speaking that felt both rehearsed and raw. Like she was revealing something, but only a sliver.

"I don't understand how you can stay friends," Camille said. "With all of them. After what happened."

Charlotte reached down and plucked a small fig from the ground, turning it slowly in her fingers. "Selena tried to leave once. After Leo died."

Camille's pulse quickened. "She did?"

"She disappeared for six months. Went off to South America. Stopped answering messages. Told Mara she was done. She wanted to live a different kind of life."

"What happened?"

Charlotte looked toward the sea. Her expression, when it finally came into focus, was something between pity and resignation.

"Rowan and Mara flew out. Met her in Buenos Aires. When they came back, Selena was with them."

"Do you think they convinced her to come back to the fold?" Camille asked.

Charlotte didn't answer immediately. "Convinced, coerced... call it what you like. But she's been different ever since. Softer, quieter. Like something was taken from her."

The breeze picked up. The scent of the fig tree grew stronger, mingled with the hint of petrichor in the air, heralding the earthy anticipation of rain. Camille wrapped her arms around her waist, suddenly cold despite the heat.

"Do you think they regret it?"

Charlotte tilted her head. "What? What happened with Leo?"

"All of it. The circumstances. The events. The tragedy of it all."

Charlotte considered this for a long time. "They regret being caught up in it. But probably not causing it."

Camille's breath caught. The clouds overhead had thickened to slate. Light fractured strangely through them, painting everything with the sickly yellow of a storm that hadn't yet arrived.

"I think you're the first person here who hasn't tried to pretend that everything's normal here," Camille said.

"It's not," Charlotte said. "But neither are they."

They sat together while the clouds folded closer. From the villa, a low hum of music drifted, an old tune warping in the breeze. Camille stood.

"Where are you going?" Charlotte asked.

"Nowhere. Just... for a walk."

~

She walked the edge of the garden and down the path that circled the outer wall of the villa. Here, the windows were small and high, shuttered tight. The wind was stronger too, and the scent had changed. Now it carried something less floral, more mineral, earthy.

She rounded the corner and froze. Alba was kneeling outside the heavy wooden door to the wine cellar, scrubbing the marble tiles with a stiff-bristled brush. Her sleeves were rolled up, her movements deliberate, focused. The stain was dark and red, faded with scrubbing, but fresh enough to glisten. The tiles shimmered beneath the water she poured from a silver bowl. The motion felt ritualistic.

Camille stepped forward. "Is everything alright?"

Alba looked up. Her eyes were calm and unblinking, the color of old stone. Her face looked cold and

"It's not the first time," she said simply.

Camille's throat dried. "What do you mean?"

But Alba turned her gaze back to the tiles and said no more. Camille took an involuntary step back. The air seemed thicker now. Charged. From inside the cellar, a faint clang echoed. Metal on stone. Camille froze.

"What was that?"

Alba dipped the brush into her bucket. "You should go now."

Camille's mouth opened, but nothing came out. She turned and walked quickly back the way she came, her heart hammering against her ribs. She didn't look back. And behind her, the clouds began to break. But the rain didn't fall. Not yet.

The library at Villa Limaccia was tucked into the west wing of the house, where the walls ran thickest and the ceilings curved like ancient cathedrals. Camille had stumbled into it looking for quiet, needing somewhere cool and far from the others after what she'd seen in the garden. The heavy wooden door creaked open into a world of dust, old paper, and shadows.

The air was scented with mildew and citrus polish. Sunlight filtered through stained-glass transoms, painting fragmented patterns of color across the parquet floor. Towering shelves groaned beneath the weight of books, their spines cracked, their pages yellowed with age.

Camille walked slowly past the shelves, letting her fingers trail along worn leather bindings. Most of the titles were in Italian or Latin. Some were blank. Others had strange symbols on their spines of crescent moons, eyes, vines. A few books had no titles at all. The silence was dense, almost viscous. She found herself walking more carefully, as if not to disturb something sleeping.

She wasn't sure what she was looking for. Maybe proof. Maybe a distraction. Maybe something, anything, that could make the feeling in this villa make sense. She paused near a bookcase half-swallowed by ivy that had pushed in from a shattered high window. The wind whispered through the broken glass like a voice half-heard. A thick, dusty tome lay open on a table nearby. It looked like some sort of family ledger, names written in slanted script. Camille scanned the pages but didn't recognize them. They seemed ancient. Generations of people who had lived here, perhaps. Or died here.

Something flickered in the shadows. She reached for a book and then hesitated. Just behind the bottom shelf, something charred was wedged between the wall and the bookcase. She crouched, heart skipping. It was a fragment of paper, edges burned, half-curled from heat. She eased it free and squinted at the faded writing. Only a few lines were legible:

"L.M. knew. The wine cellar, he said, was always the quietest place to scream."

Her blood chilled.

She turned it over. It was blank. No signature. But the handwriting was delicate, almost elegant. A journal page. She reread the line. L.M. Leo's initials. And the wine cellar. Her thoughts immediately flew to Alba, her calm voice as she scrubbed the red stain: *It's not the first time.* She tucked the page into her pocket just as the wind outside rattled the windows like bones.

Dinner was a tense affair. The dining room had been set for ten, but the table felt far too long, as though distance had grown between everyone overnight. The storm had not broken, but it hung over them, pressing against the tall windows like a held breath. Lightning flickered over the sea, casting jagged shadows across the walls.

Camille sat beside Selena, who smelled faintly of lavender and wine. Across from them, Mara and Noel laughed too loudly at something Charlotte had said. Jasper picked at his food. Rowan hadn't touched hers at all.

The candles flickered in their brass holders, throwing light into the hollows of faces. Alba moved silently through the room, her presence almost ghostly, placing platters with silent precision. Matteo was nowhere to be seen.

Soren, Max, and Jasper were in deep conversation, while Noel seemed to sit slightly apart from all of them, watching. Camille studied the others with quiet intensity, trying to decipher what lay beneath the rehearsed smiles, the hearty laughs, and the glass-clinking rituals. Selena's posture was especially stiff tonight. She wore a long-sleeved blouse despite the heat. Her hair had been carefully pinned up, but several strands clung to her temples in the humidity.

The roasted sea bass, delicate and steaming smelled incredible. Camille waited until the main course had been served before she turned to Selena.

"I found something," she said quietly.

Selena blinked. "What kind of something?"

"In the library. Behind a shelf. It was burned. It looks like a page from a journal, I think."

Selena's fork paused halfway to her mouth.

"It mentioned someone. L.M. And the wine cellar. Said it was the quietest place to scream."

Selena slowly set her fork down. Her hands trembled slightly, but she quickly folded them into her lap. The transformation in her was as instant and complete as a curtain dropping. The sound of laughter from the other end of the table faded as if muffled. Selena's face had gone pale, her eyes fixed on the candle in front of her. Her breathing shallowed.

"Are you alright?" Camille whispered.

Selena didn't answer. She reached for her napkin, dabbed at her mouth, then rose slowly. Her chair scraped across the tile, the sound sharp and final.

"I'm not hungry," she murmured, and left the room without looking back.

Conversation faltered. Cutlery paused. Even Mara's glass clinked too loudly as she set it down.

Rowan watched Selena go, her face unreadable. Then her eyes flicked to Camille.

"What did you say to her?"

"Nothing," Camille replied.

Nobody pressed. But nobody smiled either. The storm rolled closer. A single crack of thunder rattled the glass, and Alba rushed in to shut the windows. But before she could, wind spilled in, cold and smelling of seaweed and something metallic. Noel muttered something under his breath and poured himself more wine. Mara's smile was thin and strained. Charlotte toyed with her knife, her gaze far away.

Camille sat back in her chair, the burned paper heavy in her pocket. She glanced down the length of the table and felt, with certainty, that she was not the only one who had found something. They all had their pieces. But none of them were talking. She caught Jasper watching her. He looked amused. Curious. But there was something else behind his expression. It looked like cold calculation. Camille looked away.

Selena's absence lingered like a ghost. And Camille couldn't help wondering: What had she remembered when she heard the words 'wine cellar'? What had she seen or done down there? She still didn't know why she was here. But she was beginning to understand what it might cost to find out.

5

NIGHT SWIMMING

A thick fog clung to the grounds of Villa Limaccia like gauze. It coiled low over the terraces, slid down the marble balustrades, and blanketed the lap pool in ghostly vapor. The water was still, black as obsidian, a glassy mirror to the slate sky above. The air was taut with pressure, heavy with the threat of the storm that had hovered for days but refused to break.

Renata emerged onto the pool deck barefoot, the hem of her silk robe whispering across the cold stone tiles. Her hair was loosely knotted, damp with sleep-sweat. In her right hand she held a towel, folded neatly. In her left, a pair of sunglasses. Totally ridiculous to wear them in at night, but she carried them like armor.

She needed a swim. She needed the repetitive peace of it. Ever since she'd arrived, er dreams had been fragmented and jagged. Leo's face had flickered through them like a faulty film reel. First smiling, youthful, happy. Then with blood trailing from his nose, his eyes open and blank. In her dream, the others had circled him, faceless and silent. Rowan had stood among them, mouth open in a scream that made no sound.

Now, in the blue-grey hush of night, Renata moved across

the with practiced elegance that she felt didn't come as naturally as it did to Mara or even Rowan. It wasn't unusual for her to be up late. She didn't like change. It upset her sleep. Order mattered to her. Ritual mattered. Control mattered.

She dropped the towel onto the nearest chaise, stepped to the edge of the pool, and stopped. There was something floating there. A dark shape. Renata blinked, disoriented. Her brain tried to conjure a logical explanation. A pool cover. A towel. A trick of the fog and the dark night.

Then the shape shifted slightly, bumping against the side of the pool. A bare shoulder surfaced. And Renata began to scream. It tore from her like a jagged thing, sharp and animal. Her voice cracked with it, echoed off the marble walls, and disappeared into the fog. She stumbled backward, slipping on the damp stone, catching herself on the wrought-iron table with shaking hands.

~

The sound brought them all running. Jasper arrived first, shirt half-buttoned, sandals askew, his breath visible in the cold morning mist. He skidded to a stop beside Renata, who was now crouched, hands braced against her knees, her eyes wide with something close to hysteria.

"What is it?" he panted. "Ren?"

She pointed with a trembling hand. "In the water."

Jasper followed her finger, squinting through the haze. At first, he didn't register what she was pointing at. It was just a shape, half-submerged. Then, like a camera coming into focus, he saw the slack limbs, the bobbing head.

"Noel?" he called hoarsely.

No response. He dropped his towel and moved to the pool's edge.

"Noel! Shit!"

He slipped in with a splash, the cold water biting his skin, and pushed through the fog until he reached the floating body. He rolled Noel over. The sight made him freeze.

Noel's eyes were open. His mouth, slightly parted, had taken in water. One arm drifted at an unnatural angle. A bruise bloomed purple across his jawline, and his skin was the color of a flawed pearl.

"God, no," Jasper breathed. "No, no, no!"

He gripped under Noel's arms and kicked hard toward the shallow end. His breath came in ragged gasps. The water felt like molasses. As he reached the steps, strong hands reached down. Matteo.

The groundskeeper had arrived without a sound. He grabbed Noel's wrists and pulled him from Jasper's grip, hauling the body up and out with a strength that seemed impossible in his lean frame. Noel's body thudded onto the stone with a sickening finality.

Rowan arrived next, her robe clutched tightly at her chest, hair plastered to her temples. She didn't scream. She didn't even speak. She just stood there, her face pale and unreadable, lips pressed tight together as though keeping her words inside.

"What the hell happened?" she asked finally, her voice thin but steady.

Jasper climbed out of the pool, shivering. "He was floating. Face down. I think he's..."

"Dead," Matteo said, flatly. "He is dead."

They all turned to look at him. He was kneeling beside the body, checking the pulse with practiced fingers.

Rowan moved closer. "Are you sure? He could still..."

"There's no breath," Matteo said. "No heartbeat. He's gone."

Renata let out a choked sound and turned away, pressing her fist to her mouth.

Alba stood at the edge of the terrace, her white apron ghostly in the fog. She was perfectly still, hands folded in front of her, like a mourner at a wake. Her eyes locked with Mara's, who now stood on the edge of the group.

"And so it begins again," she muttered, turning away.

Nobody spoke.

Only the slow drip of water from Noel's fingers, pooling at the edge of the deck. Jasper dropped to sit on the ground, soaked and silent. His eyes were red, though whether from chlorine or shock, no one could tell. Rowan crouched beside him, one hand on his back.

Mara stepped forward now, her voice shaking with incredulity. "But he was fine earlier. Drinking. Laughing."

"Drinking yes. But not laughing," Rowan said quietly. "He was tense. Remember? He seemed jumpy. He spent most of the night just watching everyone."

Mara looked at her, frowning slightly as though that wasn't her recollection of the evening.

"Do you think he slipped? Or, maybe he..." She let the suggestion hang in the air

"No," Rowan snapped. "He didn't do this to himself."

They turned to Matteo who stood slowly, brushing his hands on his trousers. "We should call the police."

Before anyone could respond, a distant rumble of thunder rolled over the sea, its deep growl vibrating through the ground. A chill wind swept across the terrace, rustling the trees and sending a few stray leaves fluttering past their feet. Rowan shivered, pulling her cardigan tighter around her shoulders.

Then the lights around the terrace flickered. At first, it was just a brief flutter, no more than a quick pulse of darkness before the bulbs hummed back to life. But then it happened again. This time, longer. The lights dimmed to an eerie, ghostly glow. The air grew thicker, the hum of the villa's electricity struggling under the pressure.

The next flash of lightning split the sky wide open, and as it lit up the villa, the power cut completely. The stereo inside fell silent, the terrace lights fizzed out, even the dim light spilling from the villa's windows shut off.

"Dammit," Matteo muttered, his voice sharp in the stillness. "The storm's come in early. The power surge will kill the mobile signal. I'll try the landline."

He made for the villa, leaving the group staring at each other in silence. The air, crackling with the approaching storm felt heavy with the realization. They couldn't risk the coast road if the wind came in hard. It would disappear under crashing waves at the best of times. If this storm was going to bed in for the rest of the night, no help would be coming until it passed. They were alone.

"Guess we'll have to wait it out," Jasper said, his voice quieter, the weight of it sinking in.

The others exchanged looks, the tension hanging like thick fog between them. They were trapped. And with a killer among them, the hours that stretched ahead would feel endless.

Alba busied herself removing the cushions from the pool furniture, tying down umbrellas, making ready for the worst of the winds and rain. "One by one," she muttered. "They'll all be gone."

Rowan looked at her angrily. "What did you say?"

But Alba had already turned and walked away, her apron fluttering behind her. Thunder rumbled across the sky. The clouds rolled in around them, cold, like thickening fog. And at their feet, Noel's body lay still.

"We'll have to move him inside," Jasper said. "We can't leave him here."

"But the police..." Rowan began.

"No one's coming, Ro," said Jasper, his voice sounding tight and angry. "Not until this storm blows over. And I'm not leaving him out here. We're taking him inside."

Renata staggered back, as though the idea of touching him had shoved her. Her face, usually composed even under pressure, had lost all its color. Her eyes were red-rimmed, not from tears but from disbelief, like a dam holding back a flood she couldn't afford to release.

Jasper knelt beside the body again, his eyes scanning for signs of injury. "No other wounds. No more blood." He ran a hand over Noel's arms and torso, checking for broken bones or deep bruising. "Just this one on his jaw. It's bad, but it doesn't look like a fatal blow."

His voice was clinical, almost detached, but his hands shook. He had known Noel for fifteen years. They'd travelled together, covered each other's secrets, laughed until sunrise. Now, he couldn't even look at his face.

Max crouched beside him and wordlessly reached into the pocket of Noel's shorts. His brow furrowed.

"What is it?" Rowan asked, her voice taut.

Max turned the pocket inside out. "His phone is missing."

They all looked at one another.

"Maybe he took it out to dive in the pool," Rowan offered.

Jasper stood up. "He would have changed out of his normal shorts if he was going for a swim. Besides, it would be out here somewhere if he'd one that."

"Maybe he never brought it out here," Mara offered, her voice thin and unconvincing.

Rowan shook her head. "He was never without that thing. Always documenting, always watching."

"So, someone took it," Max said.

There was a long, tense silence. Renata wrapped her arms tighter around herself, shrinking inward. Her robe had slipped off one shoulder, revealing a livid bruise along her collarbone. She covered it quickly.

"I'll check his room," Rowan said. "We need to know if anything else is missing."

She left quickly, her robe flaring behind her like a shadow. The others remained still.

Another crack of lightening lit their faces.

Jasper crouched again and tugged gently at the waistband of Noel's shorts, searching for anything the first check had missed. His fingers brushed something soggy and crumpled. Slowly, he pulled out a soaked, half-folded piece of paper.

"What is it?" Renata asked, edging closer but not daring to look too directly.

Jasper unfolded it slowly, careful not to tear it. The ink had run slightly, but the message was still just about legible.

"We all drown in the truth."

Renata gasped. Mara closed her eyes. Max's jaw clenched.

Jasper read it again, then handed it to Mara. Her hands trembled and the paper stuck briefly to her fingers, as if reluctant to be passed on.

"That sounds like a threat," Max said, grimly.

"It's more than that," Jasper replied. "It's part of some sick game."

The fog churned, the clouds closing around them as if locking them all together, thick and impenetrable. Renata turned a slow circle, as if expecting to find someone watching.

Rowan returned moments later, breathless. "His room's been turned over. Not ransacked, exactly. Just... rearranged. Carefully. Nothing broken. But everything slightly off. Like someone was looking for something."

"His laptop?" Jasper asked.

"Gone."

"Of course," Max whispered. "Of course it is."

Jasper nodded.

Rowan moved to stand beside him, taking the wet piece of paper from Renata's trembling hand.

"Who the hell wrote this?"

They all stared at one another. Then Mara broke. Her composure shattering like glass.

"This isn't how it was supposed to go!" she cried, backing away. "We were supposed to come here, clear the air, drink wine, bury the past, pretend to be normal again, and then just move on with our lives." Her voice cracked.

Renata stood too, trembling. "This can't be happening. Not again."

She turned and ran, disappearing into the fog toward the house. Her footsteps echoed on the stone, too loud in the oppressive quiet.

Camille found her an hour later, barricaded inside her bedroom, whispering through the door.

"I should never have agreed to come," Renata kept repeating. "This isn't how it was supposed to go."

"Renata?" Camille asked, knocking gently. "Renata, please."

But Renata wouldn't answer and the door stayed firmly locked. The hallway was eerily quiet. Camille stood alone for a long moment, one hand still against the wood. She could hear the faint rattle of Renata's sobs from the other side. They weren't theatrical. They were small, tight things, as if she were trying to keep her fear from leaking out of her lungs.

Camille didn't move. Something about Renata's collapse frightened her more than the body by the pool. Renata was always the one who seemed in control, like she knew what was about to happen before it did. If even she was cracking...

The thought was whisked away by a huge crack of lightening, the thunder bursting right over the top of the villa. A shutter flew open, snatched by the wind. Somewhere in the distance, a splintering crack was followed by a deep, resonating thud. A branch falling, or the whole tree.

~

As Alba and Matteo busied themselves securing the house and property, the first heavy drops of rain had forced the group to disperse from the pool edge. The sea beyond the cliffs churned with grey foam, and gulls wheeled in the sky, crying out final warnings as they scurried for shelter themselves.

Matteo, Jasper and Max had carefully carried Noel's limp body inside, and now he was safely in one of the lower rooms. Locked away, but a constant presence.

Rowan stood at the window in the dining room, looking out as the storm tore the garden apart, arms folded against the chill bouncing off the window pane. Her face was drawn, her mouth a tense line of thought. Beside her, Jasper leaned on the railing, still damp-haired from the pelting rain and his dive into the pool to help Noel. His knuckles were white where they gripped the balustrade.

A low wind stirred the olive trees.

"Leo also died in a storm," Rowan said.

Jasper looked at her sideways.

"I don't remember much. But I remember the storm," she continued. "The sound of it. The smell of chlorine whipped out of the pool, the rain in the dry earth, and something... metallic. I remember Mara screaming."

She turned to him. "You don't forget a scream like that."

"I didn't hear it," Jasper replied. "I was passed out drunk, remember. Worse than useless."

She nodded slowly, eyes still on the storm. "And now it's happened again. All of us here together. The signs. The tension. The games. The silence after dark. The storm. It's like someone's trying to recreate the whole thing."

Jasper exhaled, long and low. "Why bring us all here, though?"

Rowan's voice dropped. "Maybe we're supposed to confess our part in it all. Someone here knows what really happened. They must."

And Jasper didn't reply. Because deep down, he knew she was right.

6

THE HOUSE WATCHES

Rain lashed the terrace in silver ropes, hammering the stone with a force that made conversation inside the villa nearly impossible. The shutters rattled, candles guttered, and the air hummed with the low, aching static of a storm that had finally broken.

Most of the guests had scattered, each retreating to corners of the house, as though distance could protect them from whatever was unravelling.

Camille stood at the base of the grand staircase, listening. The storm groaned against the windows, but above it, the house creaked, its timber and stone shifting like a beast in uneasy sleep.

She climbed slowly, trailing one hand along the banister, fingers skimming dust that hadn't been disturbed in years. The upper level was darker, heavier. The light from the storm was diffused through rain-slicked windows, casting watery shadows down the corridors.

Each footstep felt intrusive, like she was walking into the lungs of the villa, where breath was still and secrets lived in the walls.

She passed closed doors. Most were guest rooms, unused and silent. A few stood slightly ajar, revealing only shadows and sheets stripped from beds. It felt like the house was holding its breath.

At the far end of the east wing, she came to a narrow corridor, its wallpaper faded and peeling in places. A single painting hung crooked on the wall, showing a storm-tossed ship caught in churning waves. The eyes of its passengers seemed to follow her as she passed.

She stopped at a door that looked older than the others. The handle was brass, dulled with age. She tried it. Locked. Camille leaned in, pressing her ear to the wood. There. Muffled voices. She couldn't make out the words, but the cadence was unmistakable. A low, urgent conversation. Then... nothing. Her heart began to race. She scanned the hallway, half-expecting someone to step from the shadows. She stepped back. Her skin prickled. The hallway felt suddenly colder.

"Hello?" she called, heart thudding.

Silence. She waited. Nothing. As she turned to leave, she heard a faint click. It sounded like a latch slipping further into place. Not loud, but intentional.

She didn't look back. Her pace quickened as she made her way down the corridor, every creak beneath her feet a gunshot in the silence. She told herself it was nothing. Just an echo. A trick of the storm. But the pressure between her shoulder blades didn't lift until she reached the landing again, and even then, she couldn't stop wondering who had been standing, arguing just behind that door.

Downstairs, in the drawing room, Mara sat curled in an armchair by the fire, the flickering glow casting harsh shadows across her face. Her eyes were glassy, distant. She didn't look up as Jasper entered.

He paused in the doorway. The fire was the only light. The power was still down. Outside, the rain slammed against the French doors.

"I didn't think you'd come back down," he said.

Mara looked at him then, slowly. "I didn't want to be alone."

Jasper crossed to the bar and poured a splash of whiskey into two glasses. He handed one to her. She took it, but didn't drink.

"He told me," she said quietly.

Jasper frowned. "Told you what?"

"Noel. He told me, just a few days ago. He was going to leave here."

Jasper sat. The leather groaned beneath him.

"He seemed really upset. Said we shouldn't have come. That he couldn't pretend anymore." She laughed bitterly.

Jasper watched her carefully. Her fingers trembled around the glass.

"What upset him?"

"I don't know," Mara half-whispered. "But something, or someone, did..."

The silence between them deepened. Outside, the wind howled against the shutters. Jasper leaned forward, elbows on his knees.

"It is all a bit strange, though, isn't it?"

She turned sharply, looking at him with hard eyes.

"A bit strange? He said he wanted to leave, and now he's dead. That's more than a bit strange."

"I didn't mean that. I mean all of us being called here. I mean, who even sent out the invites? Why did we all come? It's like we're tied together by a past none of us want to even remember, let alone talk about. Maybe he got too close to something. Something someone didn't want dug up."

Mara looked down at her lap. Her voice came out as a whisper. "He always knew more than he let on."

"About Leo?"

She didn't answer. Instead, she reached into her sweater pocket and withdrew a small, folded note.

"He showed me this the day we arrived," she said, handing it to Jasper.

He unfolded it slowly.

"The dead don't stay buried here. The house won't let them."

There was no signature. No date. Jasper looked up at her, stunned.

"He didn't say where it came from?"

"No. He just laughed. Said someone was being dramatic. But he wasn't laughing later. He was quiet. Distant."

Jasper leaned back, the paper still in his hand, but said nothing. The storm thundered overhead. On the other side of the room, a candle guttered and flickered out as the house seemed to lean in closer.

~

As the day turned to evening, rain continued to pour in sheets against the villa's windows, turning the glass to warbled, shifting veils. The interior of the house grew dimmer, more cloistered. The once-elegant ambiance now felt oppressive. Shadows thickened in the corners, and the candlelight seemed to sputter and lean away from the walls.

In the kitchen, Camille lingered by the long wooden island, absently running her fingers over the knife-scarred surface. She watched Soren from across the room. He was seated by the hearth, phone in hand, thumbs working rapidly over the screen. Again.

He'd been on his phone all morning. His fingers moving

quickly, his eyes constantly glancing furtively, checking if he was being watched. It was unnerving, because the storm had knocked out the signal, so what was he typing, and to whom?

"Still no signal?" she asked finally, voice casual but loaded.

Soren didn't look up. Just shook his head and grunted, fingers still tapping out words on his screen.

"You writing a novel or something?" she joked.

He glanced at her then, his eyes dark and sharp. "What's your problem, Camille?"

She studied him for a moment. The charming calmness he usually wore like a second skin was fraying. There was tension in the set of his jaw, a stiffness to his shoulders. Even the way he held his phone looked tight, defensive.

"You just seem... upset," she said carefully.

"Upset? Of course I'm upset. One of my oldest friends is dead, and we can't even tell the police. We can't even get out of this damned villa to get help!"

Camille didn't respond. Instead, she looked toward the back door, where the wind shook the frame with alarming force.

"Do you think..."

"I don't want to talk about any of it right now," Soren snapped, cutting her off. "This isn't some detective novel. People are grieving. People are scared. I know you came to the group late. I know you didn't know Noel as well as some of us. But just leave us to grieve in our own way."

Camille felt the air shift. The warmth between them, and the tentative intimacy they'd once very briefly shared, had completely evaporated. She took a breath, trying to stay calm. It had been Soren who'd introduced her to the group in the first place. It had been him who'd invited her to join them on the holiday when Leo had died.

"I'm trying to understand. That's all."

Soren stood abruptly, pushing the stool back with a loud

scrape. "Then understand this. Whatever's happening here, whatever's going on, you'd be wise to keep you nose well out of it. Don't go digging up things that want to stay buried."

He stalked out, leaving a faint scent of cologne and something bitter behind him.

Camille remained where she was, her heart thudding hard in her chest. There had been a flicker of something in Soren's eyes before he left. Something bitter and tight, colder than frustration.

Max came in just as Soren stormed out, shaking rain from his coat and muttering. "Hell of a night out there. I think we've made the place as safe as we can. Matteo says the landline's down too, so we really are stuck here until this passes."

Camille nodded toward the hearth. "Did you hear him?"

"Who?"

"Soren. He just really snapped at me."

Max gave a grimace. "I wouldn't worry. We're all stressed. Besides, that whole 'nice guy' shtick has to buckle at some point, doesn't it?"

Camille crossed her arms. "He's hiding something."

Max raised an eyebrow. "Oh, come on, sweetheart. We're all hiding something. Even you, right?"

"What do you mean?"

"That's why we're all here, isn't it? To share our secrets. Bare our souls. Share or die."

His tone was flat, almost bored, as if the entire situation were merely an unfortunate inconvenience.

"You sound so dismissive. Noel's dead. Doesn't that bother you? Don't you want to know what happened?" she said.

Max gave a shrug, leaning against the counter. "Of course, but I deal in facts, not feelings. The fact is, Noel's dead. The fact is, we're all trapped in a villa in the middle of a storm. We're all scared. But panicking won't do us any good."

Camille turned away, jaw clenched. She didn't want Max's detached calm right now. She wanted someone to care.

"There's calm," she said. "And there's cold indifference. You're leaning toward the second."

Max looked at her, something harder flashing in his eyes. "Maybe that's how I cope with pressure. Maybe that's what's needed. It can't be full drama all the time."

His voice had sharpened unexpectedly. For a moment, Camille saw past the calm exterior. Beneath the steady hands and cool tone, Max was afraid too. He was just better at hiding it.

Behind them, Alba entered silently carrying a small box which she set on the table with a delicate thud. Without a word, she opened it up and began to unpack what looked like wine labels, faded, cracked and curling at the edges.

"What's that?" Max asked.

Alba shrugged in answer, laying the labels out on the table. Her movements were careful, almost reverent.

Camille stepped forward. "These are... old. Very old."

She sifted through them until one caught her eye. It was different. Not a label but a card. Cream-colored paper, edges slightly torn. In the center was a blood-red wax seal, cracked. Above it, the initials: L.M. Camille's breath hitched. Leo Marinetti.

She picked it up. "Alba, where did you get these?"

Alba's eyes flicked to hers, unreadable. "I found them in the cellar. They belong to the house."

"To the house?"

"To its memory. I thought you should see."

The words settled like a weight between them. Camille glanced at Max, but he said nothing. She turned the card over to see faint writing on the back. Something illegible, followed by *...truth is fermented, then sealed.*

Camille felt suddenly dizzy. Alba turned and left, leaving the box and the labels on the table. Max exhaled and rubbed the back of his neck.

"What's the matter? You look like you've seen a ghost."

"Look at this," Camille said, turning the card over again before handing it to him.

He stared at it for a moment, frowned, and then handed it back to her.

"Very poetic," he muttered. "I wouldn't read too much into it."

Camille stared down at the seal. It looked like it had been smeared in blood. And those initials. Had Leo left this? What did it mean?

"Right," max said a little too loudly. "If this storm's going to roll all day, I'm going back to bed."

And, as he walked out, lightning cracked outside. And somewhere deep in the villa, a door slammed shut.

~

By the time the storm calmed enough to allow a glimpse of the hills beyond the villa, the damage had already been done.

The landline was still dead. Matteo had discovered it when trying to call the doctor in the village. The wires, strung between trees, had been torn down by trees falling in the wind. The villa's Wi-Fi, never reliable, had vanished with the first lightning strike. And the storm had swallowed their mobile signal, leaving them stranded in a fortress of candlelight and dread.

They gathered in the drawing room, silent at first. The atmosphere was thick, heavy with things unsaid. Outside, the rain still hissed against the windows, but the thunder had retreated to a low, distant murmur.

Camille stood near the fire, arms folded tightly across her

chest. Her eyes moved from face to face, searching for someone to voice the one thing none of them wanted to say.

Max cleared his throat. “We need to talk about Noel.”

Jasper looked up sharply. “What about him?”

“About what we’re going to do. With... him. We can’t just leave him where he is.”

The silence swelled again. Mara sat curled in the armchair, her knees tucked to her chest.

“Maybe we should try walking the coast path,” Camille said softly.

“We can’t,” Matteo said from his post near the windows. “The winds are still too strong. The waves will be too dangerous to cross the boardwalk.”

“But someone will come,” Mara whispered. “Eventually, right? They’ll notice we’re missing.”

Max exhaled. “We’re not missing. We’re guests on holiday at a private estate. Nobody’s going to come looking unless one of us tells them to.”

Camille looked around the room. “We have to do something.”

“What can we do, but wait?” Jasper asked, his voice hard.

The fire popped. Someone flinched. For a moment, the sounds of rain and wind seemed to recede. The silence hung between them.

“Do you think the police will ask about Leo?” Soren said finally. The question cut the air like a knife.

“Leo has nothing to do with this,” Camille said.

“Doesn’t he?” Soren asked. “You really think they won’t see the connections? Two people dead under mysterious circumstances. The same group. Same location.”

“Noel didn’t die in the same way,” Jasper shot back.

“No, but he died here,” Soren said. “With all of us. And that will be enough for them to start asking questions.”

They all looked at each other, the cracks widening with every breath.

"Maybe that's not such a bad thing," Camille asked. "I mean, we've never really got the bottom of what really happened to him."

Max shook his head. "This is madness."

No one argued. In the end, they agreed to keep the body in the cellar, wrapped and cooled. Until they were able to leave the villa or call the police.

7

AFTERSHOCKS

The rain had stopped, but the aftermath of the storm lingered. A sullen grey sky pressed low against the jagged cliffs, clouds still clinging like smoke to the upper ridges. Below, the sea churned in long, roiling waves, crashing against the rocks with bruised fury. The villa, though it was high above the water line, still felt precariously balanced, like it was perched on the edge of something ready to give way.

The kitchen smelled of damp stone and leftover coffee. Morning light filtered weakly through the windows, diluted and colorless. The warmth from the oven hadn't yet chased off the chill. The power was still resolutely off, and every room had a dim darkness to it.

Rowan sat at the table with a mug clutched in both hands, her fingers pale against the ceramic, knuckles white. Her robe, once ivory, now looked grey in the dimness, wrinkled and soaked through at the hem. Stray tendrils of hair clung to her cheek. She hadn't slept. Anyone could see that. Her eyes were shadowed, her movements slow and hesitant, as if her very bones ached.

Across from her, Mara picked at a slice of toast she hadn't

touched in twenty minutes. She was dressed immaculately in black trousers, with a white blouse buttoned high. The cuffs of her shirt trembled where her hands rested. Her eyes darted to every sound, every shifting candle flame, every scrape of a chair leg. She was a woman trying to hold on to composure, but the cracks showed in the way she swallowed too hard, blinked too fast.

Alba moved silently through the space, boiling water, wiping surfaces that didn't need it. Her face was unreadable, her expression carved from something harder than habit. She didn't speak, didn't look at anyone, but her presence was heavy, as though she carried something more than the kettle in her hands.

Jasper paced near the back door, barefoot, his hoodie stained at the sleeves. He kept shifting between the window and the door like a caged animal. Occasionally, he'd pause, pressing a palm to the cold glass, eyes scanning the cliffs beyond. Once, he whispered something under his breath, but no one asked what.

Matteo crouched near the stone hearth, elbows deep in the innards of the satellite phone. The table beside him was scattered with its guts. Coils of wire, battery parts, thin, broken circuit boards, all laid out in a hopeless mess. His hands moved deftly, methodically, but his brow was furrowed, lips pressed in a thin line.

"This was no accident," he said at last, holding up the stripped casing. "Someone took the wiring out deliberately."

Mara looked up. When she spoke, her voice sounded hoarse. "Are you sure?"

Matteo gave a grim nod. "Clean cut. No burn marks. No sign of surge damage. Someone dismantled this and destroyed it."

"Who would even know how?" Jasper asked, voice sharp, suddenly still.

"Doesn't matter," Rowan said. "The point is, they didn't want us to contact anyone in a hurry. Even once the storm passed."

Silence fell again. The wind outside groaned against the edges of the building, as if the villa itself was listening.

Selena entered, silent and shadowed, moving like smoke. She wore a dark sweater, oversized, sleeves pushed up to her elbows. Her hair was damp, curling slightly from the humidity. There was something evasive about her gaze, something unfinished in the way she approached them. Like she didn't really want to be there at all, but couldn't help herself. She took a seat near the end of the table, not speaking.

Renata stood slowly. She looked around the room, her jaw set, hands pressed flat to the tabletop.

"Alright," she said. "We need to address the obvious."

"Which is?" Jasper asked.

Renata looked at him. "That maybe one of us is doing all this."

The words dropped like a stone.

"Cutting the phone lines. Smashing the router. Stripping the satellite phone. And let's not forget the wine cellar. Noel's room. The cryptic notes. The half-veiled threats."

"Noel's death," Rowan added quietly.

Renata nodded. "Exactly. Someone doesn't want us to leave. Or speak. Or trust each other."

Alba stopped moving. For a moment, even the clink of mugs and chairs was silenced.

Jasper stepped forward, arms crossed, his stance wide as if bracing for a blow. "You're saying someone here is a killer."

"I'm saying we have to consider it."

"And what?" Max said. "Start accusing each other? Play a little game of whodunnit?"

"No more games," Mara said with a harsh finality.

"But if we keep pretending this is all just some random series of unlucky events happening to us, we're going to be picked off one by one," Renata said. "Just like Noel."

Selena stood abruptly, her chair legs screeching on the tile. Everyone turned, but she didn't look at any of them. She just wrapped her arms around herself and headed out into the corridor, footsteps quick, echoing.

"Renata," Rowan said quietly. "You scared her."

"She should be scared," Mara said. "We all should be."

Matteo stood up, brushing his hands off on a rag, his eyes on the door Selena had disappeared through. "Until the road is clear and we can send someone for help, there is nothing we can do. You all need to consider what you will say when the police come. Because they will come. And they will have questions. About now. And about the past."

Soren appeared in the doorway, drawn by the tension. He looked around, took in the satellite phone parts, the set jaws, the empty chairs. "What did I miss?"

"A whole bunch of cracks appearing," Rowan murmured.

No one laughed. No one moved. Outside, the sea raged and heaved below.

~

The air had turned thick now. Earthy, still buzzing faintly with the static of the storm's lull. Mist hung like gauze over the villa's garden, softening the edges of the crumbling statues and wild hedgerows. The birds had not yet returned. Even the sea, though quieter, swelled with a restlessness that mirrored the unease inside the house.

Rowan moved slowly through the overgrown path leading to the greenhouse. The gravel crunched softly beneath her sandals, and her arms prickled with gooseflesh despite the lingering humidity. She didn't know what drew her out there, only that she couldn't stay inside another moment with the suffocating weight of glances, the half-whispered questions, the barely veiled accusations.

The greenhouse loomed ahead, tucked into the crook of the garden's far end. Ivy and thick vines had overtaken the roof, threading through broken panes of glass, dangling like silent threats. When she pushed open the rusted door, the hinges let out a groan loud enough to echo.

Inside, the air was warmer, heavy with the scent of damp soil and crushed rosemary. Ferns curled in corners, and long-forgotten terracotta pots lay cracked on stone benches. Beneath one of the broken windows, Matteo stood with a cigarette between his fingers, the ember a faint orange glow in the dim space.

He looked up but didn't flinch. "Couldn't sleep either?"

Rowan stepped inside, folding her arms over her chest. "No."

He didn't offer her a cigarette, nor did she ask. Smoke drifted between them.

"This place was meant to keep people safe, once," he said, voice low.

She stared at him. "What does that mean?"

Matteo flicked ash into an empty flower pot. "The villa's old. Older than any of you know, I think. It was built as a sanctuary, you know? But it long ago stopped being a place for joy or peace. Now it's just home to secrets. To whispered regrets."

Rowan shivered despite the heat. She looked away, her gaze catching on a broken table beneath a hanging plant. The sudden quiet made her heart beat louder in her ears. She could see it again, as if it were yesterday.

The wine. The music. The firelight dancing on glass. The game that had come before the end of everything.

They had all been in the drawing room, the scent of clove

cigarettes and spilled wine in the air. Leo was the loudest, sprawled across the velvet couch, his long legs tangled in someone else's. Someone, Camille, maybe, had dared him to kiss the portrait of the villa's original owner. He'd done it with a flourish and a mock bow.

"Truth or dare," Mara had said, swirling wine in a cut-glass goblet.

"Truth," Camille had whispered. Her voice always dipped when she was drunk.

"Do you think he's in love with you?" Mara had asked, nodding toward Soren, who sat by the hearth, his face unreadable.

Camille had blushed but said nothing. That was the thrill of the game: what you didn't say was louder.

Then it had been Leo's turn. He was already tipsy, his voice too loud, but his eyes were sharp with mischief.

"Rowan," he said, pointing at her with the neck of his bottle. "Truth or dare?"

"Dare," she said. She'd always hated how truth made her freeze.

"I dare you to... No, wait. I dare you to climb the banister," Leo had said. "All the way to the top landing."

Rowan had laughed. "No way."

"Then I'll do it," Leo had declared, leaping to his feet.

"No, Leo!" Jasper had said?

But Leo was already up the staircase, taking them two at a time.

"You're drunk," Rowan had said, half-rising as though she could stop him.

Leo grinned down at them from the top landing. "I'm fearless."

He set the wine bottle on the banister, then climbed up beside it.

"Leo," she said again. There was laughter behind her. A nervous, high-pitched chorus. Someone said, "He won't do it."

And then he did.

He stepped up, balanced one foot, arms out wide like a gymnast on a balance beam.

"I'm walking the line between saints and sinners," he shouted.

"Get down," Rowan had said.

"Make me."

But she hadn't moved. None of them had. She'd felt it then. An awful, quiet urge to see what would happen. Like pushing over a domino just to hear the sound.

He wobbled once. Laughed. Wobbled again, almost for show.

"You've got to live life on the edge," he called out. "Isn't that right, Max?"

Max's smile was more of a snarl.

And then Leo hurried down the last few meters and jumped off the banister with a flourish and a bow.

"Dares are always better than the truth, aren't they?" he'd shouted, laughing.

So young. So full of life.

But the next day, he would be dead. And the truth would die with him. And none of them would ever be the same again.

Matteo was watching her. She could feel it.

"You alright?" he asked.

Rowan nodded quickly. "Just tired."

He didn't press. Just inhaled deeply, exhaled. "You all came back here hoping it would be different. That you could all move on, maybe. But that's the problem with places like this. They remember what you did, or didn't do. And they'll make you remember too."

Rowan looked at him for a moment, and then turned without a word and walked back toward the house.

Her room was dim when she entered, the curtains drawn but fluttering slightly with a draft she hadn't left open. She paused in the doorway, scanning the space.

Everything was exactly as she'd left it. Except for the pillow. A note had been placed neatly atop it. Cream paper. Precise handwriting.

She stepped forward slowly, heart pounding. She unfolded it.

You saw and you said nothing. That makes you worse.

Rowan stared at the words. Her breath caught. The paper trembled in her grip No signature, of course. No clue. But someone knew. Someone else remembered that night differently.

Her knees gave slightly, and she sank to the bed, the note clutched in one hand like a match about to burn. The villa creaked softly in the silence, as if it, too, was waiting for her reaction. And for the first time since returning, Rowan began to wonder if the truth had been buried deeper than even she dared dig.

8

THE PHOTO ALBUM

The rain had returned with startling intensity, like an old grudge flaring up. Sheets of water lashed against the arched windows of the villa's library, distorting the view of the gray sea below. The sound was a constant rush and rattle that filled every pause in conversation.

Despite the downpour, the summer heat lingered stubbornly inside. The villa's thick stone walls held the warmth like a kiln, and the air was heavy with the scent of sunbaked plaster and blooming oleander from the garden. Sweat clung to the nape of Camille's neck, dampening the collar of her linen dress. Even the marble floor beneath her feet felt warm.

Camille stood near the fireplace, holding the album carefully, as though it were a living thing. The room was dim, despite the high, cathedral-like windows, and motes of dust spiraled slowly in the golden shafts of light. Books lined the walls from floor to ceiling, their spines faded and peeling. A single wingback chair stood by the hearth, where Charlotte sat curled with her legs tucked beneath her.

"You sure it was here?" Charlotte asked, reaching out to touch the worn leather cover.

"I found it in my room," Camille said. "Like someone left it for me to find it."

She knelt beside Charlotte and opened the album on her lap. The pages inside were yellowing but intact, held in place by fragile corner tabs. Photos in black and white, then fading color: laughing faces at sunlit tables, cliffside dinners, bonfires on the beach. Most of them were bathed in the long amber light of late summer, everyone squinting against the glare, hair stuck to foreheads, skin glowing with sweat and salt.

"I recognize most of them," Charlotte murmured, pointing. "That's from our second summer. The wine tasting in the hills."

Camille flipped through slowly. Her fingers paused at a page where four photos had clearly been removed, leaving ghostly outlines where the page had faded yellow around them.

"This was Leo's page."

"You're sure?" Charlotte asked.

She nodded. "I saw the photos just yesterday. You were all at the cliffs. All dressed in white."

"Oh yes, I remember. Selena made a joke about it looking like a cult. Leo laughed so hard he nearly dropped the wine."

Camille glanced at her. "You and Leo were close, weren't you?"

Charlotte hesitated. "I thought he was okay. He helped me. Back then. After what happened with my family. He didn't really fit in. But Leo saw things others ignored. And he was kind to me."

Camille nodded, remembering the first time she'd met Charlotte. A theater major with a poet's soul, quiet but not shy. She'd lost her sister to an overdose the year before they all met, and it was a fact most had tiptoed around. Leo hadn't. He'd said her name aloud, toasted her memory. That was the kind of person was, both reckless and kind in equal measure.

"He fell from the cliffs in the same spot, the next year we came here. And now those photos are gone."

"Like someone doesn't want him remembered."

"Or they don't want us reminded of the good days, before he died."

They shared a look. Footsteps echoed down the hallway, slow and uneven. Camille closed the album instinctively just as Max entered the room. He was dressed in his usual knit pullover, sleeves rolled to the elbows, hair still damp from a recent shower. Even he looked sun-flushed and weary, a bead of sweat trailing from his temple.

"Morning," he said. "Or... whatever it is now."

"Morning," Camille echoed.

Charlotte stayed silent.

Max tilted his head toward the album. "What's that?"

"Nothing," Camille said too quickly. "Just an old book we found."

"A photo album," Charlotte said at the same time. Camille glanced sideways at her, but Charlotte didn't meet her gaze. Max stepped forward slowly.

"Mind if I have a look?"

Camille hesitated. "It's mostly old stuff."

Charlotte, with a kind of quiet defiance, opened the album again and turned it toward Max. He stared down at it.

"I remember this night," he said softly, pointing to a picture of the group gathered around the villa's outdoor dining table. "Leo had just made his ridiculously potent sangria. Selena got sick from it."

He flipped a few pages. Then paused at the torn section.

"Missing pictures?" he said.

Camille watched his expression carefully. "You remember what could have been here?"

Max shrugged. "Not exactly. We all had cameras, phones.

Could've been anything. We were in our second year. It was a good year to be alive. That was the first time we all came here together. Wild."

"They were photos of all of us out on the cliffs. The White Day," Charlotte said. "Camille said she saw them yesterday."

Max looked up at her sharply. "The cliffs?"

"We were wondering why someone would tear out just a few of the pictures?" Charlotte pressed. "Why not get rid of the whole album."

Max gave her a look that could be a warning. "People get sentimental. Or paranoid. Maybe someone didn't like how they looked back then."

Camille knew Max's past well enough to know that he was uncomfortable with scrutiny. Years ago, during their third summer at the villa, he and Soren had been caught up in a plagiarism scandal that nearly cost him his place at university. Leo had covered for them. He'd even sacrificed his own chance at publication to protect Max's career. It had driven a wedge through their friendship, one that never fully healed. Not before it was too late.

Charlotte's eyes narrowed, but she said nothing.

Max offered a strained smile. "If you find any good ones, let me know. We could all use a laugh."

He turned and left as quickly as he'd come. Silence settled in his wake.

"Why did you press him like that?" Camille asked quietly.

Charlotte turned a page, eyes scanning the faces. "Because I'm done pretending nothing happened here. Max won't even go to the cliffs anymore, have you noticed?"

A sudden gust of wind blew the shutter open and a shower of fresh rain struck hard against the windows. Outside, the storm was rising again, pushing steam up from the stone terrace, and the scent of citrus trees, wet earth, and aging wood crept into the library. The harsh weather had lulled for only an hour before returning with renewed fury, as if it too refused to let the past rest.

Camille pulled the album closer.

"I think someone is trying to erase Leo's memory," she whispered.

Charlotte didn't look up. "Then we make sure he's remembered."

The library was cloaked in soft gloom, made heavier by the weight of rising humidity and renewed, relentless rain. Wind rattled the old shutters, and outside, the garden swayed in the wind like ghostly silhouettes caught mid-dance. Rain clung to the tall glass windows in thick streaks, distorting the sea into a boiling, restless smear of silver.

Inside, the air was thick with the scent of aging paper, waxed wood, and faint lemon oil. Despite the storm, summer's heat lingered like an accusation. The villa's heavy stone retained warmth like a slow-breathing beast, its air close and unmoving.

Camille remained behind, the album shut on her lap. Charlotte had gone to fetch tea.

She pressed her palms to the windowsill. The stone should have been cold, but instead, it was clammy with stored heat, like a feverish forehead. Sweat pooled beneath her dress, the linen clinging to her spine. Even the library's marble floor had lost its chill. She needed answers.

The bookcases loomed around her, floor to ceiling, the wood darkened by age and smoke. Dust furred their edges. There was a subtle skew in the symmetry. One shelf jutted a finger's width farther out than the rest. It was enough to catch her eye.

Kneeling, Camille ran her hand along the grooves between the shelves. Her nails caught a seam so fine, it was nearly invisible. Her breath slowed as she pressed gently, and the panel gave way with a dry creak like something exhaling after a long silence.

Behind the panel, tucked in a hollow cavity, was a small object. A flash drive.

She pulled it free and rubbed it clean with the hem of her dress. It was wrapped in a faded label, the handwriting shaky and almost rubbed out, but still legible under the dust: *Limaccia – Confession Night.*

Her skin prickled.

The weight of the drive in her hand felt unnatural. Small, yes, but dense with significance. Camille turned it over once, twice. This wasn't a souvenir. It was a threat. A promise. A ticking bomb.

Her breath caught in her throat. The library, once serene, suddenly felt watchful. She had the sharp, gut-deep sensation of being observed.

"Find something?"

Jasper's voice made her flinch. She spun, instinctively clutching the flash drive behind her back. He leaned in the doorway, his silhouette framed by the gold-streaked light of the hallway. His white linen shirt clung to his chest and arms, soaked through from the walk back inside. His normally tousled hair was plastered to his forehead, and droplets still tracked down his temples.

His eyes dropped to her hands. "You've been in here a while."

"I was... looking through the shelves," she said, willing her voice to remain steady. "I thought I saw something behind one of the panels. Turned out to be a secret opening. But there's nothing in it."

Jasper tilted his head. His gaze lingered too long. "You're not a great liar, you know."

Camille forced a smile. "I'm getting better."

He smiled, but it didn't reach his eyes.

"Been looking at old photos, I see. They stirred anything up?" he asked.

"They raised a few questions, for sure."

Jasper stepped into the room and cast a look toward the closed album on the table. "Questions? Or answers you don't want?"

"I'm not sure yet," she said.

He looked like he wanted to say more, but after a breath, he simply nodded and retreated. Camille watched him go, then closed the door quietly behind him.

Later, alone in her room, Camille sat cross-legged on the floor, the USB in one hand, and a printed copy of Soren's university yearbook laid open in front of her. The pages smelled like old glue and dust, and their edges curled from the humidity. Sweat glistened on her brow as she pored over the photographs, comparing them with the album from the villa.

The storm outside had darkened the afternoon into a deep, wet dusk. Thunder grumbled over the cliffs. Each flash of lightning briefly illuminated the room in cold white, contrasting the lamp's honey glow.

There it was: a group photo from their second summer. Everyone smiling, bronzed from sun and wine. Soren stood at the center, arms around two others.

And just behind him, slightly out of focus, was a boy with uneven bangs and tired eyes. Camille stared. She remembered him now. Barely. He'd been quiet. Wasn't really part of the group, but he was often there, on the side lines. Always watching, rarely joining. What was his name? She couldn't recall. But she remembered his sudden disappearance that summer. A family crisis, someone said. They never saw him again after that.

She flipped back to the villa album, looking for the photo with the boy's face scratched out. Was that him? Had he been at the villa too?

But now, as she looked for it, she realised the photo was gone too. Not just the photo, in this case, but the entire page. Deliberately cut out. Her stomach twisted. Not only had someone erased Leo's memory from the album, but they'd removed someone else, too. Someone no one had ever spoken of after that summer.

She thought of Leo's voice, years ago. His glance, his tone. "He probably saw too much," he'd said.

The thunder cracked so loudly the windows rattled. Camille reached for her laptop. She stared at the USB still clutched in her hand. Her fingers trembled slightly. *Confessions Night.* She didn't know what she'd find. But she suddenly understood this wasn't a story about one death.

It was about the ones who disappeared first. Before Leo died. Slowly, she slipped the drive into the port, and waited to find out the truth.

~

The dining room of Villa Limaccia was unusually quiet for an evening meal. No laughter. No clink of glasses. Just the howling wind outside, the crash of the angry ocean, the persistent thrum of waves crashing far below. The storm was showing no sign of passing. Wax from half-melted candles pooled in irregular shapes like tiny maps of unknown territories.

Everyone was there except Charlotte. Camille sat between Rowan and Jasper, her shoulders stiff, eyes tracking the movements around the table like a chess player anticipating a fatal move. At the head sat Mara, her face pinched, fork untouched beside a plate of perfectly roasted sea bass gone cold.

Max poured himself another glass of wine. His hand was unsteady.

"So," Mara finally said, voice brittle. "We need to talk about what happens next."

No one answered. Outside, the trees groaned in the foul wind. Somewhere deep within the house, a shutter slammed closed, making Selena flinch. She reached instinctively for Camille's hand beneath the table.

Rowan was the first to speak. "The satellite phone. Any luck?"

All eyes turned to Matteo, standing near the door, where he'd been mostly silent, his presence more like a monument than a participant. He shook his head once, gravely.

"It was gutted," he said. "Wiring torn out. I don't have the parts to fix it."

"Torn out?" Jasper echoed. "You mean someone... someone deliberately sabotaged it?"

Matteo gave him a long look, as if the answer should've been obvious. "Yes."

Selena's face paled. "And the road?" she asked.

"Still blocked," Matteo replied. "Mudslide took it out completely. Could take days to clear. Maybe more."

Max leaned forward, his tone falsely bright. "We've got food. Wine. A lovely view. Maybe we just wait it out."

"You can't joke right now," Mara snapped.

"Why not? It's either laugh or admit one of us might be a murderer."

That word hung heavy in the air.

"Murderer," Jasper repeated softly. "You think Noel was murdered?"

"He didn't drown by accident," Rowan said flatly. "His phone was missing. His room was ransacked. That doesn't sound like accidental drowning, either, does it?"

"Maybe it was a robbery," Max offered.

"In the middle of a locked down villa?" Camille asked. "You really think some stranger hiked all the way up here to steal a phone and ended up killing Noel in the process?"

Max looked away, wine glass trembling slightly in his hand.

"This isn't just about Noel," Selena said quietly. "It's about... the past. Something we did. Something someone wants us to pay for."

"Leo," Rowan whispered.

The name crackled in the air like lightning.

Mara stood abruptly. "We're not doing this. Not again."

"You said we need to talk about what happens next," Camille said, standing too. "This is what happens next. We stop pretending we're safe. Because we're not."

Jasper rubbed a hand across his jaw. "So what, we wait around for someone else to die?"

No one answered.

Finally, Alba, who had been silently clearing away plates from the sideboard, turned to face them. Her expression was unreadable, but her voice was steady.

"The house remembers," she said. "You may try to forget. But it never does."

Max barked a laugh. "Is that a threat?"

"It's a truth," Alba replied, and disappeared into the kitchen, her skirts whispering across the stone floor. As the candles guttered lower, the shadows in the room lengthened. The sea roared louder below, as though echoing the unrest inside.

Camille looked at each face in turn. She couldn't tell who was scared and who was hiding something. Maybe they were all doing both.

"Until we know who did this," she said, "None of us should go anywhere alone."

"For how long?" Max asked. "Until we all turn on each other?"

"Until we know the truth," Camille said, softer now.

Rowan stared at the dark window, her reflection blurred in the glass. "This place... it never wanted to let us go. But now it's like it didn't want us back."

Jasper poured himself a drink with shaking hands. "She's right. We should have all just stayed away."

9

CONFESSION NIGHT

The rain had become a kind of rhythm, ceaseless and insistent, as if it were trying to wash the whole villa away. It pounded against the shutters in a relentless tattoo while the sea beyond roared and rolled, unseen but ever-present, like a warning in the dark.

Inside Rowan's bedroom, the air was thick with candle smoke and the scent of old wood and linen warmed by bodies. The flickering light clung to the walls, dancing across a faded oil painting of a hunting scene, distorting the eyes of the hounds until they seemed to follow every movement in the room. Shadows huddled in the corners like gossiping ghosts.

Despite the storm, the heat hadn't broken. It pressed into their skin and settled in the hollows of their collarbones, clinging like a fever. The walls themselves seemed to sweat. The bedsheets were limp and twisted, the air unmoving even with the balcony door cracked open. The breeze brought no relief, only the scent of rain-drenched rosemary, salt, and the faint rot of something unseen and old.

They had pulled the curtains shut, blocked out the chaos of the sea beyond the glass. The USB drive, titled *Limaccia –*

Confession Night, was now plugged into Rowan's laptop. The screen glowed faintly on the desk, its pale light like an open wound in the dark room.

Camille sat closest, cross-legged on the edge of the bed, her posture alert but not tense, her expression unreadable. She had rolled her sleeves up as though ready to get on with the job. She kept her gaze fixed on the laptop screen, eyes narrowed not with suspicion, but with careful, forensic interest. Selena was perched in the nearby armchair, her back stiff, lips pressed tightly together. She held a napkin from dinner in her lap and had unconsciously twisted it into a tight coil.

Charlotte stood slightly behind her, one hand resting on the carved wooden frame of the dresser, the other resting on Selena's shoulder. She had been mostly silent since returning from the garden earlier that afternoon, and her eyes kept shifting to the closed door as if she expected someone else to join them.

Jasper leaned against the far wall, posture loose but jaw clenched. His linen shirt, rumpled and damp at the collar, clung to his chest. He ran a hand through his hair and left it there, as if unsure whether to brace for impact or start pacing.

Rowan remained standing. She was the only one who hadn't taken a seat, and something about that made the others nervous. She rested her hand on the back of the desk chair, her fingers curled into the velvet like she could crush the wood beneath it if she tried hard enough. Her dark hair had been twisted up hours earlier, but loose strands clung to the back of her neck, damp with sweat. A fine sheen coated her skin and she looked both flushed and pale at once.

The file was ready. No one said anything. The only sounds were the storm beyond the walls, the distant boom of surf below the cliffs, and the faint whirr of the laptop's overheating fan. Camille clicked play.

The footage stuttered into view, grainy and handheld, a shaky lens capturing candlelight, echoing laughter, bodies in motion. A room full of shadows and wine and youth.

Leo sat in the center. Even in the poor lighting, he was unmistakable. His narrow frame sat tense in the dining chair, his wrists tied to the arms with a red silk scarf. A second scarf was knotted around his eyes. He was smiling, but it was brittle and forced. His lips were flushed with drink, his cheeks too red. Around him, figures hovered, all laughing, jeering and encouraging.

A woman's voice rose above the laughter: "Confession Night begins!" Mara. The camera caught a brief shot of her, eyes glittering as she raised a wine glass and turned back toward Leo. There were others nearby. Rowan's own face passed briefly through frame, her smile small and uncertain. Max stood behind Leo, bottle in hand, pouring clear liquid directly into Leo's mouth.

Everyone on the screen looked golden and young. Everyone watching in the room looked pale by comparison. On the screen, Leo coughed, then laughed nervously.

"Okay, okay," he said. "One confession, right?"

"Make it a good one," someone slurred. More laughter.

He hesitated, then said, "I lied on my scholarship form. That's how I got into school."

Applause. A cheer. A toast. The sound distorted slightly. The camera dipped and rose again. The laughter became shriller, more frayed. The footage was unsteady now, as though someone had clearly been drinking when filming. The image slid to the side and landed on Rowan's face. Her smile had dropped. She was no longer looking at Leo, but at someone just out of frame. Her hands were clenched in her lap.

Camille leaned forward slightly. "You look like you wanted to stop it all," she said softly.

Rowan didn't respond. She didn't move.

"It was pretty mean, when you look at it in the cold light of day."

Back on the footage, Leo shifted in his seat. Someone else shouted, "Tell us the worst thing you've ever done to someone!" Leo's smile faltered. "I... Nah. I don't think..."

"Come on!" another voice boomed. "You want to be one of us, right?"

There was a moment. A pause where the air seemed to hold its breath.

Leo said something so quietly it was inaudible on the tape. Whatever it was, it had an effect. The laughter stopped, just for a second. The room froze as the camera stopped swaying.

"What?" Mara said, sounding angry.

Someone laughed again, shrill and high, and then someone else, unseen, snapped: "Rubbish! You don't know anything, Leo! You'll never be one of us! You'll always be a loser."

In the room, Selena gasped. The napkin twisted so tightly in her lap it tore in two.

On screen, Leo flinched. The video suddenly cracked with static. The image broke apart. And then: black.

The sound of the sea returned, louder than before. No one moved. Camille's pulse thundered in her ears. Sweat clung to her lower back, and she realized her hands were shaking.

Jasper exhaled. "Jesus."

"You didn't know about this?" Camille asked, barely above a whisper.

"I wasn't there," he said. "I had to go to Naples that night."

On the armchair, Selena stood abruptly. Her face had gone completely ashen.

"I can't do this," she whispered, and fled toward the hallway, her sandals slapping the stone tiles with uneven urgency.

Charlotte turned, as if to follow, but paused. "She'll be okay," she said, to no one in particular. "I'll go."

Camille stared at the screen as Charlotte followed Selena out. The timestamp continued to count up in the corner, but the video was over. Only static remained. The silence in the room after the screen went dark felt loud. A pounding, wordless pressure building in every corner. The air felt heavier than before, dense with unsaid things, like something had been cracked open that would never fit back the same way.

"I need some air," Max said sullenly, and headed out himself.

Rowan reached out and closed the laptop lid gently, as if she were laying a body to rest. The click echoed through the room like a gunshot. Camille sat motionless on the edge of the bed, but her hands balled tightly in her lap.

Beside her, the candle's flame wobbled in its glass, throwing distorted shadows across the walls, where the damp had started to curl the old wallpaper. The storm's energy pressed against the villa like a fever. It was stifling, inescapable.

"How was that ever considered a game?" Camille asked, her voice low and cold, slicing through the silence.

Jasper didn't reply. He stood near the far window, his back to them, one hand pressed flat to the shutter as though trying to feel the storm beyond. His other hand clenched and unclenched against his side. When he finally turned, his eyes were hollow.

Rowan stayed silent.

"Confession Night," Camille said, her mouth curling around the words like they tasted bitter. "This was always a tradition? Tie someone up and bully them into admitting things they didn't want to say?"

Rowan gave a slow nod. Her arms were crossed tightly, her whole body taut. She looked as though she were holding herself together with pure will.

"It started out as something stupid," she said. "Drinking.

Dares. Secrets. Mara claimed it was meant to make us closer. Like... burning the rot to make something stronger. But it always ended the same way. Someone humiliated. Someone crying. And the rest of us laughing too hard, too drunk to admit we felt sick about it."

"And Leo?" Camille asked.

"He wasn't supposed to be there that summer," Rowan said, barely above a whisper. "Mara had final say on the guest list. But Leo got close to Selena. He'd earned her trust. He was different."

"Different how?" Jasper asked, finally stepping back into the room.

"He cared too much," Rowan said. "He just wanted to be part of the group. He believed we were something worth belonging to. That was his mistake. That, and he didn't know when to stop pushing."

She crossed the room and pulled open a drawer. Inside was a small leather journal. She hesitated, then handed it to Camille.

"My journal from that summer. There's a page missing. Torn out clean. I didn't even realize it until this week."

Camille flipped through the pages, scanning the neat cursive. It was structured, careful. Like everything else about Rowan.

"There," Rowan said, pointing. "That entry. It's dated the day before the video."

Camille read it aloud: *Leo asked me today if he was being tested. He said it as a joke, but there was fear behind it. I told him no. I told him everything would be fine. That it was part of being accepted. I said he'd be fine. God help me, I believed that.*

A beat of silence.

"I lied to him," Rowan said. "And he trusted me. But I couldn't tell him what those nights were really like, what they were really about. I did it to protect myself."

"No," Camille said, not unkindly. "You did it to survive. Because the moment you challenged them, you'd be next."

"I could've stopped it."

"But you didn't," Jasper said bluntly.

Rowan's eyes snapped to his. "Don't act so clean in all of this."

Jasper stepped forward, his jaw tight. "I wasn't even there that night."

"No, but you were there every other night. You saw what we all did. How we kept goading him and pushing him. You laughed along. We all did." Her voice cracked. "At the end of the day, we may not have killed him. But we all helped push him closer and closer to the edge, until there was nowhere left for him to go."

There was a knock on the door. Camille opened it, expecting Selena back. Instead, Charlotte stood in the hall, her face pale, her breath shallow.

"She's not speaking," she whispered. "Selena. She's curled up in the bedroom. She won't move. Won't answer me."

Camille moved to the doorway. "Is she in shock?"

"She's in something," Charlotte said. "And I think she remembers more than she's ever admitted."

Camille turned back toward the others. "You heard the last voice on that video. The one who said Leo didn't belong." Everyone nodded.

"It was Max," Rowan said quietly. "No one else had that sneer in their voice. That edge."

Jasper looked uneasy. "You really think he meant it? That he hated Leo?"

"He hated being challenged," Rowan said. "He hated anyone smarter than him. Leo was kind. Max read that as weakness. And weakness made him cruel."

The storm cracked outside, a bolt of lightning lighting up

the room in a sharp, colorless flash. It was gone in an instant, but the echo of it clung to the air.

"What do we do with the video?" Charlotte asked.

"We watch it again," Camille said. "All of it. Frame by frame if we have to."

"Noel was filming it, like he always did. Like he filmed everything," Rowan said, sitting heavily on the edge of the bed. "I spent years telling myself I didn't laugh that night. That I didn't join in. But I might as well have. Because I stayed. Because I didn't speak."

"And now?" Camille asked.

"Now I would speak up, but I don't remember what happened."

The candle guttered again. Thunder followed. No one said it aloud, but they all felt it: whatever secrets the villa had kept buried were starting to claw their way out. And the worst of them were still to come.

~

The corridor outside the sitting room was cast in flickering lamplight, shadows stretching long along the ancient tiled floor. The stone beneath Camille's feet radiated the day's heat back into the soles of her shoes, a trapped warmth that refused to fade, even now.

Max stood with his back to her, silhouetted against the tall window at the end of the hall. He braced himself on the sill with both hands, staring out into the dark. Rain streaked the glass, but his reflection remained still, unreadable.

"You heard the tape," Camille said, her voice quiet but pointed.

He didn't turn. "Everyone did."

She stepped closer, the floor creaking beneath her weight. "Do you remember saying it?"

Max exhaled slowly, as though trying to hold back more than just words. "We were drunk," he said at last. "All of us. It was a game."

"You told him he didn't belong."

He turned then. His eyes, bloodshot and rimmed with fatigue, flicked to hers. "It was a joke."

"Was it?"

The silence stretched.

Camille crossed her arms. The candlelight caught the slight tremble in her jaw.

"I've seen you lie before," she said. "In group meetings. To professors. To Mara. But that? That sounded like something you meant."

Max's jaw worked. "You didn't know Leo."

"No," Camille admitted. "Not the way you all did. But I spent time with him too. And I've watched you all enough now to know someone in the group hated him. From the way you spoke to him then, I think it was you."

He stepped away from the window, pacing. "Leo was... needy. He clung to people. To Selena. To anyone who showed him the tiniest bit of kindness. He always wanted more. More attention. More validation. He made everything heavier than it needed to be."

"So he deserved to be tied to a chair and mocked?" she snapped. "He deserved to be pushed to the edge, to the point where life seemed pointless to him?"

Max halted, mouth twisting. "I didn't say that."

"But you stood there. And you poured the drink. And you yelled the loudest."

A new voice interrupted them.

Jasper leaned against the door frame, watching, arms folded.

"She's right. You were the worst that night. I wasn't even there and I can hear it in your voice. But it' had been building for weeks. Months even."

Max laughed bitterly. "Convenient that you weren't there, wasn't it, Jasper. You always managed to disappear at the right moments, didn't you?"

Jasper didn't rise to it. "We should go and talk to Selena."

"Why?"

"Because she's terrified," he said. "Because she looked at that screen like she was back in that night. And if she knows the truth about what happened back then, maybe it will help us understand what's happening now."

Max looked between them. At Camille's unwavering stare, Jasper's cool disappointment. Then he scoffed.

"You're all acting like this is some Agatha Christie play, pointing fingers, rearranging chairs. But don't forget, we all had a part in that night. Leo included."

Camille flinched. "What the hell does that mean?"

"It means he knew what he was getting into inviting us all here," Max snapped. "He played innocent, but he was calculating. He confessed nothing. All he did was hide his threats better. He said exactly what he knew would hurt. He manipulated sympathy. And when it backfired..."

He stopped himself, breathing hard, sweat standing out on his brow despite the cool marble beneath their feet.

Camille's voice was like ice. "You're rewriting history."

"I'm surviving it," Max said. "History should stay firmly in the past, where it belongs."

Then he turned and walked away, footsteps echoing down the long corridor until the shadows swallowed him whole. For a moment, neither Camille nor Jasper spoke.

Then Jasper said quietly, "That didn't sound like a man with nothing to hide."

Camille turned back toward the flickering hall. "No. It sounded like a man who's afraid."

"Of what?"

She didn't answer right away.

Then, softly, "Of being next."

As if summoned by the thought, a loud crash rang out from somewhere upstairs. A door slamming, something falling, a sharp echo that bounced through the walls like a cry for help. They both flinched. And then they both ran.

10

THE SECOND FALL

The storm had returned with a vengeance. The sound that had called them upstairs had been a door blowing open in the wind, a table falling. Slowly, reluctantly, they had all peeled away to their rooms, to bed, but not to sleep.

At first the mist had crept in silently, stretching thin fingers across the terrace and whispering through the shutters like it was trying to be let in. Then, just before midnight, the sky fractured with a sound like the earth itself cracking open. Thunder rumbled so deep it shook dust from the high ceilings. The sea below, already wild, rose up in anger again, hurling itself at the cliffs as if trying to claim the villa stone by stone.

Rain struck the windows in hard sheets. Shutters banged The walls and roof of the house groaned with every gust, as if remembering things long buried. But then, another noise rose. Something tortured. Terrified. A scream.

It sliced the night open. High and sharp, human and real. It was a scream meant to summon witnesses.

Rowan sat upright in bed, heart thudding against her ribs. The air was thick. Her nightdress clung to her damp skin and the sheets were twisted, slick with sweat. The candle on her bedside table had burned out hours ago. Her phone was dead. There was nothing but black.

She threw back the covers and felt her way to the door, not bothering with slippers or robe. She fumbled through the hallway, guided by flickers of lightning that bled silver through the cracks in the shutters.

Outside her room, Charlotte emerged, barefoot, robe drawn tight. Her eyes were wide and frightened.

"That was Mara," she whispered.

Rowan didn't wait to answer. She was already moving. Downstairs, others were gathering in the gloom like moths to flame. The glow of candles began to pepper the darkness. Camille, face pale and drawn, gripping a lighter; Jasper, with a candle held high like a torch; Matteo, already half-dressed, flashlight in hand; Alba, emerging from the kitchen wing with her long braid over one shoulder, a single taper candle between her fingers.

Mara's absence was instantly noted, until a creaking door opened near the stairwell and she stumbled out, disoriented and visibly shaken.

"I heard it," she said, breathless. "It came from below."

Soren and Selena were missing. That detail settled on the group like dust. Camille's eyes flicked toward the staircase with uncertainty, wanting to run back upstairs, away from the cellar. But the urgency dragged them downward.

The stone steps to the lower level were slick with humidity. As they descended, the air grew heavier, pressing against their skin. It smelled of wet limestone, old barrels, cork rot and something else. Something more intimate and grotesque. The scent of copper. Of blood.

The wine cellar loomed at the end of the corridor, door ajar. Mara stood just outside it now, her hand braced against the wall, her other arm wrapped around her middle as though holding herself together. Her face was pale and slick with sweat, her eyes fixed on the doorway like she couldn't look away.

"Mara," Rowan said, stepping carefully toward her. "What is it?"

Mara's lips moved but no sound came. She simply lifted her hand and pointed. Rowan stepped through the door. The moment she did, she smelled it. Metallic. Sharp. Human. She knew before she saw.

The candles wavered and the flashlight beam landed on the stone floor. Max. He was splayed across the flagstones, one leg twisted unnaturally beneath him. His eyes stared at nothing. His mouth hung open, tongue lolling. Blood seeped from a heavy wound on the side of his head. Wine had spilled across the floor from a shattered bottle nearby, mixing with blood in a spreading pool that glistened with every flicker of light.

The room swam. Charlotte gave a sharp cry and staggered back. Rowan clamped a hand over her mouth.

Mara trembled. "He... he screamed. I was in the hallway. I thought I heard something. A punch. Or a thud. I came as fast as I could."

Matteo pushed through them all, down the stairs, and crouched beside the body. He checked Max's wrist. His fingers moved to Max's chin, lifted it slightly, feeling for a pulse. The motion was gentle, but matter-of-fact. He had done this before.

"He's dead," Matteo said.

Outside, thunder cracked again, rattling the floor.

"The house is closing in," Alba said softly. "Someone moving in its shadows."

Alba moved through the stunned group with uncanny calm. Her presence, usually unnoticed in the background of the villa's rhythm, now drew every eye. She stepped into the thick, iron-sweet air without hesitation, skirts brushing the wet stone. Her bare feet made no sound as she reached the body.

The wine cellar was suffocating—hot with storm-thick humidity, the candle flames guttering in the stale air. No one spoke. Not even Camille.

Alba knelt beside Max's sprawled body. She did not flinch from the blood, or the grotesque gape of his throat, still filled with shards of broken green glass. She placed her candle on the floor beside him, the halo of flickering light illuminating the whites of his wide, lifeless eyes. Her thin lips moved, whispering soft words in Italian. The cadence was old. Lyrical. Not prayer. Something older than that.

Camille strained to listen.

Rowan stepped closer. "What is she saying?"

Matteo, who stood just behind them, arms folded tight across his chest, shook his head.

"It's not meant to be translated," he said flatly.

"What does that mean?" Camille asked, but he said nothing more. His face, always unreadable, had closed in further, as though a gate had slammed shut behind his eyes.

Alba pressed her palm gently against Max's shoulder and murmured the last word as if into his skin. Then she leaned forward and gently closed his eyes with her fingertips.

Rowan lowered her gaze, something flickering at the edge of her vision.

A glint of silver, just beneath the hem of Max's crumpled shirt. Pinned to the fabric by an old corkscrew, driven deep.

She walked forward and knelt beside him, carefully pulling it free.

A folded scrap of paper, stained with wine or blood, the edges warped from damp. The corkscrew had pierced through the center like a dagger. She opened it. Thick black ink bled across the grain. No signature.

He who laughs the loudest, falls the hardest.

She read it aloud, voice cracking slightly. A ripple passed

through the cellar. Not physical, but emotional. Shock, fear, and then, recognition. Someone behind her exhaled sharply.

Mara staggered backward, her hand pressed against her chest like she'd been struck. She made a strange choking noise, then turned abruptly and collapsed against one of the wine barrels. Her body slid to the floor, fingers clutching at the wooden slats.

"He was supposed to protect us," she said hoarsely. "He promised."

Rowan turned sharply. "What do you mean?"

Mara shook her head, curls plastered to her damp forehead. "I can't..." She buried her face in her hands.

"Mara," Rowan knelt in front of her, gripping her wrists gently. "Who promised what?"

But Mara collapsed again into a heaving, sobbing mess. A silence stretched taut between the rest of them. Camille looked up at the others with a growing sense of dread. Jasper was there, Mara, Charlotte and Rowan all gathered together on the stairs. Selena, Soren, and Renata were absent.

"We'd better check on the others," she whispered.

"Where are they?" Jasper asked.

"Probably still in their rooms," Camille replied. "But be carefully. Let's go in pairs."

"I'll stay with Max," Mara said, her voice small.

Jasper took Rowan's hand, pulling her back slowly.

"We'll go find Soren," he said.

Camille moved toward the cellar door, motioning for Charlotte to follow. When they were out of earshot of the others, Camille turned to her.

"You've been very quiet," she said. "But you know something."

Charlotte hesitated. Her eyes were glassy with unshed tears.

"I shouldn't say anything. Selena. She told me not to stir up the past. Not here."

"Charlotte," Camille said, her voice low. "People are dying. First Noel, now Max. If you know something, you have to tell me. I can help"

Charlotte wrung her hands. "It was a long time ago. Years. We were all drunk. It was just after Leo had fallen. Or maybe just before. It's so hard to remember. Everything was such a blur."

"Go on," Camille pressed.

"I saw them. Mara and Max. They were in the courtyard, fighting. Whispering, arguing in low voices like they didn't want anyone to hear. I was going to say something, to stop them bickering, but then Max shouted at her. I remember it exactly. He said, 'You think the villa won't give it up eventually? We should've burned it, not buried it.'"

Camille blinked. "Burned what?"

"I don't know," Charlotte said. "But Mara looked terrified."

Camille stepped back, heart beating faster. The walls of the cellar suddenly seemed closer. The air tighter. The villa wasn't just keeping secrets. It was suffocating them with them.

~

Once the others had been roused, they all gathered back in the cellar. Matteo and Alba had covered Max with a sheet, the ends draped into the pool of blood and wine. Mara was sitting on a box, distant and lost.

Matteo stood, determined. "We cannot leave him down here."

"Where will we put him?" Rowan asked. Her voice was flat. Exhausted.

Matteo's eyes flicked toward Alba. The older woman gave the barest nod.

"We will move them both to the chapel," Matteo said.

Rowan felt her skin crawl.

"The chapel?" she said, frowning. "I didn't think that was still standing."

The small chapel sat behind the villa, a ruin overgrown with ivy and hidden by the lemon grove. Its roof had partially collapsed years ago. No one had stepped inside in over a decade.

"Most of it is still fine. And the ground there is colder," Alba said. "The shadows hold tight."

No one argued. Not because they agreed, but because no one had a better idea. They carried Max's body between them. Mara followed, apparently too shaken to help. Charlotte led in silence, holding a lantern that barely pierced the downpour outside. They would bring Noel later.

The night was ink-black. The rain was heavier now, warm and relentless. They moved through it like shadows, down the rear path slick with mud and leaves, past the citrus trees that groaned under the weight of the storm.

The chapel stood crooked, its stone facade coated in moss. The door sagged on its hinges. Matteo kicked it open. The air inside was fetid. Earthy. Still. They laid Max's body on an old wooden bench beneath the broken stained-glass window.

Rowan stepped back, her clothes soaked, her skin shivering with something colder than water.

As they turned to leave, Camille caught sight of something in the far wall, behind the disused altar, where the plaster had flaked away. A smear of black. Something not quite shadow. She moved closer.

There, half-hidden behind a wine rack that had been dragged in from the cellar long ago, was a patch of wall scratched over and over. Deep gouges in the plaster. Letters carved into the plaster. Raw and angry.

She crouched, trying to read the words:

I WAS HERE. THEY ALL WATCHED.

She turned toward Rowan, who had remained behind as the others had filed out.

"Rowan," she whispered. "Look."

Lightning strobed again. For a moment, the whole chapel lit up, illuminating the scratches with horrifying clarity. And in the silence that followed, Rowan felt not just the chill, but the weight of something left behind.

They left the chapel quietly. No one spoke as they walked the narrow path back to the villa, the only sound the hissing rain and their own footsteps squelching in the mud. The night had thickened, pressing down like a wet towel. Even the lemon trees stood still now, the wind having moved inland to seek other things to torment.

Rowan was the last to re-enter the villa. As she crossed the threshold, she turned back once, staring into the darkened garden. The chapel was gone from sight, swallowed whole by storm and shadow.

Inside, the air was warmer again. Thick with damp, sweat, and the smell of old stone. Someone had lit more candles, dotting the dining room with golden flickers that made the shadows dance on the walls like they were whispering secrets. No one wanted to return to their rooms. Not after what they'd seen.

Not with the knowledge that Max's body lay stretched on a rotting bench beneath a broken stained-glass Jesus. And Noel's now beside it.

So, they gathered around the long dining table that had once played host to wine-fueled dinners, laughter, toasted memories. Now, the chairs were pulled close, as though proximity could keep something darker at bay.

Matteo poured them each a glass of Grappa from a dusty decanter he'd retrieved from a high cabinet. Rowan took a sip. It burned down her throat like fire. She didn't cough. She welcomed the heat. Mara clutched her glass with both hands, elbows braced on the table. Her knuckles were white. Her eyes, red-rimmed and far away, were locked on nothing. A shadow of the woman who had once swept through rooms with a cocktail in one hand and power in the other.

Charlotte sat beside Camille, occasionally drumming her fingers on her knee, grounding herself. Jasper leaned back in his chair, unreadable, one leg crossed over the other, watching everyone like a poker player waiting for someone to show a card too early.

Selena and Renata had pulled their chairs closest of all, gathered together like conjoined twins, clinging on to each other for comfort and safety.

"I can't believe he's gone," Rowan said, looking around them all.

"He was killed," Matteo said, putting the Grappa down. "That blow to the side of his head either killed him outright, or made him fall to his death."

"But who?" Rowan half-whispered.

Camille nodded. "Whoever left that message. Not just for Max. For all of us."

Charlotte whispered, "He who laughs the loudest, falls the hardest."

Renata let out a brittle breath. "It's cruel. All of it. Someone... someone's playing a very cruel game."

"Just like we did," Jasper said quietly. "To Leo."

The silence that followed was worse than any shouting. Rowan looked at him, frowned, and tilted her head as though trying to see more in his face. But there was nothing.

Camille leaned forward. "You think that's what this is? Revenge for the way you all treated Leo? Who would want that now? And who call us all here to get it?"

Everyone's eyes drifted, slowly and uncertainly, toward Mara.

She stiffened.

"I didn't invite anyone," she said, too quickly.

Rowan's voice was low. "You said he promised to protect us. That it would stay buried. What did you mean?"

Mara blinked rapidly. "He did. Max... he promised that if we came back, he'd protect all of us. But now..." her voice broke. "Now he's dead, and Leo's ghost runs around this house like a curse, taking all of us down with it."

The candlelight trembled as someone shifted. The flame danced across the woodgrain of the table.

Camille pressed gently, "What was he supposed to protect us from, Mara?"

"I don't know," Mara whispered. "Not exactly."

"That's not good enough," Jasper said. "Because whatever it is, it's coming after us, one by one."

Matteo took a long sip of Grappa and stood slowly.

"The house always remembers," he said. "And it's not done with any of you."

They watched him walk into the hall, the candle in his hand casting a distorted silhouette up the staircase. His words hanging over them like a prophecy.

11

THE MESSAGE IN THE WALL

The storm was finally gone. It had slipped away sometime between the last candle guttering out and Alba's quiet footsteps returning to the kitchen. No fanfare. Just silence. An eerie, absolute stillness that settled over Villa Limaccia like a velvet cloth pulled tight.

Outside, the sea stretched grey and endless, soft waves whispering along the rocks below. A breathless calm. No birdsong. No wind. Even the trees in the orchard were motionless, their soaked leaves limp and heavy with secrets.

Camille stood barefoot in the hallway, one hand braced on the cool plaster wall as she listened. The villa had taken on a new quality since Max's death. Even the building seemed more alert, like it was listening back. Watching.

Camille turned toward the stairwell just as Rowan appeared, hair damp, face drawn, a throw blanket clutched around her shoulders.

"You're not sleeping either," Camille said softly.

Rowan gave a humorless smile. "Can any of us afford to sleep anymore?"

They didn't need to ask where they were going. Both women

moved through the villa in silence, past the scorched embers, glistening in the hearth, past the burnt-down candles, the half-finished glasses of Grappa still resting on the table like reminders of a vigil no one chose to keep. They stepped over the threshold of the cellar stairs.

The stone steps were damp beneath their feet, the air already cooler, denser. The cellar was sealed. Matteo had locked the door after they returned from the chapel, muttering something about keeping the energy in, or out. Camille hadn't caught the exact words.

But she'd slipped the key from its hook when no one was looking. Rowan didn't ask where she'd gotten it. They unlocked the door together.

Inside, the cellar was exactly as they'd left it. The air hung heavy with the sour scent of spilt wine, the floor still stained. The bottle shards had been pushed into a corner, glinting softly in the grey morning light. A low mist clung to the floor as if reluctant to let go of the night.

Camille led Rowan to the back wall. The wine rack was still there, its heavy wood frame half-collapsed, one side leaning against the damp plaster. Camille crouched and ran her fingers along the cracks, nails catching in uneven lines.

"This is where I saw it," she whispered. "Behind here. When the lightning flashed last night. I swear I saw something scratched into the wall. And then, when I saw that message in the chapel, I knew I had to come back and find it."

Rowan crouched beside her, the blanket slipping from her shoulders. Together, they gripped the edges of the rack and heaved.

It groaned against the floor, resisting like it didn't want to be moved. But with effort, it scraped aside enough to reveal the wall behind. Camille ran her hands over the mottled surface. The plaster was soft in places, weakened by time and damp. Dust drifted in the air. It tasted like stone and old ash.

And then her fingers touched a groove in the plaster. Faint. Crooked. She shone the flashlight onto it. There, etched deeply, as though with trembling hands were the unmistakable words:

I WAS PUSHED. L.M.

Camille froze. She reached out, ran her fingertips over the words, tracing them.

"Leo?" Rowan said.

Camille sat back on her heels. Her breath was uneven. Camille stared at the words. "Everyone said he jumped."

Rowan's voice was barely audible. "That's what we were told. It's what we assumed. But what if someone knew different? What if they lied?"

Behind them, the cellar door creaked. They spun around. Alba stood in the threshold, her face still and pale, candle in hand.

"You shouldn't be here," she said, stepping forward slowly, her eyes fixed on the message. Her candlelight trembled on the wall. "The house wants to give up its secrets to you, but it will bring you nothing but harm."

"Do you think Max found this? Before he..." Camille said, but she couldn't bring herself to finish the thought.

"You think that's why he was killed?" Rowan asked.

"Out," Alba said, shuffling them towards the stairs and the door above. "This is a bad place."

The candle in her hand flickered again. Camille turned slowly back toward the wall.

"She's right. We should leave. We're not just in danger because of the past. But because someone's trying to keep it buried."

Rowan stepped closer. "And they'll kill us all to do it."

Far above them, somewhere in the villa, a single piano key

struck. Soft. Isolated. And impossibly deliberate. The three of them looked up. Alba did not blink.

"The house knows who's next," she said.

Camille and Rowan looked up as Jasper came out onto the terrace, drink in hand, and sat down beside them. Mara was standing by the edge of the pool, staring at the water. Out of earshot, but still there.

"What does it mean?" Jasper asked as they told him about the message in the cellar wall.

"I don't know. Do you think it means he was pushed to behave as he did? Pushed to kill himself?" Camille asked.

"Or pushed to his death," Rowan said, darkly.

"Leo wasn't as innocent as you think," Jasper said.

Rowan's eyes narrowed. "Don't."

"He manipulated people," Jasper ignored her warning. "Said some awful things to Selena. And to Max. Stirred things up. He knew how to play the outsider. But he was closer to the inside than anyone realized."

"You're blaming him for his own death," Rowan said, stunned. "After what we just found carved into the wall."

"He didn't carve that," Jasper said. "Come on. That's a hoax. Or do you think he'd fall of a cliff and die, and then somehow back to the basement just to scrawl some melodramatic message that you'll accidentally find ten years later?"

His gaze bore into Rowan's. "Pull yourselves together. Someone's toying with us."

She hesitated. Camille sighed. And in that breath of silence, the truth hung heavy and pregnant until Jasper gave a sharp laugh, bitter and hollow.

"Jesus. We've been through enough. We need to get out of here. Away from here. Away from each other."

"Yes," Rowan said, bitterly. "But we can't. We're trapped here."

He stared at her for a long moment, then turned and walked back up the stairs without a word. The echo of his footsteps faded into silence.

Camille shifted. Mara ran her toe across the top of the water by the pool, and then walked slowly over to where they were sitting. She took a deep breath, but didn't speak for a moment.

"You have to understand. It was never meant to go as far as it did."

"The confessions?" Camille said, eyes hard. "Or the bullying?"

"Or Leo's death?" Rowan snapped. "First Leo. Now Noel. And Max. How many bodies will it take before we stop calling what happened that summer an accident?"

Mara's shoulders slumped. She looked younger in the dim light. More human. But also more fragile, as if finally stepping out from behind a decades-old mask. Camille studied her.

"You knew more than you ever admitted," she said. "You and Max. Maybe even Soren. You all made a decision back then to bury the truth about how hard you had pushed him. About how cruel you had been. That must have been a heavy guilt to carry."

Mara didn't deny it.

She only whispered, "We were scared." Mara looked down at her hands.

Then, quietly, she said, "I saw Leo leave the terrace that night. I left him for a while, and then followed. I heard him talking, but I heard no reply. I heard him shout. But I didn't go to him."

"And no one asked where he'd gone?" Camille asked.

"We were drunk," Mara said. "We didn't ask about him that

night. We wanted him to stew on what had happened. By the morning, it was too late."

"And so you hid the truth," Rowan said. "Said he'd been depressed. Not himself."

They stood in silence, three women facing each other.

"We need to talk to Selena," she said. "If Leo told anyone else anything that night, it would've been her."

Rowan nodded. Mara remained still and quiet. But her silence now felt more poignant than ever.

12

SOMETHING BENEATH THE SURFACE

The atmosphere in the villa had thickened into a tense, oppressive wall. The silence that came with the morning light was not peaceful. It was heavy with the heat of withheld truths, of breath stilled in chests. The kind of silence that comes after something breaks and you're waiting for the sound of the next fracture.

The morning sun felt too bright after so much darkness, glaring across the stone terrace's bleached whites and golds. It reflected off the limestone in painful flashes, shimmering in puddles left by the rain, now steaming slowly under the fierce Italian heat. Cicadas screamed in the trees above, their chorus relentless, oppressive, as if they too were straining under the weight of the day.

Camille stood barefoot on the terrace overlooking the cliff, her skin already slick with sweat despite the early hour. The stone beneath her feet was hot, as though the storm had never happened. As though the villa had simply held its breath, endured, and now was ready to burn.

Below her, the sea looked dark and uninviting. The surface sparkled with the usual Mediterranean calm, but beneath it, the tide twisted strangely, a slick undercurrent tugging at the rocks in irregular pulses. There was no wind, and yet the waves kept lapping higher, biting at the rocks like something eager to reclaim.

Soren was swimming.

He moved through the water in long, deliberate strokes, carving a slow arc through the cove like he had all the time in the world. His bare shoulders gleamed, the water beading on his back like glass. From this height, he looked peaceful. Almost godlike. Detached.

Behind her, the doors to the villa groaned open. She didn't turn.

"I see he's already had his morning absolution," Selena said, her voice low, dry.

Camille glanced over her shoulder.

Selena looked tired. Her hair, normally pinned back, hung loose around her face. She wore a sundress that clung to her skin in the heat, and dark glasses that hid her expression.

"He doesn't look like someone whose two closest friends have just died," Camille murmured.

"Because he never really mourns," Selena replied. "He skips that part. It's too messy. Too... human."

Camille said nothing. The sun beat down on her shoulders. She felt the salt in the air drying on her lips.

"I used to admire that about him," Selena added after a moment. "His ability to move on. To shut doors. But now..." she trailed off.

Soren turned in the water and floated on his back for a moment, staring straight up at the sun as if daring it to burn him.

"You don't believe it was an accident, do you?" Camille asked quietly. "Leo's death."

Selena was silent.

"That's why you came back here, isn't it? To find out?"

"I wanted the truth," Selena said. "I brought a piece of my own to share."

Then she reached into the woven bag slung over her shoulder and pulled out a small folded piece of paper. Her fingers trembled, just slightly, as she passed it to Camille.

"I shouldn't have this," she said. "It was meant to be destroyed. But I was sent it, and I kept it."

Camille unfolded it slowly.

It was a scanned copy of a coroner's report, yellowed slightly with age. The name at the top: Leo Marinetti. The rest was clinical, brutal, and shocking.

Cause of death: Blunt force trauma to the back of the skull. Significant damage.

Injuries consistent with a fall or significant assault.

Conclusion: Inconclusive. Investigation required.

Camille looked up. "Where did you get this?"

Selena didn't meet her gaze. "I got a call from a girl who worked at the coroner's office. She'd found my number in Leo's things. She said there were... anomalies. She sent me this."

"And you said nothing?"

Selena's jaw clenched. "I was afraid."

"Afraid of what?"

"What if Leo was killed? What if whoever did it found out I had proof?"

Camille stared down at the report again. Her stomach twisted.

"The police questioned us all, but they said it was suicide. Or an accident. They closed the case."

"He didn't fall," Camille said. "He was pushed. I'm sure of it."

Selena didn't answer.

A splash echoed from below. Soren had climbed out of the water and stood on the rocky edge of the cove, his body glistening in the sun. He moved slowly, toweling off, utterly unbothered by the heat or the silence or the dead friends lying in the chapel.

Camille folded the paper and slipped it into her pocket.

"Why now?" she asked. "Why give this to me today?"

Selena took a breath, and for the first time, Camille saw something crack beneath the surface. A deep, old guilt.

"Because I don't think the house will let us leave until the truth comes out," she said. "But someone here is trying to make sure it stays buried, even if that means burying all of us with it."

Soren reached the top of the winding cliffside steps just as they turned. He draped the towel across his shoulders and gave them a wry smile.

"Morning," he said lightly. "Perfect day, isn't it? The storm cleared everything out."

Camille didn't speak. He nodded toward the sea.

"Water's warm. Calmer than it looks. You two should join me."

Neither of them moved. Soren's smile dimmed slightly.

"You're making that face, Camille. The one where you've already decided I'm guilty."

"Maybe because you are," Camille said.

Soren tilted his head, amused. "Of what, exactly?"

Selena crossed her arms. "You tell us."

He turned to her. "You're still clinging to ghosts."

"You had it in for Leo ever since the plagiarism thing. But he helped you."

"That's what you think, is it?" Soren spat. "That Leo helped me? Leo tried to ruin me."

"That's not true," Selena said. But she didn't sound so sure.

"Really? Why don't you ask Mara. I'm sure she remembers what he said that night. What he said he knew. What he was going to do."

No one said anything for a moment, the tension and mistrust hanging between them like lead. Soren stepped forward slightly, close to Camille's face.

"You don't know what Leo was like, Camille. You never saw his true face. He wasn't some tragic saint. He knew how to manipulate. How to twist things to get what he wanted."

"That's not a reason to kill someone."

"I didn't kill anyone," Soren snapped. "But maybe someone else wanted to stop him before he could ruin more lives."

The silence that followed was deafening. Even the cicadas seemed to pause. Selena stared at him. "So, you admit he was threatening you."

Soren smiled, but it didn't reach his eyes. "I admit nothing."

He turned and walked past them into the villa, the heat rising off his skin like steam. Camille let out a slow breath.

"He's hiding something," she said.

"Of course he is," Selena replied.

They both looked back toward the sea as a dark wave crashed over the rocks.

~

They were still trapped at the villa. Not because they wanted to be. They had no choice.

The power had returned sporadically across the morning, flickering like a nervous pulse before dying again. It offered a glimpse of hope. But the landlines were still dead. The satellite phone remained useless. The cellular signal, always unreliable in this cliffside pocket of southern Italy, had now vanished entirely.

No one had left the grounds since the storm passed. No staff had arrived. No maintenance vans. No delivery trucks. The long, dusty road leading from the villa into the hills remained untouched. The track beyond it buried by a mudslide.

Even the olive farmer who normally checked on the orchard once a week hadn't come.

They were surrounded by wilderness: scrub-covered hills to the north, dense forest to the east, and jagged cliffs on the south and west sides where the sea carved into the stone like a forgotten god's hand.

Camille had asked Alba, quietly, why the villa was built in such an isolated place.

"It was commissioned during the war," she'd said. "Not as a home. As a sanctuary. For men who didn't want to be found."

Rowan later explained that the estate had been bought by Leo's family generations ago. It had been a place of political refuge, then a reclusive artist's retreat, then finally leased to exclusive clients as private rentals. No records. No neighbors. No staff who stayed longer than a season unless they knew how to keep quiet.

The isolation wasn't an accident. It was by design. Which meant that right now, they weren't stuck by misfortune. They were trapped by intent.

Camille stood at the kitchen window, arms crossed tightly over her chest, watching the olive trees sway beneath the sun. The heat had settled into everything. The tiles were warm beneath her feet. The stone walls radiated the memory of fire. Her clothes stuck to her skin. The house smelled faintly of citrus and old wood and the sour edge of anxiety.

Alba moved quietly behind her, placing a few remaining tomatoes on the counter. A small bowl of olives. One loaf of bread, already hardening at the edges.

"That's it?" Camille asked, not turning around.

Alba hesitated. Then, with a quiet sigh, she said, "Fresh supplies will last another day. Maybe two. After that, we improvise."

"No one's coming, are they?"

Alba didn't answer immediately. Then: "They will clear the road soon enough."

Camille turned to face her. "You've lived here most of your life. Doesn't anyone check in more regularly?"

"This villa doesn't encourage visitors," Alba said. "Guests come by invitation only."

A few hours later, they gathered on the terrace.

Rowan, Jasper, Charlotte, Selena, Soren, Renata, Camille and Mara. The all looked like hollowed out versions of the people they'd once been.

The heat was brutal. The sea shimmered far below, its surface deceptively serene. But everyone knew the water churned beneath.

"What do we do?" Rowan asked.

"Wait a bit longer," Soren said casually, sipping from a sweating glass of white wine. "We're cut off, sure, but not forever. A boat will pass. The road will get cleared. Or the signal will return."

"We have two dead men in the chapel," Camille snapped. "And no way to tell anyone about it."

"That's assuming we want to tell anyone," Soren replied, flashing a tight smile. "This group's pretty good at burying secrets."

Charlotte stared at him. "What the hell is wrong with you?"

"Only pointing out the obvious," he said. "We've obviously been brought back here to play this little game out to its conclusion."

"You think this is a game?" Selena asked quietly. "Noel's dead. Max too. That's no game."

"It just feels like someone has got the wrong end of an old and messy stick, and now they are playing with us, wanting us to think we're in some kind of a horror film where we all get picked off one by one."

Jasper shook his head. "They're dead, Soren. That's not a prank. That's not hysteria."

Silence fell. The heat pulsed in waves off the stone. Alba lingered behind them, gently swooshing a brush across the tiles.

"This place was not made for comfort. It was made to contain."

They turned to her. She continued softly, "I've seen guests come and go. The ones who stay longest are the ones who think they can outsmart what lives here. But this villa has a memory. A way of pressing into people. Forcing them to look inward."

Camille met her eyes. "And what does it remember about us?"

Alba's voice dropped to a whisper. "Everything."

The group broke apart not long after. Everyone returned to their corners of the house. Except Camille. She stood alone on the terrace again, the sun scorching her shoulders, her mouth dry.

Soren had gone back to the pool. She could see his towel left behind, draped neatly over a chair. A short while later, he reemerged in swim trunks, gliding across the terrace like he belonged here more than anyone. He passed her without looking. And that's when she saw it. The scar. Thin, pale, and old. Just under his collarbone.

She had never noticed it before. Not even in the brief but passionate relationship they'd shared. She stepped forward.

"What happened to your chest?"

Soren paused, toweling off, then turned with a fluid smile.

"Childhood accident," he said lightly. "Fell off my bicycle. A piece of broken bottle cut me. Stupid thing."

She didn't answer. She only looked. He noticed.

"You're staring."

"You never had that scar."

His smile dimmed. "I've always had it. You just never noticed."

Camille narrowed her eyes. Behind them, the kitchen door creaked. Alba stood just beyond it, arms folded. But her eyes weren't on Camille. They were locked, unblinking and cold, on Soren.

13

THE ROOM THAT SHOULDN'T BE

The villa didn't sleep. Not really. At night, when the cicadas had quieted and the moonlight pooled in blue puddles across the flagstones, Villa Limaccia shifted. The walls creaked softly, as though adjusting their posture. The old glass of the windows whispered under pressure. There was a rhythm to it. It was a living, breathing architecture that exhaled sighs no one wanted to claim.

Rowan stood barefoot in the corridor, her nightdress clinging to her damp skin.

She didn't remember getting up. Not fully. She remembered dreaming of a bright light, a door yawning open, her own footsteps echoing somewhere that wasn't quite real.

But now she was here. Again. The same place. The same door. She'd woken three times this week in front of it, each time with the taste of copper in her mouth, her heart thudding like a fist against her ribs. The first night she'd chalked it up to the stress, the second to wine. But now? This was something else. She was being called here.

The east wing was meant to be sealed. Matteo had said so. The plaster near this particular door was cracked and bloomed with salt damp, the air colder than the rest of the house. The corridor narrowed here too, as if the villa had grown weary of welcoming guests and was trying to squeeze them out. It felt older, darker, as though it belonged to a different building entirely.

And she always ended up at the same door. Heavy oak with no handle. Just a blackened keyhole and iron hinges swollen with age.

Rowan reached out, almost without meaning to. Her fingertips hovered, then touched the wood. It was warm. She pulled back. It felt wrong, that warmth so deep in the house. There was no radiator, no sunlight, no explanation. Yet it felt as though something lived behind the door. Something breathing.

She leaned in. And then she heard it. Movement. Soft and rhythmic shuffling, like someone pacing in slow, deliberate steps. Her breath caught. She pressed her ear to the door. The scent of scorched wood met her nose. Beneath that, metallic and damp, like iron or blood. Then the whisper came, faint and delicate.

"Still here."

Rowan staggered back, her shoulder catching the wall. The words hung in the air, fragile as smoke. She turned and ran, barefoot and breathless. She didn't stop until she reached the warmer light of the main corridor, where a half-burnt lantern flickered beside a dusty vase. There, she leaned against the wall and listened to her own pulse scream in her ears.

The silence behind her was now absolute. As though the walls had never spoken at all.

~

By morning, the summer sun had returned, unapologetic in its brilliance. It burned the villa's white stone walls, drenched the lemon trees in syrupy light, and turned the olive leaves to liquid silver. Birds shrieked from somewhere unseen, and the scent of salt and bougainvillea clung to the terraces like perfume. But inside, the memory of that corridor hadn't faded.

Rowan pushed her coffee aside and stared at the condensation on her glass. Across the table, Camille studied her with quiet concern.

"You look like you've been up all night," she said.

"I have," Rowan admitted. "I think I've been sleepwalking."

Camille frowned. "Again?"

"I keep waking in the same place. Outside a door in the east corridor."

"The sealed wing?"

Rowan nodded. "There's something about it. The air's wrong. It's warm. And... I think I heard something last night."

Camille leaned in, the sun painting honey across her collarbone. "What kind of something?"

"Whispers," Rowan said. "And footsteps."

She expected disbelief. Maybe even a smile, but Camille just looked at her steadily.

"I tried the door yesterday," she said. "It didn't open, but... you're right. It was warm."

Rowan blinked. "You didn't say anything."

"I thought maybe I was imagining it." Camille tilted her head. "I'm not anymore."

A long silence passed between them. The fan above them hummed. A wasp buzzed near the bowl of fruit slowly turning over-ripe in the sun.

"Let's go back," Camille said.

"To the corridor?"

She nodded. "Together."

Midday dulled the edge of fear. The house filled with movement again. Selena and Matteo had struck out to see if they could find a way through to the village. Jasper was out on the cliffs. The villa breathed in sunlight, its walls stretching. Its secrets folding just out of reach.

Camille and Rowan walked barefoot to the east wing, wrapped in a shared silence that clung to them like the heat. The stone floor grew cooler the further they went. Shadows swallowed the corridor in long teeth. When they reached the door, they stopped.

The light here was bruised. Pale and strange, filtered through a long window caked with salt. It hadn't changed. There was still no handle. Still no sound. And the keyhole glared back like an evil eye.

Camille approached first, her breath shallow. She touched the wood. It was still warm.

"Someone's been in there," she whispered.

"Or still is," Rowan said.

They waited. Then Camille, without a word, knocked three times.

At first, nothing. Then, slowly, deliberately, a faint creak. The door didn't open. But something shifted behind it. As if the villa had inhaled. And then the whisper again. Faint. Almost childlike.

"Still here."

Camille stepped back. Her heart wasn't racing. It was slowing. As if preparing for the worst. She knelt and looked through the keyhole. What she saw made her breath stop. Inside, the room was dark, lit only by a crack of sunlight from a high window. On the far wall, a mural. A fresco. Old, with peeling paint, but intact. It showed people. Twelve of them, dressed in ceremonial robes, laughing, raising goblets. But in the corner, standing slightly apart, was a thirteenth figure.

He wasn't laughing. He wasn't toasting He stood with his face half in shadow. Looking straight out of the mural at her. Leo. Camille drew back, her breath shallow.

"What did you see?" Rowan asked.

"A painting," she said. "Of us. With Matteo and Alba. And Leo. It was like a last supper."

That night, Camille couldn't sleep. She returned to the library, drawn by something she didn't understand. Alba was there, placing wood into the hearth like someone performing a ritual.

"I need to ask you something," Camille said.

Alba looked up. Her eyes were tired, but kind. "Ask."

"The east wing. Has anyone... ever lived there?"

Alba hesitated. Then said, "Long ago. Before the war, it was the servant's wing. After that, it was where the family lived when they stayed. After Leo... it was abandoned. Strange things started happening there. People hearing voices. Seeing figures. The door was sealed. Matteo says it's superstition."

"And you?"

"I think old places remember," Alba said. "Especially when truth stays buried and the lies walk free."

Rowan appeared behind them, a sketch in her hand.

"I found this," she said. "In one of the old ledgers. It matches the mural."

Camille took the sketch. It was charcoal, faded. Twelve figures laughing. A thirteenth in shadow. His face blurred.

"I think they were recreating it," Rowan whispered. "Summer after summer. Without knowing it."

Camille looked at her. And knew. The villa hadn't caused the deaths. But it had kept the memory of them alive, waiting for someone to finish what was started.

Later, alone in her room, Camille opened her journal. She tried to draw the face of the outsider. Each time, it changed. It started as Leo, then became Jasper, Max, then herself.

She stared at the messy final image and whispered, "Still here."

From somewhere in the house, a door creaked softly. And the wind carried laughter that wasn't natural. Not anymore.

14

THE FORGOTTEN ROOM

The east wing of the villa felt different. It always had. Even in daylight, it seemed reluctant to reveal itself. Each shadow here felt deeper, every floorboard groaning louder than it should. The plaster smelled faintly of damp and time. As Camille followed Selena up the narrow staircase, she felt it again: the sensation that something here was resisting them. Like the house was tightening around its own ribs, unwilling to let this part of itself breathe.

Behind them, Jasper kept a steady pace, his steps heavy, his expression taut with exhaustion. He hadn't spoken much since that morning's confrontation with Rowan. His silence felt heavier than the air.

Selena stopped at the end of the corridor. The hallway was narrow, choked with cobwebs and stale heat. Old family portraits lined the walls showing men in outdated military uniforms, women in black lace, all unsmiling.

Camille wiped her forehead with her sleeve. Sweat pooled at her collarbone. The villa held the heat like a furnace now, sealing it inside thick stone walls, offering no breeze, no relief.

"This way," Selena said.

She stepped around a long linen-covered mirror that leaned against the wall. Behind it stood a small wooden door with a rusted iron keyhole and an antique brass handle. A faint cross had been scratched into the wood near the top, now barely visible beneath layers of dust.

"This was the old family wing," Selena said. "They sealed it years ago. Said it wasn't needed anymore."

"How did you find out about it?" Jasper asked. "I didn't even know this part of the house existed."

Selena gave him a look that wasn't quite a smile. "Leo brought me up here. Said it was the only place in the house that felt honest. Like family. But he didn't want me to tell the rest of you, in case you came in and trashed it."

She reached into her skirt pocket and pulled out a small, tarnished key.

Camille raised an eyebrow. "Where did you find that?"

"It's always been a jar of rosemary in the kitchen."

Jasper blinked. "You're joking."

"I'm not."

She turned the key in the lock. It clicked and the door groaned open.

The smell hit them first. Mildew, dust, rusted iron, and old paper. The air inside was dense and unmoving. For a second, Camille imagined she saw the dust flinch as the light crept in.

The room was small and cramped. A single narrow window let in a sliver of sunlight, which sliced across the warped floorboards. A rusting iron bed frame leaned against the wall, its mattress long gone. A narrow dresser stood lopsided in the corner, one drawer missing entirely. Faded wallpaper peeled like dead skin from the walls. But it was the stack of boxes that drew their eyes.

Cardboard, brittle with age, stacked in the corner beneath a yellowed linen sheet. Camille moved first, pulling the cloth free.

Dust exploded upward in a ghostly bloom. She coughed, waved it away. Four boxes. Each marked in faded ink:

YEAR ONE

YEAR TWO

PHOTOS

PRIVATE – LM

Camille's throat tightened at the last one. Jasper reached into the top box and pulled out a handful of photographs. Smiling faces. Summer tans. Parties on the terrace. Late-night games, drinks raised mid-toast. Camille leaned in.

There he was. Leo. Always on the edge of the frame, never quite center screen. His hair sun-bleached, his smile cautious. In one photo, Max had an arm around him, both laughing. In another, Mara stood beside Leo at the dinner table, leaning away as he turned toward her. In another still, Rowan sat with Leo on the edge of the pool, legs dangling, a bottle of wine between them. Camille flipped one of the photos over.

Confession Night. July 3rd.

She exchanged a glance with Jasper. His face was unreadable. Selena opened the second box. It was filled with folded notes, scraps of paper, university flyers, and cocktail napkins with scribbles in pen. All of them fragments of another lifetime.

"Leo kept everything," she said softly.

Camille reached for the final box marked PRIVATE – LM. It was heavier than the others. Inside, wrapped in old linen, was a rusted lock box. Like a small safe, it was padlocked though the latch corroded with age.

Jasper crouched down beside her. "We need something to cut this."

"Let me," Selena said.

She stepped outside and returned a minute later with Matteo.

He entered silently, like he'd been expecting this moment. He didn't ask questions. He just lifted a small pair of bolt cutters from the tool roll he carried. With two sharp crunches, the lock snapped open.

The lid squeaked as Camille lifted it. Inside were a number of notebooks. One spiral-bound. A leather diary. A small wooden box. And at the very bottom, a printed university ID card. Camille pulled it out and stared.

Leo Marinetti. Age nineteen. Sociology and History.

He looked younger than she remembered him from the photos. Bright-eyed and unsure. The photograph taken before the courses had started. Before he'd met them all.

Jasper picked up the leather-bound journal and opened it to the first page. He read in silence, then passed it to Camille without a word. The handwriting was neat, deliberate.

I was never supposed to bring them here. They weren't the kind of people to be invited to a place like this. I asked them because Selena wanted me to. She said it would be good for me. That the others would see that I wanted them to like me. That they were family.

But families don't laugh when you cry. Families don't laugh when you bleed.

Camille flipped through several pages, loaded with observations about the group.

Max is the loudest in the room. Laughs too hard. Always watching for weakness. Told me once that kindness was a liability.

Mara. She's beautiful. Cold and dangerous, but so beautiful. Tries to pretend she's in control, but she's just terrified of being ordinary.

Rowan. The quiet, *gentle soul. But there's something behind her eyes. Like she's watching a version of herself she doesn't recognize anymore. Still waters.*

Jasper. Alright. Not as cruel as the others. But not brave enough to stand up to them either.

Then, further along, a section dated July 1st:

Max cornered me by the chapel last night. Said if I told anyone what I saw, or what I knew, I'd regret it. He didn't say it like a warning. He said it like a promise.

I want to believe Selena didn't know. I want to believe Rowan would help me if she really knew me. But I'm starting to think they're all part of it. The circle. The pact. And that I'm not the first they've driven to the edge.

I'm scared. Not of being here. But of being here with them.

Camille closed the journal, her fingers trembling slightly. She looked up. Selena's face was pale. Jasper stood and walked to the window. He stared out over the north garden, jaw clenched. They'd all read the words. They'd all seen Leo's thoughts.

"We have to show the others," Camille said. "This changes everything."

"No," Selena whispered. "It doesn't change it. It confirms it."

"But what if one of them did take things too far. Doesn't this add to the evidence? Doesn't this suggest he was scared before he died?"

Matteo, who had stayed near the door, spoke for the first time. "This is why this part of the house was kept closed."

"If he was scared of us, of the group," Jasper said. "Perhaps we should be too. I mean, I was away that night, and you weren't part of the group properly at that stage, Camille. But Selena, you remember what it was like in the days after he died."

Selena nodded.

"I thought we were all just shocked. I mean... we were just shocked. But there was a lot of talk of covering up the confessions nights. Not talking about what had gone on that holiday. Or before."

Camille turned back to the box. At the very bottom, something shimmered faintly beneath a layer of dust. A silver chain. She lifted it gently. A small silver medallion hung from it, worn down by time and touch. It had Leo's initials scratched crudely into the back.

She clutched it in her fist. Camille stood completely still, the silver chain tangled in her fingers, Leo's initials faintly pressing into her palm.

The room had grown colder somehow, though the heat of the day still pressed thick against the villa's walls. It was the kind of cold that came from a sudden revelation opened wide. A cold that settled on the chest, just between the ribs, and refused to let go.

She met Selena's eyes. "He was going to tell someone's secret. He knew something terrible."

Selena nodded faintly. "But he never got the chance."

Jasper, still facing the window, said nothing. He was breathing heavily, trying to control his feelings, but Camille could see his hand clenched into a fist at his side.

Behind them, the floor creaked. They turned instinctively. Matteo still stood in the threshold.

But there was a tension in his shoulders now, a flicker of emotion behind his dark eyes that hadn't been there before. Something sharp. Personal.

"You should go back to your friends," he said, his voice low but unwavering.

Jasper took a step forward. "We need answers."

Matteo looked past him to the open locker, the scattered photos and papers, the silver necklace still clutched in Camille's hand.

"You have them," he said. "If you know how to read them properly."

Camille studied him carefully. "You knew all this was here all along?"

He didn't deny it.

"You could have told us."

"It's family business. Not for you."

Matteo exhaled through his nose and stepped into the room fully, letting the door fall shut behind him with a dull thud.

"You're playing a dangerous game," he said quietly. "Digging in this house. Pulling apart the bones."

"You think we don't know that?" Camille said. "Max is dead. We're trapped. Someone is orchestrating all of this."

Matteo's jaw tensed. "Yes. But you'll achieve nothing turning over stones you don't understand."

"You're not making any sense," Selena said. "Why don't you just tell us what you know?"

Matteo looked at her. And then he looked at Camille.

And he said, "Leo was my cousin. And he was killed. By one of you. Or all of you. The house just wants the truth."

The words hung in the air, thick and sudden and impossibly heavy.

Camille blinked. "What? Your cousin?"

A long silence stretched between them.

Camille's mind reeled. "So you've known from the beginning. About us. About Leo."

"Yes," said Matteo. "It was me that invited you all here. The house needs answers. The truth needs to be exposed. And Leo needs to rest."

They stared at him in shocked silence.

"I don't know what happened," Matteo said. "But I know he brought you all here when he wasn't supposed to. And he left in a body bag, while everyone else went home with suntans and secrets."

Jasper's fists unclenched. "Why didn't you say something before? All this time. You let us sit around that dinner table. You watched our friends being killed. You knew..."

"I watched," Matteo said. "Because I needed to know which of you was lying."

Selena stared at him. "You think one of us killed him."

"Not one of you three, no," Matteo said. "But one of the others. And they'll keep doing it until there's no one left that knows their secret."

The room was silent again.

Outside, the wind picked up for the first time all day. A hot, dry gust that rattled the cracked window frame and sent dust spiraling through the narrow beam of light.

"Did you kill Noel? And Max?" Jasper asked.

"No, I swear. I just want the truth. Justice for my cousin. You can't tell the others what you know. One of them... at least one... is a killer."

Camille's voice was barely a whisper. "Who?"

Matteo looked at her. And in his eyes was something she hadn't seen since they arrived. Grief. Deep and weathered, but still unbearably raw.

"I don't know," Matteo said. "But I know Leo was scared. He sent me a message two days before he died. Said he'd found something. Said it would ruin them."

"Ruin who?" Jasper asked.

Matteo looked between them.

"He didn't say. Just said they were hiding something terrible. Something they'd done a year ago. Something about another boy. Ben? Leo thought he could use it to make them accept him. Or maybe protect himself."

Camille's thoughts raced. "Ben? The kid that disappeared from university. The one who had a breakdown?"

"He never said any more. Just that they made him feel sick. And that he had proof of what they really were."

Selena took a shaky breath. "Why didn't you go to the police?"

"Because he died, and I didn't know any more than I've just told you. You all gave statements. Everyone agreed it was a fall.

There was no evidence. No motive. No one wanted to pursue it. Apart from me, and I couldn't. I didn't know how."

"And now?" Camille asked.

"Now," Matteo said, "I think Leo is making sure his story doesn't stay buried. The house keeps showing me more and more. Things he'd hidden. Secrets he was keeping."

He turned to the locker, picked up the spiral-bound notebook, and thumbed through the pages like he'd done it before.

"He was meticulous," Matteo murmured. "Always writing. Always watching."

Jasper stared down at the floor. "He wasn't one of us."

"No," Matteo said. "But he really wanted to be."

Camille suddenly remembered the look on Leo's face in those photos. The way he hovered at the edges, always smiling just a little too hard. Wanting so badly to belong.

"He died because they rejected him," Matteo said. "Or because he got too close."

Selena stepped forward. "What do we do now?"

Matteo looked up at her. "Now you can all stop pretending none of this matters. And you make your friends tell the truth."

Jasper's expression darkened. "What if none of us know the whole truth?"

"Then you'd better find it," Matteo said, stepping back toward the door. "Before whoever is trying to silence you wins for good."

And with that, he left the room, closing the door behind him with a final, echoing click.

15

FIRE AND GLASS

A shadow of the storm returned just after dusk. Not with the chaos of its predecessor, no sharp thunderclaps or jagged lightning bolts crashing down, but with a slow, rumbling menace, like something old stirring beneath the skin of the world. The clouds pressed low, the sky thick and angry. And the heat, far from breaking, only grew heavier.

Rain came in waves, lashing the windows in uneven bursts. The glass panels rattled in their frames. In the east wing, a loose shutter thudded over and over against the crumbling stone, like a heartbeat just slightly off rhythm.

Inside the villa, the walls seemed to shrink. Every corridor darker. Every breath heavier. They'd gathered again in the dining room. Matteo had summoned them. Not by force, but with a quiet authority no one dared defy.

Camille sat at the long table, her fingers pressed to the dark wood. The surface was sticky from the heat, and her palms had started to sweat. She could feel the folded coroner's report inside her notebook like a ticking clock, pulsing with quiet urgency. She hadn't shared it with the whole group yet, but she wondered if that moment approaching.

Jasper sat beside her, his posture rigid, his jaw set. He looked older than he had a week ago, wearier. His shirt was rumpled and sweat darkened the collar. He kept adjusting the sleeves like he couldn't get comfortable in his own skin.

At the head of the table, Soren sat with his usual detached composure, swirling wine in a glass with idle precision. He hadn't said much since that morning, but his silence was loaded now. Watchful.

Rowan stood by the tall windows, her arms crossed over her chest. A strand of hair clung to her cheek. Her face was drawn, haunted. She looked like someone preparing to step into a fire.

Mara entered last. Her dress was damp from rain and clung to her frame. Her eyes were ringed with fatigue, but her chin was lifted in that way she always did. Like defiance was the only thing holding her together.

Alba slipped in behind her, settling into the shadows by the wall. Matteo already stood there, silent and still, his arms crossed like a sentinel. No one spoke at first. Until Jasper did.

"We need to talk. All of us." His voice was rough and strained, but firmer than usual.

Soren smirked. "That's all we've been doing lately, isn't it?"

"No," Jasper said. "We've been circling. And lying. And pretending."

A tense silence followed. The rain intensified.

Camille glanced around the table. "We all know what this is. We were all called back here together. Now two more of our friends are dead. And someone, maybe even someone in this room, is responsible. If we keep pretending Leo's death was an accident, or bad luck, and that Noel and Max are some twisted coincidence. Well, we're all going to end up dead."

"Or," Soren said lazily, "We're just playing right into someone's plan. Someone who wants us to turn on each other."

"And who would that be?" Selena asked, her voice sharp. "Because it wasn't Noel. And it wasn't Max."

"Unless it *was* Max," Soren said, shrugging. "Maybe he started this because his guilt finally cracked him. Maybe he left the notes. Then offed himself to make us look guilty too."

"That's disgusting," Camille said. "He was murdered."

"We don't know that."

Rowan turned away from the window. "Yes, we do."

All eyes shifted to her.

She moved slowly to the center of the room, rain still tapping behind her like fingers on glass. Her voice was quiet, but unshakable.

"I've been keeping something from all of you. And I'm done."

Mara tensed. "Rowan..."

Rowan held up a hand. "Don't."

She looked to each face in the room. "It was the night of the last game. The final Confession Night."

"Leo was blindfolded," she went on. "Tied to the chair. Everyone laughing. Everyone drunk. Max was leading it, wasn't he? Pushing him. Humiliating him. Then Leo said something that made Max go quiet. Something about knowing the truth. And Max... changed. He shoved him. Hard."

The room fell still.

"The chair tipped. Leo hit the floor. His head hit the edge of the table. He started crying, saying he couldn't see straight."

Jasper swallowed hard. "And then?"

"Max dragged him out," Rowan said. "Said he'd help. But Max never came back. I found Leo in the kitchen, cleaning the blood off his head, but he was okay. He said Max had gone to bed."

Camille felt her chest tighten. "So, he hit his head before the fall from the cliff. That makes sense. Did no one go and check on Max?"

"We were drunk," Rowan said. "We thought it was just more drama. But later... well, by then it was too late."

Mara's voice cracked. "You're remembering it wrong."

"No," Rowan said. "I'm not."

"You're rewriting history," Soren snapped. "You always do this. You make yourself the martyr."

"No, I'm not. I saw you and Max later that night. Coming back from the cliffs," Rowan said flatly.

Soren stood. "That's a lie."

"I saw you," Rowan said.

Silence. Thick and searing.

Soren leaned forward. "That's convenient, isn't it? Your word against mine and a man who's already dead."

"I'm telling the truth," Rowan said.

Jasper turned to her. "Why didn't you tell me? Or the police?"

"Because I thought he fell," she said, her voice breaking slightly. "I had no reason to think otherwise. And if I told the police you'd been up there, it would only make things worse."

"You were right," Soren said darkly. "It has."

Camille looked around the room. "What if this isn't just about Leo?"

Everyone froze.

"What if someone else knew what Leo knew? What he was threatening to tell everyone."

Camille's heart pounded as she said it, knowing how dangerous threatening to expose this truth could be.

Rowan's voice dropped. "We need to stop looking for shadows and start owning what we did. The part all of us who were here played."

Soren exhaled sharply. Camille watched him closely. And in that moment, for just a short breath, he looked afraid. The lights flickered. Then held. Outside, thunder cracked. Glass shuddered in the frames and upstairs, somewhere in the east wing, a door slammed. Hard.

The argument was still hanging in the air, sharp, tense, and unfinished, when the sky cracked open. It began with a flicker. Just a ripple of movement beyond the tall windows, something fast, arcing through the night like a comet on fire.

A sudden, blinding flash lit the entire eastern side of the villa. Then came the sound: a single, concussive *boom* that shook the floor and rattled the wine glasses still sitting half-drunk on the table. The gas tanks that ran the heating system had just been struck by lightning.

The conservatory exploded. Glass shattered in every direction, raining inward like a storm of razors. A fireball bloomed outward in a roar of heat and smoke, licking the arched hallway, illuminating it in violent orange. The windows pulsed and cracked, the air pressure in the room changing so suddenly it knocked Camille backward.

She hit the stone floor hard, her ears ringing. The heat was immediate, the old wood of the villa catching fire like a dragon exhaling into the corridors of the house.

For a second, there was only the cacophony of cracking wood, falling beams, and shattering glass. Then: screams.

Rowan was shouting Selena's name. Jasper pulled himself upright, blood on his temple from a flying shard.

Camille's head spun. She forced herself up to her knees. The eastern hallway was already filled with smoke, curling in thick, serpentine waves.

"Selena!" Rowan screamed again, her voice high and splintering.

"She went to get wine!" Mara cried, staggering up from behind a toppled chair, eyes wide with horror. "She would have been coming back through the conservatory!"

Matteo didn't wait. He was already sprinting through the doorway, throwing his shoulder into the half-open door that led toward the glass corridor. The heat slammed into him like a wall.

"Stay back!" he shouted over his shoulder.

No one listened.

Camille followed him, only for a few feet, but far enough to see what he was running toward. The conservatory was an inferno. Where once there had been elegant whitewashed arches and a glass ceiling revealing stars and sea beyond, there was now a gaping maw of fire and smoke. Flames danced along the beams like they were feeding on memory itself. The floor was littered with the remains of furniture and broken glass.

And in the center of it all, collapsed and unmoving, was Selena.

She had been flung across the floor. Her arm bent at an unnatural angle, her leg pinned beneath a section of a collapsed beam. One side of her face was streaked with blood. Shards of glass protruded from her shoulder, but her chest still rose and fell in shallow, rapid breaths.

Camille's heart seized.

"Stay back!" Matteo bellowed as she started forward. "It's not stable!"

He was already there, though, grabbing Selena's limp body beneath her arms, lifting her with a strength that didn't match his frame. The fire crept closer. Glass cracked and dropped from the iron supports above, shattering just inches from his legs.

He staggered back through the arch, smoke curling around

him, Selena slumped in his arms, blood trailing behind them on the floor.

"Move!" he barked as he crossed back into the dining room. Jasper and Rowan scrambled to pull back chairs and clear a space. Matteo laid Selena down on the tile, his breath heaving. Camille dropped beside her.

"She's alive!"

"But barely," Matteo said, checking her pulse, then beginning to pull the largest shards of glass from her shoulder. "We need clean cloth, for pressure, go! Quickly!"

Alba was already at the doorway, her apron flung aside, bringing a wet towel and strips of linen. Her face was ghost-pale, but her hands were steady. She knelt and took over, pressing the towel against Selena's bleeding side.

"We need a doctor," Rowan gasped, voice shaking.

"There is no doctor," Alba said. "There's only us."

Soren stood apart from them all, as if untouched by the chaos. His wine glass still sat on the table, intact. He hadn't moved since the explosion.

"We have to get help," Jasper said, standing. "We'll carry her. Hike out through the olive groves."

"In the dark?" Matteo said sharply. "With smoke in your lungs, no supplies. You'll all be dead by morning."

Camilla looked back at the smoldering wreck of the conservatory, and something strange caught her eye. She pointed to the archway leading into the conservatory corridor, now blackened, scorched at the edges. Something glinted on the far wall, half-hidden by smoke and soot.

She stepped toward it carefully, coughing into her sleeve. As she got closer, the shape became clear. A dagger. Long, ancient-looking, the hilt curved and dark with age. It had been driven deep into the plaster wall, pinning something beneath it: a piece of paper, burnt at the corners.

Camille ripped it free, her heart in her throat. The message was scrawled in thick black ink:

TRUTH BURNS. LIES ROT. LET IT ALL FALL DOWN.

She turned slowly. The room behind her was filled with smoke, fear, and silence. She held up the note. But no one spoke.

Rowan knelt beside Selena again, brushing damp hair from her temple. "She doesn't deserve this."

"None of us do," Camille said.

Mara folded her arms across her chest. Her hands were shaking, and her face had gone pale beneath the smudged makeup. "Well, it's never been about getting what any of us deserve, has it?"

"Maybe it's time," Matteo said.

They turned to him. He was looking at the note. At the dagger. His eyes were unreadable. Soren finally spoke.

"If you ask me, this doesn't feel like revenge anymore. It feels like some kind of purification."

"What does that mean?" Camille asked.

"It means someone thinks they're righteous," he said. "That they're doing something holy. Cleansing the rot."

Rowan shook her head. "Or they just want us to suffer."

Camille studied Soren. The way he stood so still. The way he hadn't run. Hadn't flinched when the strike hit. And beside him, Mara, hugging herself, her eyes darting toward him, not quite meeting his gaze.

A flicker of realization crept in. Camille took a step back. They were aligned, the two of them. Not overtly. Not openly. But she saw it now. The shared silences. The exchanged looks. The glances when no one else was watching. They had a secret.

And maybe it was one they shared.

"Why are you so calm?" she asked suddenly, staring at Soren.

He raised an eyebrow. "Excuse me?"

"You haven't asked how Selena is. You haven't moved. You haven't said one word about the fact the house just exploded."

He smiled faintly. "I've learned not to panic. That's all."

But his voice was far too smooth.

Jasper cut in quickly. "We're wasting time. Someone needs to get help. Before she dies, too."

16

THE PACT

The power came back with a groan. Lights snapped on with a faint crackle overhead, casting long, pale beams through the smoke-stained corridors. The sconces in the hallway buzzed softly. One of the chandeliers in the lounge flickered uncertainly, throwing fractured shadows across the gilded ceiling. Somewhere deeper in the house, a mechanical hum stirred—an ancient refrigerator, maybe, or the water pump stuttering awake after hours of silence.

But the light brought no relief. If anything, it sharpened the edges of what had already broken.

The heat hadn't lifted. Instead, it had deepened and was now heavy with the metallic tang of smoke, the acid sting of scorched wood, the coppery trace of blood. The fire was out, but the air still tasted like ruin.

Selena remained unconscious in one of the guest bedrooms, her pale skin now made ghostly under the electric light. Her face was slack with exhaustion. A dressing of gauze wrapped her temple, already stained rust-brown. Her breathing was shallow but steady, and one hand curled faintly at her side as though still gripping something unseen.

Alba had not left her side. She sat in a straight-backed chair by the bed, her apron still streaked with soot and blood, her hands folded tight in her lap. A bowl of cold water sat beside her, a rag resting within. Every so often, she dabbed Selena's forehead and whispered something too soft to hear.

Elsewhere in the villa, the rest of them gathered in the lounge.

The room was wide and grand, with high vaulted ceilings and furniture that spoke of another era: velvet chairs, a cracked leather chaise, oil portraits that stared down from shadowy frames. Rain traced slow lines down the windows like fingers dragging across glass.

Jasper sat hunched forward on the settee, his white shirt wrinkled and damp at the collar. His brow was furrowed, a smudge of soot still clinging to one temple, his hair stuck to his forehead.

Across from him, Camille curled into an armchair, legs tucked beneath her. Her skin still bore faint streaks of ash; one wrist was bandaged from a shard of glass. Her eyes, rimmed with exhaustion, hadn't left the screen in nearly an hour. Her usually neat hair was knotted back in a bun, strands clinging to her neck with sweat.

By the window, Rowan paced slowly, barefoot. Her hem was darkened with soot and rain, her arms wrapped around herself in a gesture that was less about warmth than protection. Her nails, bitten to the quick, tapped absently against her forearm.

Mara stood off to the side, not fully in the circle of light. Her silk blouse was rumpled, her mascara smeared beneath one eye. A single drop of blood stained her sleeve, a remnant from Selena's evacuation. She held a glass of whiskey untouched, her posture like a dancer caught in freeze-frame. She looked poised, but brittle.

Soren lounged in one of the high-backed chairs, legs

crossed, one arm draped lazily across the armrest. He looked untouched by the night, his clothes pristine, his cufflinks gleaming. But Camille had noticed earlier the way his hand trembled slightly when he thought no one was looking.

No one spoke at first. They didn't need to. The fire hadn't just damaged the conservatory, it had scorched something in each of them. The room was thick with the smoke of suspicion. Of things left unsaid. Finally, Jasper broke the silence. His voice was hoarse.

"She could have died."

His words fell flat, as if spoken in a language the others no longer spoke. Rowan flinched, stopping mid-pace.

Camille shifted. "She still might," she said quietly.

No one argued.

"She was just getting wine," Renata whispered, her voice frayed. "That's all. Just wine."

The silence that followed was heavy. It was Camille who finally moved. She reached beside her chair and picked up the old laptop they'd pulled from Max's locked box. The one Matteo had forced open with quiet precision. The machine was dusty and slow, but the files on it... They'd spoken volumes.

Camille passed the laptop to Jasper, who opened a file folder marked "Correspondence from July 2015."

"Look at this," he said.

He turned the screen toward the others. Rows of emails stretched down the display, most dated nearly a decade ago. At first, they seemed benign. A bunch of school records, university admin threads. But one exchange stood out: short, encrypted, deliberately buried.

Soren's name on the sender line. Max's on the reply.

Subject: "The Problem with words."

Camille read aloud.

"We need to make sure the committee sees it our way. Can you plant the draft in Leo's folder?"

A few lines down:

"Already done. I'll handle the whispers. You handle the 'proof.' This ends with him gone."

And then:

"If anyone asks, he plagiarized from my thesis. I'll back it up. Just make sure the files are corrupted enough that he can't prove otherwise."

No one moved. Rowan sank slowly into the chair beside Camille. Soren stared, slack jawed.

"That's fake. It has to be," he said, darkly.

"It's not," Camille said. "Max encrypted it. But not well enough."

"You tried to destroy him," Rowan whispered.

Soren offered a humorless smile. "I protected what mattered."

"What mattered to you," Jasper said. "You sabotaged his degree You tried to make sure he'd be kicked out. And all he did was protect you. He took the hit, so that you could carry on with your lies."

"He wasn't safe," Soren said. "He was obsessive. Manipulative. You don't know the things he said. The threats he made."

"He was a teenager," Camille snapped. "And you hurt him. You destroyed him. All he wanted was to be your friend. You just hated that he was smarter than you."

Mara turned her face away.

Camille stared at her. "You knew."

"I didn't," she said. Then, softer, "Not at first. And not all of it."

"What did he say to you?" Rowan asked.

Mara's eyes closed. "He told me he loved me. He said... he

said unless I agreed to be with him, he'd tell them all what he'd found."

Jasper frowned. "And what had he found?"

Mara shook her head. "He wouldn't say. He just smiled like he knew how the story ended."

Soren stood. "We're not going to solve this tonight."

"No," Camille said, rising too. "But we can start being honest."

Soren met her gaze. "Honesty's dangerous."

"Lying's worse."

The overhead light flickered once. Then steadied. From down the hall, the sound of a door creaking open. All of them turned toward the sound. Alba appeared in the doorway.

Her face was pale, her apron damp. Her voice was quiet—but filled with weight.

"She's gone."

They stood in unison. Camille's pulse thundered in her ears. They'd been waiting for news. But not this news. Camille was already running. Jasper pushed off from the sofa, following Alba with heavy steps. But Rowan remained seated. Still. Frozen. Her heart pounded. Not just from fear. From something more insidious. Memory.

Because while they'd all been waiting for Selena to come round, deep down, Rowan had known she wouldn't. She wasn't the first innocent victim of this villa's malice. And the story didn't begin with Leo's death. It didn't begin that summer. It started the summer before, in a study hall that reeked of coffee, secrets, and ambition.

She could still feel the heavy air of the library archives, the scent of worn paper and mildew-soaked velvet curtains. The way the shadows stretched between the tall stacks like arms reaching for something they'd once held.

She had found Leo there often. He was always hunched over,

scribbling obsessively in a lined notebook. His hair fell into his face, and he'd barely look up when someone passed. He was brilliant. Unnervingly so. Professors had begun to talk about him. He quoted things no one remembered reading. Corrected visiting lecturers. Challenged Soren in seminars with a polite but surgical precision that made other people squirm. Made Soren snarl.

And he had an eye for things that were broken. And that was the problem. He didn't just notice errors, he exposed them. Lecturers recycling theses. Department favoritism. Misattributed citations. He didn't do it maliciously, not at first. But there was something relentless in the way he sought truth. Like he couldn't help it. Like it was an addiction.

One day, he walked into the student union with a USB drive and a knowing smile.

"I found something," he said to Max.

Rowan had been there. Sitting with them. Watching from across the table, her coffee growing cold. Leo had that bright, amused look in his eyes.

Max had laughed. "What kind of something?"

"An old draft," Leo said casually. "A thesis. The one Soren submitted his second year."

Rowan remembered the exact moment Max went still.

Leo leaned forward. "It's nearly identical to the one Ben Perri published last year."

Max's face had paled. Rowan hadn't understood at first. She thought Leo was bluffing. He wasn't.

Over the next week, whispers started in the faculty offices. Someone had submitted an anonymous tip. There were murmurs about academic misconduct. A review committee. Soren's name began to circulate. Quietly, at first. Carefully. Nothing official. Then, one night, Rowan heard voices from outside her door. Max and Soren. Their tones sharp. Furious. Panicked.

"Do you want to lose everything?" Soren hissed. "Do you know what my family will do if this comes out?"

Max had said something about damage control. About flipping the narrative. About getting rid of Ben… And something about making Leo look unstable.

And suddenly, things changed.

Rumors spread again. But this time about Leo. That he'd stolen papers. That he falsified citations. That he was trying to take others down to elevate himself. Professors began to watch him with unease instead of admiration. And Ben, who'd been on the edge of their group, and who'd always been quiet and studious, disappeared. Soren said he'd had a family crisis. Max said he'd had a breakdown. No one questioned it. And then it was Leo's turn.

Rowan remembered the day Leo found out. He stood at the base of the campus chapel steps, holding a letter in his hand. It was a formal notice of academic review. He looked… betrayed.

"It's not enough to be smart," he told her. "You have to be quiet and pick your friends wisely."

She didn't know what to say. So, she said nothing. And the guilt of that silence still echoed in her bones. Later that week, Leo stopped coming to lectures.

Then came the invitation to the villa.

And with it, a fragile hope. Leo's belief that maybe, if they came, if he played their game, if he smiled and shared toasts and secrets under the summer sun, he could claw his way back into the group. Into control.

But by then, they'd already decided he didn't belong. Not just because he knew too much. But because he made them feel small.

And now, all these years later, with Selena lying pale in the guest room and smoke staining the walls, Rowan finally saw the whole picture. Not just of the night Leo died. But the rot that had started before that. The thing they'd tried to bury under heat and wine and time.

And the part of herself that had helped bury it.

She stood slowly. She didn't need Selena to tell her what happened because she already knew.

~

Rowan didn't follow the others to Selena's bedside. She stayed in the lounge, her hand resting on the scorched back of the velvet armchair, the silence inside her now louder than the fire had been. Camille returned first, her face pale and jaw tight, and stood in the doorway, waiting for Rowan to look up.

"She's gone," Camille said, voice low, her face streaked with tears.

Rowan nodded once. But she didn't move. She couldn't. Camille stepped into the room and Jasper entered behind her.

"Maybe Alba is right. Maybe the house wants us to tell the truth or die hiding," he said, grimly.

Rowan turned to face them both. The light from the chandelier cut harshly across her face, catching the sweat beading at her temples, the strain pulling at her eyes. Her voice shook, but not from fear. From something deeper. Resignation.

"I was told to stay quiet," she said. "But this has gone too far."

Camille stared at her. "Who told you to stay quiet, and what about?"

Rowan looked toward the doorway. Soren stood there. Leaning against the frame with deliberate ease, as if he'd known his name would arrive before he did.

He smiled faintly. "You say that like it was a threat."

Rowan didn't answer. Jasper moved beside Camille, his expression darkening.

"Was it?"

Soren pushed off the doorframe and stepped into the room. "Rowan made her own choice. We all did. No one held a gun to anyone's head."

"You held something worse," Camille said. "Power. Fear."

Soren's jaw flexed. "Leo made choices too."

"He was a *kid*," Camille snapped. "He was isolated, outnumbered, manipulated."

"He was a *liability*," Soren said, louder now. "A narcissist with a savior complex. Always watching, always calculating. He wanted to expose everyone. He *enjoyed* it. You think he was innocent? You think he didn't know exactly what he was doing?"

Camille stepped forward. "He was *murdered*."

"Don't say it like that."

"Why not? Because it forces you to admit the truth?"

Soren's voice cracked. "He wasn't a victim. He was a grenade. And you're all acting like he wasn't the one who pulled the pin."

The words hit the room like a detonation. Jasper didn't wait. He lunged. His fist connected with Soren's jaw with a sickening *crack*. Soren stumbled back, crashing into the antique side table, the lamp on top toppling and smashing at his feet.

"Jesus Christ!" Mara shouted, rushing into the room.

Camille stepped between them before Jasper could lunge again. "Enough!"

Soren straightened slowly, blood blooming at the corner of his mouth. His eyes burned, not with pain, but rage.

"You think you're better than me?" he growled. "You didn't stop it. None of you did."

"You *started* it," Jasper said, voice shaking. "You, Max and Mara. Always creating the environment for fear and loathing."

Soren wiped the blood from his lip and turned to Rowan. "You're quiet now. How convenient."

Rowan stared at him. "I kept your secret. You made me believe I was protecting everyone. That Leo would destroy the group if he spoke."

"You were protecting everyone," he said simply.

Camille's voice cut through the rising storm. "You mean: he would've exposed the fact that your thesis was plagiarized. That Max doctored files to cover you. That Mara seduced him to keep him quiet."

Mara froze. "That's not fair."

Camille turned. "Isn't it?"

"I didn't seduce anyone," Mara said, voice trembling. "I was trying to protect us."

Camille stared at her. "Protect who, exactly?"

The question hung in the air like smoke. From the hallway, slow and uneven footsteps echoed, coming closer. Alba appeared, her expression unreadable.

"We need to move her body, too," she said softly. "Whenever you're ready." And then she was gone.

The silence that followed was dense with fury. Rowan sank into the chair, her head in her hands. Jasper stood, fists still clenched, his breathing ragged. Mara crossed to the shattered lamp and picked up the largest piece of glass, running her thumb across the jagged edge, then stopped.

"This isn't going to end in an apology circle," she said, voice low.

Jasper laughed bitterly. "No, it's more likely to end in a morgue."

She looked at him, eyes narrowed, laying the glass shard carefully on the table.

17

THE LOVERS' DIVIDE

The upper terrace was soaked in moonlight and silence, a vast plane of mottled limestone still steaming faintly from the evening rain. Water pooled in shallow dips between the tiles, reflecting fractured images of the moon and the towering cypress trees that lined the perimeter. It was as if the villa itself had taken a deep, uneasy breath and was now holding it.

The balustrade that rimmed the terrace stood cold and damp under the silver light, its carved stone balusters gleaming slick with rain. A faint breeze stirred the wet vines trailing down from the pergola overhead, rustling the leaves in a whispering language that didn't comfort so much as unsettle. The scent of lemon blossoms hung faintly in the air, mingled with ash and salt and the faintest trace of something sulfur as an echo of the lightning still embedded in the stone.

Camille stepped out into this quiet expanse with bare feet, her soles pressing against the warm, uneven stone. The quiet was jarring after the last few hours of panic, accusations, and smoke. Her breath formed a small ghost in the air before her, though the night was not truly cold, only heavy, dense with the tension that hadn't been dispelled by rain.

She wasn't surprised to find Soren already there.

He stood by the far edge of the terrace, leaning against the damp railing with the easy arrogance of someone who never feared falling. A tumbler of amber liquid glowed faintly in his hand, catching the moonlight like a false gemstone. The wind moved through his hair, and despite the chaos of the day, he looked eerily composed—shirt unwrinkled, cufflinks still in place, as if untouched by the fire, the screams, the smoke that had soaked into everyone else's skin.

"You followed me," he said, without looking.

"You left a room full of accusations," Camille replied. "What did you think I'd do?"

He turned slowly, lifting the glass in a casual salute. "I thought you'd come looking for a villain."

"I didn't have to look far."

Soren tilted his head, and his smile was razor-thin. "Still playing detective, then?"

Camille took a step closer, her arms crossed tightly over her chest. "You're not denying any of it?"

"I'm just tired," he said, turning back to the sea. "Tired of guilt masquerading as justice. Tired of ghosts dragging their chains through every conversation. We were children. We made so many mistakes."

Camille's voice was cold. "Murder's not a mistake."

Soren's jaw twitched, and his eyes flicked to her with something sharper than annoyance. "Leo wasn't murdered."

"You and Max tried to destroy him before he even arrived," she said, taking another step. Her feet splashed lightly in a shallow puddle, the sound oddly loud in the silence.

"He was unstable anyway," Soren said, his voice hardening. "He wanted chaos. He didn't want to belong. He wanted to be better than us. He wanted to win."

Camille's stare didn't waver. "So you made sure he never had the chance."

Soren exhaled, a slow and calculated breath that steamed in the cooler night air. He sipped from his glass, then leaned forward to place it gently on the railing. "You're emotional. Understandable. This place brings it out of people. But you're letting it cloud your judgment."

"No," Camille said. "You're trying to gaslight me."

A gust of wind moved across the terrace then, rustling the vines and sweeping a scattering of fallen leaves across the stone. In the distance, the sea churned softly against the base of the cliffs, quiet now, but restless.

"You've been unravelling since the minute we all arrived," Soren said. "Digging through drawers, whispering with Matteo, dragging Rowan into your little theories."

"I'm trying to keep people alive."

"You're trying to rewrite a story that already ended."

Camille had just opened her mouth to reply when a voice cut through the darkness.

"She's right to, though."

Jasper.

He emerged from the shadows of the terrace entrance, his face streaked with the remnants of smoke and exhaustion. His shirt was wrinkled and damp, sleeves rolled to the elbows. He looked like he hadn't slept in days, but his eyes were sharp and focused.

"I've looked through everything on that old laptop," he said.

Soren's smile faltered.

"There were messages," Jasper continued. "Deleted ones. Between you and Max. You thought they were gone. They weren't."

Camille's breath hitched. The cold stone beneath her feet suddenly felt miles away.

"We found enough to prove a coordinated attack from both of you," Jasper said. "Requests for silence. Instructions to orchestrate his silence."

Soren's face changed. The casual charm drained from his expression, replaced by something harder and sharper.

"You think that means anything?" he said slowly. "You're trying to make ghosts scream louder than facts."

"You lied," Camille said. "You lied about everything."

And then Soren's voice dropped. "You want someone to blame, Camille? Maybe look in the mirror."

"What?"

"You're the one who brought out the yearbook. Who knew where to dig. Who found every note and every photo at the exact right time. You think we don't see what this really is?"

He stepped closer, and the chill Camille felt had nothing to do with the wind.

"You weren't part of our circle. Not then. You arrived after the blood had already dried, and you've spent every minute trying to get to the bottom of what happened."

"That's enough," Jasper said, stepping between them.

But Soren's eyes were wild now. "What if she's the one who sent the letters? What if she's been behind all of this?"

"You're grasping," Camille spat. "Trying to deflect the blame."

"No," Soren said, "I'm surviving."

Rowan stepped out into the moonlight. Her eyes were wet. Her shoulders hunched. But her voice was steady.

"None of this matters," she said softly. "Unless we survive the night."

A hush fell across the terrace. Below them, waves broke softly against stone. Somewhere deep inside the house, a door creaked. And high above, a cloud passed away from the moon.

Camille stared at Soren as if seeing him clearly for the first time. The light from the moon had sharpened every line of his face. His cheekbones seemed cut from marble, his smile a flicker of something that had once resembled charm. But not now. Now it looked like armor. A mask. And beneath it, she saw what she hadn't dared acknowledge until this moment: the glint of someone who didn't just lie, but who shaped the lie, crafted it into a weapon, and handed it to you with a kiss.

The air around them thickened. Not with heat anymore, but something else. Something colder. Camille's breath came shallow as the realization crystallized. He hadn't encouraged her to come here because he needed her. He'd brought her because he *needed someone*. A distraction. A shield. A possible scapegoat.

"You knew," she said softly, the words tasting like acid. "You knew this trip could go wrong."

Soren blinked. "Excuse me?"

She took a step back, her voice growing steadier. "You brought me here because I didn't know the history. Because I wouldn't see what the others already suspected. You thought I'd be grateful, that I'd defend you. I'll go if you go, you said. Now I see you just needed cover."

His smile didn't waver, but something in his eyes shifted. Just slightly. "You're being paranoid."

"No," she whispered. "I'm finally seeing straight."

He approached her, slow and measured, as if trying not to spook a wild animal. "Camille. You're upset. Everything's been so intense. Selena, Max, Noel, the storms, the stress... It's all making you see patterns that aren't there."

The softness in his voice made her flinch. The condescension was laced with a venom she could finally taste.

"You're doing it again," she said. "You're trying to twist it. To make me question myself. But I'm done doubting my instincts."

She turned and walked toward the far edge of the terrace, needing space, air, anything to keep from screaming. The wind had picked up again, sweeping her hair across her face in fine, salt-heavy strands. Below, the cliffs loomed, jagged and unforgiving. The sea churned in slow, seething movements, lit silver by the moon.

She had felt so close to him once. Trusted him. Even admired him. But what had she really known? Every tender moment. Every long gaze. Every time he'd touched her face and told her she was the only one who saw him. Had all of it had been carefully placed? Not affection. *Calculation.*

Camille pressed her palms against the stone railing. It was slick, still damp from earlier rain, and cold despite the warmth of the day still lingering in the terrace tiles.

She didn't turn when she heard him approach behind her.

"I didn't bring you here to hurt you," he said.

She let out a bitter laugh. "You didn't bring me here to protect me, either."

"I didn't know it would go this far, but I didn't set this up."

"Didn't you?" She turned, eyes blazing. "You knew Leo died under suspicious circumstances. You knew the truth about the tapes. You knew Max had enemies. You knew how fragile all of this was, and you still said we should come anyway."

He opened his mouth, but she didn't let him speak.

"Because if something went wrong," she continued, "you could point to me. The outsider. The new girl who just *happened* to find all the evidence."

"That's not fair."

"No," she said. "It's not. But it's true."

For a moment, the only sound was the rustling of the vines and the distant crash of a wave.

Soren stepped closer, voice low and urgent. "I didn't want any of this to happen. I just wanted it to go away. For the past to stay buried."

Camille stepped back. "You can't bury what you never owned. You can't run from what you never faced."

He looked at her, and for a fraction of a second, something flickered in his expression. Was that regret? Panic? Or was it just another layer of performance?

She would never know.

"I'm done," she said. "With this. With you. With all of you."

"You're overreacting."

That did it.

She stepped in close, her voice shaking, not with fear, but fury. "Don't you *dare* tell me how to feel. Don't you *dare* reduce this to my emotions."

Soren flinched slightly, and the illusion cracked once more.

"You don't get to hide behind your logic and charm anymore. You've been playing chess with real people's lives, and I won't be another piece on your board."

She turned and walked toward the staircase leading back into the villa.

"Camille..." he called after her.

But she didn't look back. Each step she took was like shedding skin. The weight of him, of his voice, his touch, his web of words. It all fell away with the steady rhythm of her feet on the stone.

When she reached the door, she paused to steady herself. She looked out one last time across the terrace. Soren stood alone now, his expression unreadable in the dark. The wind tugged at his shirt, the fabric rippling like a flag of surrender that hadn't quite been raised.

"You're more dangerous than I thought," she said softly. "And not just because of what you did, but because of what you convinced me not to see."

Then she stepped through the door and let it close behind her. The click of the latch was sharp and final.

Inside the villa, the hallway stretched quiet and empty. The scent of burned wood and lemon oil lingered in the air. Faint candlelight flickered from sconces. The whole house felt like it had shifted, just by a few degrees, but enough to throw everything off balance.

Camille stood there for a long moment, letting her heartbeat slow. She had lost something up there on the terrace, her illusions, her closeness to Soren, but she had gained some clarity too. She was on her own here. But at least now, she *knew*.

18

CHARLOTTE'S SILENCE

Morning crept into the villa like it didn't belong there. Dew glistened on the windowsills, refracting pale light into fractured lines across the marble floors. The sky above the cliffs was cloudless, a radiant blue, but the sea still churned, restless and thick, as if it remembered what the night had taken.

From outside, the villa looked calm again. Elegant. Untouched. But within, its bones ached with secrets. The library was still locked. Matteo had locked it himself that morning, turning the key with a quiet finality, sealing off the place where too many questions had surfaced too quickly. The dusty shelves, the server panel, the half-burned photograph album—none of it could be trusted anymore.

Camille stood in the west wing corridor, staring through the open shutters. The garden below steamed under the returning heat, the wet stone paths dark and glistening. Somewhere nearby, a cicada clicked to life in the lemon trees. She felt something behind her before she heard it.

"Charlotte," she said without turning.

The woman froze in the corridor, her soft shoes silent on the tile, but her posture tight, like a deer in the crosshairs. She looked as if she'd tried to sleep but hadn't made it far. Her eyes were puffy and red-rimmed, her shoulders hunched under a too-large linen cardigan. A black hair tie drooped from her wrist. Her hands were clenched into fists.

Camille turned, slowly. "Will you walk with me?"

Charlotte didn't move at first. Then, with the hesitancy of someone approaching a grave, she nodded.

They walked in silence, barefoot across warm tiles, past empty rooms and echoing hallways, until they came to the secluded side veranda tucked beneath a tangle of bougainvillea. The stone bench there was cool and shaded, the air scented faintly with rosemary and dust.

Camille sat. Charlotte remained standing.

"I know you saw something," Camille said gently. "I think you've been carrying it a long time."

Charlotte's eyes flicked toward the sea. "I thought if I stayed quiet, it would disappear. That someone else would come forward. That someone else would tell the truth."

Camille waited.

"I didn't even mean to be there," Charlotte whispered. "It was late. Everyone was drunk. I'd gone to the kitchen for water. I heard voices... arguing."

She shifted, her hands twitching at her sides. "I thought maybe someone was sick. I followed the noise."

"To where?" Camille asked.

Charlotte hesitated. "The corridor outside the music room. You know the narrow one, behind the tapestries? There's a window overlooking the wine cellar staircase."

Camille nodded, heart beginning to pound.

"I heard Leo first," Charlotte said. "He was shouting. Not angry, but frantic. Like he was trying to stop something. And then I heard him say, 'I have the proof. I know what you did. You can't hide anymore.'"

Camille leaned forward. "He had something?"

Charlotte nodded, eyes distant. "A recording. He said: 'The whole thing's on tape.' He was gripping something in his pocket."

"And who was with him?"

Charlotte exhaled shakily. "Soren. Max. Both of them. Soren looked... blank. Just watching. But Max kept pushing. Laughing. Saying things like 'Who's going to believe you?' and 'You think this'll change anything?'"

Camille's breath caught. She felt a chill despite the warm air.

"You've kept this for years?"

"I was scared," Charlotte admitted. "I spoke to mara about it, and she got so cross with me. She made it clear I wasn't supposed to be involved. And Soren..."

"Soren what?"

Charlotte's lips trembled. "He cornered me. Later that night. Said I'd had too much to drink. That I must have misheard. That my memory was unreliable. Then he smiled. He told me it was better to forget. Safer."

"And you believed him?"

"No," Charlotte said. "But I knew I had no choice. I had to stay quiet."

Camille reached out and took her hand. It was cold and damp with sweat.

"You're not alone anymore," Camille said softly.

But as the breeze shifted through the veranda vines, Camille wasn't so sure. What if that tape was still here somewhere? What would it tell them? What were Soren, Max, and mara hiding from them all, and had it really been damaging enough to kill Leo over.

Camille stretched, her mind frazzled. The summer sun was relentless. It pressed down on the villa with the intensity of an accusation, turning the white stone walls into mirrors of light and trapping the air beneath a glassy dome of heat. The garden paths steamed with the aftermath of the morning's dew, and the citrus trees drooped under the weight of their own fragrance. Insects buzzed low and lazy through the lavender, their hum a background to the uneasy stillness that had settled across the grounds.

Charlotte watched her with wide eyes. "I should've said something. I should've taken the recorder, or said something after Leo fell."

A soft voice interrupted them.

"Camille."

Alba stood in the archway, framed by trailing vines. Her apron was folded neatly over one arm, her face unreadable. But in her other hand, she held a small velvet pouch. The kind used for jewelry, or precious things meant to stay hidden.

Camille crossed to her slowly. "What is it?"

Alba offered the pouch without speaking. Camille took it, heart racing. The weight was unfamiliar. She untied the drawstrings and reached inside. Metal. Crushed. Small. A mini tape recorder.

She looked up sharply. "Where?"

"In the old chimney flue," Alba said. "Behind the bricks. Matteo found it this morning while clearing ash from the hearth in the south drawing room."

Charlotte stepped forward, staring. "That's it. That's the one Leo always had."

Camille's hands shook as she turned the device over. The casing was warped and heat-damaged. The buttons melted slightly. But the cassette inside was old, transparent, but still there.

"Does it still work?" Camille asked.

Alba nodded. "Matteo tested it. Most of the tape is distorted. But the last few seconds survived."

Camille felt her mouth go dry. "What's on it?"

Alba met her gaze evenly. "Come."

They walked together through the villa's now-silent corridors, past the locked library, past the shuttered doors of the wine cellar. The air was thick with sunlight. Dust floated in golden slants through the windows. Outside, the world seemed endless, beautiful, alive.

Inside, it was suffocating.

Matteo's workshop was a cluttered, shadowed room near the garage, he had connected the recorder to an ancient set of speakers. Camille, Charlotte, and Alba stood in silence. Matteo pressed play. A low hiss filled the air. Then Leo's voice.

"If anything happens to me..." His voice cracked. "Tell Matteo. Tell my cousin. Please." Then static. Then silence.

Camille's chest tightened. Leo had known. He'd known who might save him. And he hadn't made it. She looked to Charlotte. Her face was wet now, tears sliding down her cheeks, quiet and unacknowledged.

Camille looked back at the recorder, then at the window beyond, where the sunlight burned through the vines like fire.

"Is there anything else?" she said softly.

"No," Matteo said. "But he wanted me to know the truth and I will find it."

They stood there, the four of them, with the ruined evidence and the ghost of Leo's words still echoing in the warm, golden air.

And above them, somewhere deeper in the villa, the others remained unaware. But not for long. Because this time, the truth wasn't just rising. It was burning.

19

THE FINAL PACT

The dining hall was candlelit again. The long table stretched between them like a bridge no one dared cross. Thick linen runners curled slightly at the edges, frayed from heat and time. Dust glimmered faintly in the candlelight, catching on the tips of old wine glasses, still smudged from the night before. No one had eaten. Silverware sat untouched, plates cold. The scent of rosemary, lemon peel, and charred wood clung to the air.

The candles burned quietly, their flickering reflections trembling in the dark eyes of the people seated around the table. It should have been a gathering of friends. Instead, it looked like a tribunal. Or a wake.

Matteo stood at the head of the table. The tape recorder sat before him, its casing cracked. He had been silent for minutes, his hands flat on either side of the device, as if waiting for one last breath before exhuming the past.

Rowan sat across from him, posture rigid, face pale. Her hair was still damp from a cold shower she hadn't dried properly. Beside her, Jasper leaned forward, arms braced on the table, his knuckles white.

Camille sat to Matteo's right, her stomach a twisted knot, her eyes locked on the machine. She could hear her pulse in her ears. Charlotte was at the far end, folded in on herself, barely visible behind her long cardigan and unspoken grief.

Mara sat beside her, shoulders squared, lips pressed tight. She hadn't spoken since entering the room. But her eyes darted constantly, first to Matteo, then to the recorder, then to Camille, then back again.

Alba hovered in the background, her hands clasped in front of her apron. Her expression was unreadable. Only her eyes betrayed the deep weight of what she knew. Matteo looked around the table.

"I need you to understand," he said. His voice was low, steady. "This doesn't explain everything. But it matters."

He pressed play. The hiss of static. A pause. Then Leo's voice, soft, broken, and full of dread.

"If anything happens to me... tell Matteo. Tell my cousin. Please." Another hiss. The sound of shuffling. Then silence. The tape clicked to a stop. No one moved.

It wasn't long. Barely a breath in the expanse of what they'd lost. But the rawness of it, his voice, still alive in that single moment, cut sharper than any confession.

Camille felt tears prick at the corners of her eyes. She blinked hard and said nothing. Jasper cleared his throat, but the sound cracked in his chest. Charlotte stared down at her hands.

It was Mara who spoke first.

"God," she whispered, then louder, "God, he *sounded* like a child."

"Because he *was*," Rowan said, voice thick.

Mara looked up, eyes wide, wet. "We were children. All of us. We were young and drunk and stupid and scared. That night was chaos. You all know it. Leo wasn't murdered. He slipped. It was dark, we were shouting, no one meant..."

"Stop," Rowan said, her voice a blade.

Mara flinched.

Rowan leaned forward. "Don't do that. Don't soften it with excuses."

Mara's voice broke. "We didn't push him."

"No," Rowan said. "But we let it happen. We stood by while Max lost control. We stood by when Soren told us to lie. And we let Leo die believing no one was on his side."

Jasper spoke, voice low. "And now someone's making sure we don't forget."

The table fell into silence again.

The candle flames guttered slightly in the breeze from the open windows. Outside, the sun had turned harsh again, casting long shadows across the polished floor. The heat was relentless, creeping in through stone and mortar, wrapping around ankles, sticking to the back of necks.

"We need to talk about what comes next," Camille said finally. "Someone's killing us. Three are already dead. Two of them murdered. Who's next? Who's doing this?"

"It could be anyone. It could be Matteo. He's Leo's cousin." Mara asked, her voice defensive, desperate.

Matteo didn't react.

Camille shook her head. "No. I think he's the only one who's actually trying to *help*."

"But then who?" Charlotte whispered.

Mara's eyes darted to Rowan. "What about Alba?"

Alba's expression didn't change.

"I've buried more than one body on this land," she said softly. "But not like that. Not the way Max and Noel died."

A beat of silence.

Camille leaned forward. "We need to face the fact that we're all in danger."

Jasper ran a hand through his hair. "We need a plan. We're cut off, the phone's useless, we don't know who to trust."

"And food is running low," Alba said. "The storeroom is nearly empty. I told you three days ago."

"We're running out of time," Matteo said, his voice dark. "And you're right. Whoever did this wants more than revenge. They want justice on *their* terms."

Camille looked around the table. "Then we have to expose the truth. All of it. No more games. No more secrets."

Mara's laugh was brittle. "You think confessions are going to stop this?"

"No," Camille said. "But lies definitely won't."

The table was silent once more. Only the candles moved, their flames curling like breath, wavering toward the ceiling.

"Then let's start from the beginning," Rowan said. "From confessions night. From the night Leo died."

Everyone looked at Mara and she, for once, didn't look away. The recorder clicked off again, a final punctuation mark to Leo's voice, a whisper from beyond the grave that now hung thick in the air. No one moved. The heat had intensified, a heavy, oppressive weight that seeped into their bones and blurred the edges of the room. The candles sputtered gently as if recoiling from the truth. Outside, the sun loomed low and molten over the cliffs, turning the world into gold and shadow. Mara wiped her hands down her thighs, trying to hide the way they trembled.

Matteo stepped forward from the head of the table, the quiet force of him more imposing than any raised voice.

"That's not enough," he said. "We've all listened. We've heard Leo. But now it's your turn. Each of you have something to say about this. Each of you has a truth to tell."

Rowan raised her head. "What do you mean?"

"I want it written," Matteo said. "In your own hand. A confession."

The word fell like a match in a room full of dry wood.

"A *what*?" Mara spat.

Camille sat upright. "You want us to confess to what happened?"

"To what *really* happened," Matteo said. "No more of this he said, she said. No more shifting blame. No more secrets. I want every one of you to write down what you saw, what you did, what you knew."

"That's insane," Mara said, standing suddenly. "You want evidence? Against ourselves? That could destroy lives!"

"No," Camille said. "We already did that. Ten years ago."

Mara glared at her. "You're not even one of us. You don't get to come in here and play judge."

Camille stood too. "No, I'm not one of you. And thank God. But I am here now, and I've seen what you buried. I've seen what your lies cost. If the police won't reach us in time, then we have to make our own justice. And that starts *now*."

Matteo didn't take his eyes off Mara. "You want to save yourself? Start with the truth."

Mara's jaw clenched. "I won't put anything in writing."

"That says enough," Jasper muttered.

She turned on him. "Don't you dare."

Charlotte flinched at that. The table was a minefield now, and the heat in the room was suffocating, not just from the weather but from the pressure. The weight of the past pressing down like it had nowhere else to go.

Matteo turned to Alba. "We'll need paper. Pens."

Alba nodded once and disappeared through the door.

Camille could feel the shift now. The air of passivity that had hung over them was gone. They were no longer helpless. They were no longer waiting to be punished. They were going to uncover every dark, festering truth, even if it meant destroying themselves in the process.

"What if there's more evidence out there?" Jasper said

suddenly. "There *has* to be. That recorder survived. Who knows what else Leo left behind?"

Camille looked at him. "You're right."

Matteo returned to the head of the table. "We split."

The word sent a fresh ripple through the room.

"One group stays here," he said. "Finishes their confessions. Alba watches over them. No more secrets."

"And the rest?" Rowan asked.

"We search the villa. The land. Every room, every tunnel, every outbuilding. But we do it together."

Charlotte finally spoke. "There's an old cistern behind the west grove. Leo used to say it was haunted."

Jasper nodded. "And the root cellar. We never opened it."

"There's also the chapel attic," Alba said, returning with a leather-bound notebook and a handful of pens. "But the stairs are narrow. One at a time."

Mara sank slowly back into her seat, the blood drained from her face. "This is madness."

"This is *justice*," Camille said.

"Justice doesn't bring back the dead."

"No," Rowan said. "But it might save the living."

They divided quickly.

Matteo, Camille, Charlotte, and Jasper would search the grounds, starting with the cistern and the chapel attic. Rowan, Soren, and Mara would remain behind under Alba's watch to write their accounts.

"No one leaves their group," Matteo warned. "No one disappears."

"Or what?" Mara snapped.

"Or we assume you have something to hide."

A silence settled over them, taut and terrible. Outside, the sun had begun to dip toward the horizon, setting the sea ablaze.

The air thickened with the sharp scent of drying herbs and hot earth. Somewhere, a bird shrieked and then fell silent.

Camille turned to Jasper as they made their way down the corridor toward the gardens.

"Do you think Mara's hiding more?"

He didn't answer for a moment.

Then: "I think we all are."

Behind them, Alba stood in the dining hall, arms folded. She watched the remaining three as they stared at their blank sheets of paper.

Mara didn't touch her pen. Rowan stared at the flame of a candle and said quietly, "We weren't stupid. We were scared. And we let fear kill someone." And this time, no one corrected her.

20

THE CHAPEL

The path to the chapel twisted through the woods like a secret that didn't want to be found.

It was barely more than a deer track now, overgrown with brambles and browned nettles, winding between gnarled olive trees whose shadows seemed to clutch at their ankles. A hot wind moved sluggishly through the canopy above, whispering through dry leaves like gossip passed too late.

The sun was punishing, burning down from above in a cloudless blaze, but here in the woodland hollow, the light turned strange, refracted through branches and misted with the salt-heavy air that drifted up from the cliffs below.

Charlotte could hear her own heartbeat over the crunch of twigs beneath her sandals. Every now and then, Matteo would pause, glance behind him, and continue without a word. He had a direction in mind. She wasn't sure she wanted to arrive.

Then the chapel emerged, abrupt and wrong, as though the trees had birthed it. It slouched at the edge of a cliff, partially hidden by ivy and the rubble of its own decay. One side of the building had caved inward, revealing the skeletal bones of a roof long since consumed by time. Black scorch marks streaked the stone around what had once been stained-glass windows. Fragments of ruby and cobalt still clung to the edges, glinting like embedded shards of accusation.

A twisted iron cross stood half-buried in the dirt before the chapel's door, bent as if by force, or fury, or both.

"Jesus," Jasper muttered behind her. "It looks like something out of a nightmare."

"It's worse up close," Matteo said, and ducked through the arched doorway without hesitation.

Inside, the air changed. It was cooler, yes, but heavier too. Still and silent. As if it hadn't been disturbed in years. A low dampness crept through the stone, carrying the smell of mildew, soot, candlewax and dried flowers long since withered to dust.

They stepped through puddles of shadow.

Broken pews were scattered across the nave, some overturned, others charred black. The altar, once bright marble, had been blackened by flame, its carvings obscured beneath layers of soot and melted wax. Rows of candles, long since burned out, had spilled across the floor in patterns too deliberate to be accidental. The wax had hardened like lava over the flagstones.

On the far wall, faded scrolls still clung under cracked wax seals. And among them, more symbols: the serpent eating its own tail. The same as on Leo's wine labels. Over and over. Sometimes with initials beside them. Sometimes with names that had been scratched away.

Charlotte felt her breath catch in her chest. They fanned out, stepping carefully. Matteo's boots echoed in the silence, the sound sharp against the soft hum of the wind through the ruined beams above. Jasper was the one who found the loose stone.

A hollow clunk beneath his foot drew their attention. Matteo knelt, brushed away the debris, and worked the corner of the flagstone free.

Beneath it: a rusted metal box. Charlotte held her breath as Matteo pulled it free and set it gently atop the scorched altar. Even unopened, it radiated weight. Not just physical, but psychic. Like the pressure in the air before a lightning strike.

Matteo pried open the rusted lock. Inside was a leather-bound journal, its cover warped by time but still intact. A photograph, curling at the edges. And a sealed envelope marked *Alba*, the ink still visible despite the years.

Charlotte picked up the photo with trembling hands.

She recognized them all. Herself, Rowan, Noel, Soren, Mara, Max. And Leo. But Leo's face had been violently scratched out, over and over, until the paper had torn, and behind it, a hole gaped like a wound.

On the back, Leo had scrawled: *The summer we stopped pretending.*

Something inside her buckled. Matteo opened the letter and read aloud.

"If I disappear, it won't be an accident. You were right about them. They play loyalty like a game. They made me believe I was the problem. I wasn't. I just saw too much. They're scared of truth. And scared people are dangerous."

The silence after was unbearable. Charlotte sank onto a collapsed pew. Her breathing was shallow, irregular.

Jasper stepped forward, unsure. "Charlotte?"

She didn't look up.

"I didn't want to protect them," she said at last, voice thin. "That's the truth. I wasn't loyal to anyone. I just wanted to forget."

"Why?"

She looked at the photo again. "Because remembering meant admitting I *let it happen*. Not actively, not violently, but through silence. We stood around while Max tore him down. While Soren whispered lies. While Mara deflected and joked and reminded us that no one would believe Leo anyway."

Her voice cracked.

"Leo was the only one brave enough to say the truth aloud. And we made him pay for it."

She pressed her palm to her mouth, her eyes brimming now, red and raw. "I told myself I didn't know what was coming. That I couldn't stop it. But I did know. And I didn't want to stop it. Because if Leo kept digging, he would've dragged all of us into the light."

She looked up at Matteo.

"I was relieved when he disappeared. Relieved when they found him dead. I didn't question the story. That he'd fallen, or jumped. And that's what I have to live with."

Outside, the sun had dipped behind the cliffs, and the light through the broken roof beams turned from gold to amber to bruised violet.

Matteo didn't say anything. He reached down, closed the lockbox, and held the letter with reverence.

"This isn't the end," he said. "It's the beginning."

And somewhere inside the cracked walls of that forgotten chapel, something shifted. A weight loosened. A silence lifted. But the wind that slithered through the broken stones carried the scent of coming danger.

21

BLOOD AT THE THRESHOLD

Evening settled over the villa like a slow, suffocating breath. The sky above the cliffs had gone from brilliant blue to bruised violet, streaked with ribbons of deep orange that stained the water below like fire bleeding through silk. The sea roared louder now. No longer rhythmic and soothing, but harsh and uneven, crashing against the rocks with the fury of a thing kept too long in silence.

Camille stood in the entry hall, every hair on her arms prickling. The wind had returned, sharp and salt-laden, seeping through cracks in the villa's old stone bones. It carried with it something colder and more metallic. A scent she hadn't noticed before, one that made her throat tighten and her pulse skip. Blood.

She didn't see it yet. But her body had already recognized what her eyes hadn't caught.

She turned toward the massive front doors, and stopped. They were ajar. Just slightly. Earlier, Matteo had closed them with deliberate care, sliding the inner bolt across. Not that it could stop anything, but it had given the illusion of containment. Of control.

Now, one door hung open by a few inches, and from the hallway, the candle flames nearest the entry were dancing wildly in the pull of the breeze.

Camille approached slowly, her feet silent on the marble. The weight of the air pressed against her chest like wet wool. Everything felt just slightly tilted, as though the villa itself had shifted its footing.

She reached the door and eased it open fully. Then she saw it. A smear of red on the stone step. Dark. Thick. Fresh. The air turned instantly colder around her. Not a spatter. Not the dry rust of an old wound. This was *wet*. Recent.

Camille crouched, reaching out, but stopped short of touching it. Instead, she hovered her hand above the surface. It glistened faintly in the dying light. Still warm. Still *alive*, in a way.

Behind her, the soft shuffle of steps broke the silence.

"Camille?" Alba's voice, even and low, from the shadows.

Camille didn't turn. "We're not alone."

Alba came up beside her. Her eyes dropped to the blood.

"Matteo locked this door," she murmured. "From the inside."

"Then someone opened it from *inside*," Camille whispered.

Alba nodded, then without hesitation, slipped off her shawl, folded it neatly, and said, "I'll fetch some gloves. No one else touches this."

Camille nodded as Alba vanished into the villa's dim interior. She stepped outside.

The wind hit her harder now, rising with each second, tugging at her clothes and lifting strands of hair across her face. She scanned the stone path, eyes narrowing as she spotted it.

A faint trail of footprints. Smeared, barely visible, leading away from the front door and around the villa's side, toward the cliff and the trees beyond. She followed the steps.

The trail was erratic, as though the person had stumbled.

Every few feet, there was a drop. A swipe. A toe drag. Then a sharper smear, as if someone had braced a hand against the stone.

The path narrowed as it curved around the villa's edge. Tall cypress trees leaned in like sentries. The wind hissed between them, and below, the sea thundered louder, closer now. The trail led all the way to the chapel. The old ruin squatted against the cliffside like a waiting mouth.

Camille had seen it earlier that day, shadowed by overgrowth, a place of secrets. But now it looked different. It looked *hungry*. She slowed, moving carefully toward the arched threshold. And stopped. There on the step just before the doorway, was a *pool* of blood. Not a streak. Not a trace. A pool.

Still wet. Thick and slick in the failing light. It glimmered darkly, and the way it had spread, almost circular, told her it had not come from a moving wound. Someone had stood here. Or fallen. But there was no body. Just blood. And silence.

She stood frozen for a long moment, heart pounding like a warning drum inside her chest. Then she stepped forward.

Inside, the chapel was cloaked in gloom. The roof beams clawed at the sky above, framing the last light of the sun like a dying flame. The air was cooler here, but it held a weight of something unsaid. A staleness that didn't belong to any one death—but to many.

She followed the smear of blood across the flagstone. Barefoot prints. Small. Maybe a woman's. Maybe Charlotte? No. Charlotte had been with her all afternoon.

She moved deeper, toward the collapsed pews and the scorched altar. The quiet was total, except for the high, thin sound of the wind squeezing through the broken walls.

Then she saw it. On the wall, written in broad, shaking strokes of blood:

"ONE OF YOU KNOWS THE TRUTH."

The message bled down the stone like it had been scrawled in desperation. The last letter trailed off, a thin downward streak like the person had dropped mid-word.

Camille's breath caught in her throat. Behind her, almost too suddenly, came a footfall. She spun, her heart slamming against her ribs. Charlotte stood in the archway, ghost-pale and backlit by the burning horizon. She clutched a flashlight, the beam low, as if afraid of what it might reveal.

"I saw the door," Charlotte said. "It was open. And then..."

Her eyes locked onto the pool of blood on the threshold. Camille stepped between her and the wall.

"Don't look."

But it was too late.

Charlotte's eyes widened. She made it two steps forward before turning abruptly, clutching her stomach, and retched.

Camille was there in a heartbeat, pulling back her hair, steadying her.

"I'm sorry," Charlotte whispered, voice thick with fear. "I thought... I hoped it was over."

Camille looked back toward the message.

"It's not," she said.

They stood in the broken chapel, the sea below howling and the wind shrieking through the trees above. Blood on the stones. A message left in desperation. And a house waiting for the next confession, or the next casualty.

Camille steadied Charlotte outside the chapel, one hand braced on her back, the other gripping the flashlight Charlotte had dropped.

The sea roared louder now, as if the cliffs themselves were groaning under the weight of what had just been discovered. Wind tore through the trees, rattling the chapel's bones and carrying the salt-and-metal scent of blood further into the night.

Neither of them spoke.

Camille's mind was still spinning. The footprints, the blood, the message: *One of you knows*. It wasn't just a threat. It was a condemnation.

Behind her, a sound: the soft crunch of gravel under cautious steps. Camille spun around. A small circle of warm orange light bobbed into view, slowly illuminating the broken archway.

Mara. She appeared from the trees like an apparition, her white blouse soaked through with sweat and seawater, lantern clutched tightly in trembling fingers. Her face was ashen, lips parted as though she was still catching her breath.

"I saw the door open," she whispered. "I saw your shadows and..." Her eyes dropped to the threshold. The pool of blood. "Oh, God."

Mara staggered forward, pressing a hand to her mouth.

Camille stepped into her path. "What are you doing out here?"

Mara's eyes flicked to Charlotte, still hunched and pale, her body shivering despite the heat.

"I realized you were both gone. And the front door was swinging open."

"So, you followed us?"

"I thought someone might be hurt. I thought maybe..." Her voice caught.

Camille studied her closely. Her pupils were wide, too wide. Her hands were shaking badly. "Are you high?"

"No," Mara snapped, offended.

Charlotte let out a whimper as she tried to stand straight. Camille caught her arm again, but Charlotte pulled away.

"I'm fine," she murmured, "I just need air."

"You've got plenty of that," Camille muttered. "It's answers we don't have."

The three of them stood in the chapel's entry, wind battering their hair and clothes. The message still loomed behind them, scrawled in fresh blood on stone.

ONE OF YOU KNOWS.

Camille turned back to it, eyes narrowing.

"It's not about fear anymore," she said. "It's a performance. A reckoning. Someone's building toward something. Some grand finale."

"Or someone's unraveling," Charlotte whispered.

"No," Camille said. "Not unraveling. Planning."

She didn't wait for their replies. She turned, motioning them back toward the villa.

The trail back was harder now. The wind fought them. The path was darker. Somewhere, a bird shrieked in the distance and then fell silent.

The villa loomed like a fortress as they approached, gold light flickering through the windows, but no sound, no movement. It was too quiet. Camille's skin crawled.

Inside, the stillness seemed greater. They each went their separate ways, Mara heading upstairs, Camille towards the kitchen, and Charlotte back outside to the terrace. None of them had spoken on the way down the hill, and none of them had anything to say now.

An hour later, Camille walked outside with a rising feeling of dread. She'd gone upstairs to check on Charlotte and found her room empty. Moving quickly through the house, she checked the kitchen, the guest rooms. Nothing. No one had seen her since they got back from the chapel.

As she opened the French doors leading to the pool. The wind howled through. A lounge chair was tipped over. A single towel fluttered across the tiles. But no Charlotte.

"Perhaps she's run," Jasper whispered, following close behind.

"Not after what she saw. She wouldn't leave us," Camille replied. But the weight of her own words settled like stones in her stomach. They regrouped in the lounge. Camille felt the room spinning.

"She was with us," Mara said. "She stayed down here when we got back from the chapel, but she was with us."

"What if someone *took* her," Rowan said.

Alba locked the front doors with a heavy clank. "If they did, they moved fast. And without sound."

Camille's heart thudded. *Or Charlotte ran. Or Charlotte was lured.* Either way, the message had changed. First: One down. Then: Two more must drown in truth. Now: One of you knows. Now there was no body. Just blood. And silence. The killer was no longer waiting for confessions, but creating them, one by one.

22

VANISHING POINT

Dawn crept across the cliffs like a ghost dragging a veil of mist. The first light did not bring comfort. It didn't spill golden and warm across the villa. Instead, it filtered through layers of fog, casting a pale silver sheen across the stone paths, the scorched roof tiles, and the sharp crags of the cliff's edge. It was the kind of morning that made you speak in whispers.

Camille stood in the villa's front courtyard, arms crossed tightly over her chest. The air was clammy and sharp, and even in her sweatshirt, she could feel the cold clinging to her skin. The others emerged one by one, their faces hollowed by worry and a restless night.

No one had slept. Charlotte was still gone.

The blood on the chapel threshold had dried by now, dark and rust-colored in the early light. Camille couldn't stop picturing it. Not just what it meant, but how *quietly* it had arrived. No sound. No scream. Just a disappearance. And a message.

You were supposed to watch her.

The thought circled back again and again. It had wormed

into her during the long hours before dawn, growing heavier with each tick of the antique hallway clock.

Camille turned as Matteo joined her. He was already dressed, boots on, a flashlight strapped to his hip even though the sun was up. His jaw was clenched, and he carried a long walking stick he'd fashioned from a broken tree branch.

"We check the cliff path," he said without preamble.

Camille nodded. "If she didn't go willingly, someone took her there."

Or I let her go without noticing.

Jasper and Rowan joined next. Jasper looked half-shaved, his collar stained with salt. Rowan's expression was drawn and hollow.

Alba handed Camille a thermos of tea and pressed her fingers briefly to her wrist before stepping back inside. No words. Just the press of a pulse.

Matteo led the way. The group walked in silence, save for the occasional scuff of a heel on gravel or a snapped twig beneath a boot. The cliffside pressed in around them, mist swirling through the trees, scenting the air with damp stone and pine needles. Camille's thoughts drifted toward the sound of the sea. She'd never known waves could roar this loudly without a storm behind them.

As they reached the path behind the chapel, Camille's foot caught on a root, and she stumbled slightly. Matteo reached back instinctively and steadied her with a firm hand.

"Careful," he murmured.

She nodded once. "Sorry."

But in truth, she wasn't just tired. She was afraid of what they'd find. And of what they wouldn't.

Her mind flashed with images: Charlotte's pale face as she read the blood-written message. The tremble in her voice. The way her body had folded, not from weakness, but from something much more final.

You should have stayed with her. You should have checked again.

Matteo knelt suddenly and pointed. A partial footprint. Barefoot. And smeared.

Camille crouched beside it, her fingers curling over her knees.

There was no mistaking it: someone had walked this way, bleeding.

Rowan stepped back. Jasper said something low under his breath, but Camille barely registered it. She was listening now. The wind had teeth this morning. It whistled between the trees, lifting strands of her hair and setting her nerves on edge.

Then Jasper called out.

"Here."

He was holding something, high in the morning light. A scarf. Pale blue silk.

Camille's breath caught. Rowan stepped forward slowly, as though the air itself had grown heavy.

"That's Charlotte's. She wouldn't have dropped it," Rowan said. "Unless she wanted us to follow."

Camille nodded. That was something. A sign. *Maybe* a sign. They pushed forward together. And then they reached the overlook. The mist thinned just enough for the world to open below in an expanse of cliffs, wet rocks, churning sea.

Matteo crouched near the edge. "Something was dragged," he said. "Or someone slipped."

Camille's legs locked. The image came unbidden: Charlotte, stumbling. A scream swallowed by wind. Hands. Whose hands? Grabbing at her. Or pushing.

She turned to Jasper. "Do you see anything down there?"

He scanned the rocks below, then shook his head.

"No. But that doesn't mean she's not down there."

Camille stepped away from the edge. She was shaking now. Not from cold, but from the surge of something she hadn't allowed herself to feel.

Guilt. Deep and sharp and still rising.

Because you didn't watch her.

The trail here was broken. The brambles behind them twisted like nerves frayed to snapping. There were no more signs. Matteo tied a red ribbon to a branch.

Camille stared down at the scarf, twisted in her hand.

"She left it for us," she whispered. "She left a thread."

They turned back toward the villa. And behind them, the sea screamed louder than ever. The mist had thickened again by the time they began the walk back to the villa. It clung low to the ground, curling around ankles and shrubs, softening the edges of everything until it felt like the world itself was trying to disappear. Even the sea, so loud before, now seemed muffled behind the white veil.

Camille walked at the front, her fists tight at her sides. Charlotte's scarf was still in her hand, damp and limp. She no longer cared that it might be evidence. She held it like a tether. Something to keep her grounded while her mind whirled.

Charlotte didn't run. That much I know.

She could still see the look on her face in the chapel. The terror that wasn't just fear but realization. Charlotte had known something. And now, she was gone.

The wind pressed harder against the cliff path, carrying with it the scent of salt and something coppery, metallic. Camille tasted it on the back of her tongue and shivered. Then Matteo stopped walking. They were halfway up the trail, not far from the bramble-thick bend just before the tree line.

"What is it?" Jasper asked, stepping closer.

Matteo didn't respond at first. He crouched, gently parting the thorny undergrowth with the tip of his walking stick.

"Something caught the light," he said quietly.

Camille stepped forward, just as he reached in and pulled something free from the tangle of stems and dew-drenched leaves.

A bracelet.

Silver. Simple. Delicate. The kind that clinked softly when it moved, that left a faint impression on the skin beneath it when worn for too long. One of the links had been twisted, as if it had snagged or been pulled hard.

Rowan's breath caught. "She wore that every day."

Camille nodded, her voice barely a whisper. "It was her mother's. She said it was the only thing she kept from her childhood."

Matteo held it out on his open palm. "Then she didn't leave it willingly."

His tone was certain. Absolute. He shifted his weight and peered more closely at the ground. Drag marks. The earth had been disturbed. Thin streaks ran through the mud and gravel, barely noticeable unless you were looking. But Matteo was looking.

He followed the trail with his eyes, then his body, moving slowly beside it as it veered away from the overlook and toward the denser trees beyond.

"They didn't throw her off," he said. "They took her back."

Camille felt the bottom of her stomach drop.

"Back where?"

Matteo didn't answer. Because none of them knew. They walked in silence until they reached the garden steps, where Alba stood waiting in the early sun. Her face was harder now, set into something older and deeper than weariness. When Matteo held up the bracelet, she didn't react.

Camille stepped forward. "Have you seen this before?"

"Yes," Alba said softly. "It was Charlotte's."

"We found it near the path. And drag marks."

Still no reaction.

It was only when they began to climb the steps toward the villa entrance that Alba spoke again, so quietly that Camille had to stop walking to hear her.

"This happened once before," Alba said.

They all turned.

"In this house," she continued. "A girl vanished. And they pretended she never existed."

The silence that followed was a vacuum.

"What are you talking about?" Jasper asked. "Who?"

Alba looked toward the chapel. "Her name was Evelina. She worked here. Almost fifteen years ago. She was a cleaner. Young and quiet. A gentle girl."

Camille's voice was barely audible. "What happened?"

"One night she didn't come back from her shift. They said she must have run away. But I saw her that afternoon. She was crying in the wine cellar."

"And no one investigated?" Rowan asked, aghast.

"No one wanted to. Not then. The guests were important people. Influential. They said it would cause scandal. That it was best left... unspoken."

Matteo's face darkened. "Was Leo here then?"

Alba nodded. "He was younger. But yes."

"Did he know her?"

"They talked. Sometimes. I think he tried to help her."

Camille's mind reeled. "Why didn't you tell anyone?"

"I did," Alba said. "But they didn't listen."

They stood in stunned silence. Camille looked at the bracelet again. It felt heavier now, loaded with the weight of two disappearances instead of one. One buried under decades of silence. One happening in real time.

"We need to go back to the chapel again," she said.

Rowan shook her head. "What for?"

"I don't know," Camille snapped. "I feel like she might have tried to get back there."

Camille felt it in her bones. Charlotte wasn't far. She just wasn't *free*. And someone was counting on them never finding her.

23

THE BROKEN BELL

The midday sun hung like an executioner's lamp, unflinching and merciless above the cliffs. No breeze stirred. The air had thickened into something soupy and metallic, laced with brine and the bitter tang of scorched stone. The mist from that morning had burned off, leaving behind a hard-edged heat that shimmered off the rocks and made the villa shimmer in the distance like a mirage.

They walked without speaking. Matteo led, his stride sure but heavy, as if each step toward the chapel cost him something. He didn't look back. His face, shadowed beneath the brim of his sun-faded cap, was set in a grim mask. A walking reckoning.

Camille followed closely behind, her skin slick with sweat beneath her linen blouse, her throat dry from too much sun and not enough water. The salt wind stung her eyes and lips, but she barely noticed. Her pulse was pounding too loudly in her ears.

Rowan walked with her head bowed, shielding her eyes from the glare. Her shoulders were hunched, arms folded tightly across her stomach as though trying to keep something broken from spilling out.

Jasper trailed behind, his shirt dark with sweat across the back, fists clenched as he scanned the tree line for movement. His jaw was tight, his mouth a hard line. He didn't say a word.

Mara brought up the rear, sunglasses perched uselessly on her head, one sandal dragging slightly in the gravel. She looked sunstruck, disoriented, her cheeks blotchy with heat. Her hair clung to her temples in wet strands, and she kept glancing back toward the villa as though something might call her home.

The trees whispered around them, cicadas screeching overhead like static from a broken speaker. The air was so thick Camille could feel it pressing against her lungs. Every breath took effort. Every step forward felt like an argument with gravity.

They emerged from the grove, and the chapel stood before them. It hadn't changed, not really, but in the blistering light of noon, it looked more skeletal than ever. A hollow thing. A mouth pried open by time and left to scream silently into the void.

The ivy that clung to its stone bones was limp with heat, the leaves browning at the edges. The scorched archway they'd passed through days before now yawned black and gaping in the white light.

There was no wind. Even the sea, which had been a constant companion, seemed to fall away beneath them, its roar muffled by distance and dread.

Camille stepped inside the chapel and was immediately struck by the furnace-like heat trapped within the stone walls. The air was thick with dust, with heat, with something deeper and older, like mildew and wax, like secrets fermented for too long.

The nave was silent. The candles they'd once seen were now just pale, crumbling stubs. But the air smelled different. Not just of earth. Of iron and blood. She saw Matteo pause ahead of her, just as he reached the collapsed rear chamber. And then she knew.

He stopped moving entirely. His spine straightened, then bent, almost imperceptibly, shoulders curling forward, arms slackening at his sides.

Camille felt a sick twist low in her stomach. She moved forward. Rowan followed, already shaking her head, as if saying *no* before she even saw.

The rear chamber had once been a sacristy, maybe, a storage space for relics or sacred garments. Now it was rubble and heat and shadow.

And Charlotte.

Her body lay crumpled at the foot of the broken altar. The silence in that room grew immense. Crushing. The curve of her back. The loose fall of her arm. The way her head turned at an impossible angle, her neck bent too far to be natural. Her curls were tangled with dirt and dry leaves, skin washed pale under the glare. There was no blood. No visible wound. But her mouth had parted in a small, surprised O, and her eyes were shut in a kind of stillness that made Camille's stomach lurch.

Matteo moved slowly to her side. He lowered himself to his knees like a man praying or surrendering. One hand hovered over Charlotte's hair, shaking. Then he rested his fingers on her temple.

His face broke. Camille heard the smallest exhale, like glass cracking under pressure. Matteo's shoulders folded forward, and he pressed his forehead to the floor beside her, silent but trembling. Rowan made a small, gasping sound and turned away, pressing her face into the crook of her elbow.

Jasper stepped forward, his voice catching. "Oh, God."

Mara stood in the doorway, eyes wide and unblinking. Her arms hung limp by her sides. She didn't step forward. She didn't move at all. Camille crouched beside Matteo. Her legs felt numb.

Charlotte's skin was still warm. There was something about that that made it so much worse. She hadn't been gone long. On the stone beside her body lay a piece of folded paper, the corner weighted down by a jagged piece of shattered glass.

Camille picked it up slowly. The ink bled slightly, like it had been scrawled too fast. "This time, no silence." The words hit like a hammer.

Camille read them again, her lips moving soundlessly. Three murdered. Four dead.

Noel. Max. Charlotte. And poor Selena.

Rowan, who had returned to lean in the doorway, let out a sound between a sob and a curse. Matteo stood slowly. His face was a mask of grief and fury. He said nothing. There was nothing to say.

Camille swallowed hard. "She was scared before she vanished. She knew something. She said Leo wasn't the only one who saw too much."

Matteo's eyes flicked to the note.

"This isn't revenge," he said. "This is penance. And we haven't even paid it all yet."

The chapel had grown hotter. The shadows shorter. But still, it felt like they were being watched. The silence after the discovery of Charlotte's body was a living thing. It clung to the rafters of the ruined chapel, thick as the heat, stretching over them with an awful sentience. Even the cicadas had stopped. Even the wind had died. The world seemed to hold its breath as the remaining group stood around the broken altar, faces shining with sweat, streaked with grief and suspicion.

Then Rowan broke.

With a wild, keening cry, she stumbled back from the doorway, one hand raised as if to ward off something invisible.

"We're being played!" she shrieked. "Don't you see it? This isn't about Charlotte, or Leo, or some missing cleaner, or Max, or Noel. This is a performance. A setup!"

Jasper rounded on her, his voice like gravel. "Is that what you call murder? A performance?"

Rowan's hands trembled as she wiped at her face. Her hair stuck to her temples in sweat-damp strands, her eyes glassy and bloodshot. "It's certainly designed to have an effect. Leaving her here like this, I mean."

"Enough!" Matteo barked, his voice like thunder against stone.

The chapel fell quiet again, save for their stifled breathing. Camille was still on her knees beside Charlotte, her fingers trembling. She wasn't listening to the others now. She was staring at Charlotte's right hand, where the fingers were curled tightly beneath her chest, hidden in the dirt.

Gently, she reached over, lifting Charlotte's hand, trying not to cry. Something small was clutched in her lifeless grasp. Folded, torn, smeared with earth and something darker. Camille eased it free. A scrap of paper. Ripped but familiar. It was the corner of a page. Slanted handwriting. A single letter: a looping "R."

Camille's breath caught. It was from a journal. Rowan's journal. She turned slowly. Rowan was standing in the rear of the chapel, hands clasped in front of her, face pale. She looked like a figure carved in salt. Camille held up the scrap of paper.

"Rowan," she said quietly. "Is this from your journal?"

Rowan didn't move.

Mara stepped forward. "What?"

Camille's voice was careful, clear. "Rowan said a page had been ripped out of her journal. But this was in Charlotte's hand. She died holding it."

Everyone looked at Rowan. She didn't flinch. She didn't deny it. She didn't say a word.

Rowan's eyes filled with tears. "I didn't know what to say. I was... ashamed. I wrote things in there. Things I couldn't admit."

"Did Charlotte read it?" Camille asked. "Did she find something you didn't want known?"

Rowan looked away. "I don't know."

Camille rose, brushing dirt from her knees. "Charlotte was trying to say something with this. Whatever she saw in your journal, she thought it mattered."

Rowan's mouth parted. Then closed. Then parted again.

Matteo turned from Charlotte, his grief sharpened now to suspicion. "What was in it, Rowan?"

Silence.

"Names?" Mara asked. "Dates? Details about Leo's death? Or... what he thought he knew?"

Rowan swallowed hard. "I don't know. Maybe. I wrote about everything. I had to. It's how I survive."

Jasper stared at her like he'd never seen her before. "And then you lost it? Why didn't you say anything?"

"I was scared someone would use it against me."

Mara laughed once, bitter. "You think this is about *you*?"

Camille raised the paper again. "Charlotte risked everything to keep this. Whoever took your journal, whoever planted this on her, *wanted us to see it.* And now she's dead."

Rowan stepped back. "I didn't kill her."

"But you were silent," Matteo said. "And silence is what's causing all of this."

Outside, the sun pressed down harder. Inside, the chapel was an oven of grief and accusation. Camille looked at the stone beneath Charlotte's body. At the broken altar. At the blackened wax. At the scorched seal etched into the floor. The serpent. Again.

"Whoever's behind this," she whispered, "knows every corner of this house. Every memory we tried to bury. And now they're digging them up, one by one."

Rowan wiped her eyes. "We're all doomed, aren't we?"

Camille looked at the note again. *This time, no silence.*

"Yes," she said. "Unless we stop pretending."

24

ECHOES IN THE WALLS

The villa was quieter than it had been in days. Not peaceful. It was never peaceful, but it felt drained. As if the place itself had exhausted its breath screaming. The marble corridors still bore the smudges of blood, the scent of smoke still curled faintly beneath the citrus cleaner Alba had tried to use. But the screaming had stopped. The crying. Even the accusations had slowed.

Camille wandered through the upstairs hallway barefoot, the sound of her steps softened by old rugs and older silence. Her body ached with tiredness, the kind that lives in the bones, not the muscles. It was late, but she couldn't sleep. None of them could, not properly.

Charlotte's body had been moved. Wrapped carefully, covered respectfully. But her absence left a shape behind. A hole in the air. Every time Camille passed the guest bedroom Charlotte had stayed in, her eyes darted toward the cracked door. She didn't know why she kept checking. Maybe part of her hoped it had all been a nightmare. Maybe a sliver of her still expected Charlotte to be inside, brushing her long hair, half-smiling, half-sad, like she always was. But the door was dark. And the bed hadn't been slept in.

That night, it was Jasper who found her, pacing the hallway like a ghost.

"I can't do this anymore," he said, his voice rough, his eyes hollowed out like he'd lost days to grief.

Camille nodded. "Me neither."

They didn't speak again for a few minutes, just walked side by side, like they were afraid that stillness would let the house catch up to them.

After a while, they ended up in the wine cellar, sitting on the stone steps in the cool dark. Someone, probably Matteo, had cleared the broken glass, but the stain remained. A dull rust smear across the floor, like a wound that refused to clot.

Camille stared at it, her arms wrapped around her knees. "Do you think it was always going to end like this?"

"No," Jasper said. "I think it was meant to end ten years ago. But none of us were brave enough to finish it."

He rubbed a hand across his jaw. "Do you remember that night Leo jumped?"

She looked at him.

"He didn't jump," she said.

Jasper flinched. He hesitated. Then nodded, just once.

"I wish I'd been here. I wish I'd known how far they'd push him."

Camille didn't respond. She didn't need to.

Later, as they headed back upstairs, something strange caught Camille's eye. A draught, pushing out from a seam in the wall. She paused, turned back.

"Wait."

Jasper frowned. "What is it?"

She pressed her hand against the wall. It felt... uneven. Cold air drifted from a crack along the plaster.

"Help me," she whispered.

Together, they pushed. The panel shifted with a groan of age. Behind it: a hollow space. And inside was a small, rusted wall safe. Camille reached in, hands trembling, and pulled free a thick folder bound with brittle leather ties. Jasper held a flashlight over it.

Inside were letters. Dozens of them. All addressed to someone named *Chiara Marinetti.*

Leo's sister. Camille flipped one open. His handwriting was spidery, uncertain.

Chiara,

I don't know how to tell you this. They don't like me here. I thought I'd finally found people I belonged with, but... something's wrong. I heard them talking. They think I'm spying. I think someone read my journal. I'm scared. I don't want to tell you too much, just in case this is ever found. But if anything happens, please don't believe I chose it.

Jasper cursed softly.

"Why didn't he send these?" Camille asked.

"Maybe he never had the chance."

They opened more letters. Each one darker than the last. Fear creeping in around the edges. Desperation building like storm clouds. And a recurring name. *Mara.*

Camille's throat tightened. Leo had trusted her. More than anyone. And she had used that trust as a blindfold.

That night, Rowan sat with Alba in the dim drawing room, a single lamp casting amber over the worn rug.

"I keep thinking we missed something," Rowan said. "Like a final piece of the story that would make everything make sense."

Alba poured a splash of grappa into Rowan's teacup. "You didn't miss anything. You just weren't ready to hear it."

Rowan looked at her. "What do you mean?"

Alba hesitated. "There's something you should know."

She stood and crossed the room to the fire grate. Reached into a vase no one had touched in years.

From it, she pulled a worn audio tape.

Rowan blinked. "What's that?"

"I found it when I was cleaning the year after Leo died," Alba said. "It was stuck behind the chimney grate. I didn't know what to do with it. I thought maybe... maybe it wasn't mine to hear."

Rowan took the tape in shaking hands. The label was water-damaged, but one phrase was still clear. *Tell Matteo.* Her breath caught. She ran upstairs, barefoot, adrenaline driving her. Camille and Jasper met her on the landing.

"You need to hear this," she said, voice shaking.

Together, they found Matteo in the kitchen, sitting at the table, his hands wrapped around a cold mug of coffee. They played the tape. Static. Then Leo's voice. Faint and panicked.

If you find this... please tell Matteo. He's the only one who knew me before I changed. Before I tried to fit in. I don't want to die. I don't want to be part of this anymore. I think... I think they're going to make me disappear. They say it's just a game, but it's not. It's punishment. It always was.

The tape ended. Silence fell like fog. Camille sat back, eyes wide with tears. Matteo swallowed hard, his face pale.

"I should have protected him," he whispered.

"You still can," Rowan said. "By helping us end this."

In the middle of the night, a cassette player began to hum. No one had pressed play. And from somewhere inside the villa walls, a sound echoed back. Not just a voice. A laugh. Light and cruel. Familiar and fading.

25

THE LOCK-IN

The villa's great room had grown stifling with fear. Even with the shutters drawn, the noon heat found its way in, turning the air thick, weighty, impossible to breathe. The temperature clung to them like a second skin, mixing with sweat, guilt, and old ghosts. It was the kind of heat that made tempers short and secrets slippery. The kind of heat that baked silence into bone.

Matteo turned the key in the front door with an echoing *clunk*. He slid the iron bolt across with slow finality. The sound rang out like a death sentence in the cavernous hush.

"No one leaves," he said, his voice low and hoarse with grief. "Not until the truth is laid bare. Not until the killer has a name."

Camille stood at the far end of the long walnut table, her hands braced on the polished surface. Sweat glistened along her collarbone. The wine rack shadows climbed the walls behind her like ribs of some beast about to devour them. She stared at each of them in turn, her breath measured, her control razor-thin.

Jasper moved restlessly near the fireplace, pacing with sharp turns. His shirt was damp, sleeves rolled to the elbows, his expression a cocktail of rage and disbelief. The veins in his neck stood taut.

Mara sat perched on the edge of the chaise lounge, legs drawn in, arms crossed tightly beneath her chest. Her lipstick had faded, but the tension in her mouth was bright and raw. Her left hand trembled.

Rowan stood near the heavy velvet curtain, part of her body swallowed in shadow. Her fingers dug into the fabric like it might hold her up. Her wide, unblinking eyes reflected more than just fear—they reflected the helplessness of someone being closed in from all sides.

Soren sat at the table, opposite Camille, his eyes boring into her constantly. Renata stretched out on a settee in the corner, a silent shell of herself.

Alba leaned quietly against the mantle, her apron still dusted with flour, the only one who hadn't shifted since Matteo locked the doors. But her eyes, dark and sharp, missed nothing.

Camille spoke first.

"Four of us are dead. That leaves six of us. Unless someone else is hiding in the walls, the killer is *here*."

Jasper nodded tightly. "And they've been watching. Waiting."

"And eliminating," Camille added. "In a very specific order."

She stepped around the table and began pacing slowly, as if building momentum.

"Noel. Max. Charlotte. All three were directly connected to what happened that summer."

Mara's voice was flat. "That includes all of us."

"But those three?" Camille turned, eyes narrowing. "They held pieces of the truth. Noel helped plan the confessions night. He brought the blindfold, the rope. Max kept the tapes. Charlotte recovered them. Rowan, you were the that night too."

"And?" Rowan asked, her voice low, brittle. "You think I'm next?"

"I think you're lying," Jasper said before Camille could speak. "About the journal. About what you remember. About what you've buried."

Rowan's voice cracked. "I'm not lying. I'm scared."

"Everyone here is scared," Camille said sharply. "But that's no longer enough."

Mara stood abruptly, the chair creaking behind her. "All of us standing here pointing fingers is getting us nowhere."

Matteo crossed his arms, his eyes fixed on Mara now.

"You've been playing angles since the moment we arrived. Trying to keep the group happy. Distracting people when things get tense. But underneath it, you're nervous. Always watching who's watching you."

"Because I feel like I'm going to be next," Mara hissed. "Why aren't you looking at him?"

She pointed at Matteo.

"Think about it," she continued, voice rising. "Who's the one who lives here year round? Who knew exactly where to look? Who's the one with a blood connection to the only person who *really* knew the truth?"

Matteo's mouth didn't move for a beat.

Then: "I've been here longer than any of you. If I wanted you dead, you'd be dead."

"Charming," Mara muttered.

But Alba stepped forward then, her voice cutting through the room like the ring of glass on tile.

"No," she said. "It isn't Matteo."

Everyone turned.

Alba's face was unreadable, but something burned in her eyes, something fierce, almost defiant.

"It's one of *you*. And I know which one."

A heavy, electric silence fell. Camille's stomach flipped.

Jasper stiffened. Rowan let out a strangled breath. Mara blinked like she'd been slapped.

"Who?" Jasper demanded.

Alba took one step closer. Her lips parted. "The person who..."

The power died. Everything went black. There was a metallic *pop* and then complete silence. No fan overhead. No echo from the outdoor fountain. Just dead air. Someone gasped.

"Alba?" Camille called, her voice cutting through the dark.

But Alba didn't answer.

"Where is she?" Mara asked. "She was *right there*."

Jasper fumbled in a drawer, pulling out a flashlight from the emergency box Matteo had shown him days ago. He flicked it on. The beam pierced the dark, just a narrow cone of light, but Alba was no longer in its path.

Camille turned in a slow circle.

"She couldn't have gone far."

"She couldn't have gone *anywhere*," Matteo said. "The door's locked."

"Unless someone unlocked it," Jasper murmured. "Or unless someone else has a key."

Footsteps. Soft, fast, retreating down the corridor to the east wing. They weren't loud. But they were distinct. Running.

Jasper snapped his head toward the sound. "That way."

The beam swung wildly. No one was there. But the far hallway door hung open. Camille didn't wait. She ran. Jasper behind her, Matteo close on his heels. Mara stumbled forward and then stopped, frozen in place. Rowan pressed against the wall as they passed, her face pale, mouth working but producing no sound.

The hallway was darker still, windows shuttered, sconces dead. The smell of candlewax and salt hung thick. A breeze stirred, unnatural in a house so tightly closed.

"Alba!" Camille called. "Are you here?"

Silence. Then a door creaked open. Somewhere deeper in the house. Not ahead. *Below.*

26

THE CONFESSION

The emergency lanterns flickered like dying stars. Camille could hear her own heartbeat as she stood at the top of the cellar stairs, looking down into darkness that seemed to stretch endlessly below. The villa above was hushed and watchful. Down here, it felt like descending into the belly of something that had long ago stopped breathing.

The main power was gone. The overhead lights were useless. The sconces held dead bulbs. The old stone walls glistened with moisture, reflecting what little light the lanterns gave off, just enough to cast warped shadows along the corridor.

Behind Camille, Jasper drew in a sharp breath.

"Still think we should split up?" he muttered.

She didn't answer. The air was colder now, and thick with damp, with old cork, mildew, earth and metal and memory.

Matteo had warned them about the lower floors when they first arrived. "The basement floods sometimes," he'd said. "Don't go down without a light. It's easy to get lost."

Now, even the emergency lights were failing. They moved forward slowly. Jasper took the lead, flashlight angled low. The beam carved through the gloom like a scalpel. The wine racks rose on either side, towering over them like sentinels, their glass necks gleaming like eyes. Bottles stood crooked in their dust-covered rows, labels peeling, some cracked open and forgotten.

Camille's sandals echoed faintly on the tile. Her fingers brushed the stone wall to steady herself, dampness coating her skin.

"Whoever took Alba," she whispered, "might still be down here."

Jasper grunted. "Or whoever killed Charlotte and the others."

The words hung between them like a spider's thread, thin, but impossible to ignore. They turned left at the row of Bordeaux crates, past the shelf with the loose beam. The air shifted. Colder. Closer. Like something was pressing in around them. Camille saw it then, a glint on the floor, blackened at the edges.

She crouched. It was a school ID, edges burned, the plastic warped and curling. Her fingers trembled slightly as she brushed it clean.

"Leo Marinetti," she said softly.

Jasper came to her side, crouching to see it.

"Why burn this?" he asked. "Why not throw it away?"

"To make sure it couldn't be shown to anyone," she murmured. "But someone couldn't quite let it go."

Camille slipped it into her back pocket. Her breath steamed faintly in the cold. Then, noise. A soft scuff. The clink of glass. They both froze. Camille's eyes darted to the dark end of the corridor, the old servants' entrance, bolted shut, hadn't been touched in years. Or so they'd thought.

Jasper swung the flashlight toward the sound, but it caught only dust. Then, high above them, a *slam*. A door upstairs. And someone was running. Camille and Jasper bolted for the stairs, taking them two at a time.

Upstairs, the hallway was breathless with heat and stillness. The silence had grown thick, broken only by the thump of retreating footsteps, soft and quick, echoing off old wallpaper and stone.

Rowan ran barefoot, nightgown fluttering like a ghost behind her. She didn't know what had possessed her to run. Only that everything had changed. Alba's near-confession. The lights going out. The way Jasper had looked at her, cold and flat, as though he could already see the noose tightening around her throat.

She tore through the east wing, deeper into the oldest part of the house. The hall narrowed, cluttered with disused furniture, stacks of boxes, a broken wardrobe. Paint peeled along the doorframes. The villa moaned beneath her feet.

Behind her, another set of footsteps was approaching. Mara. Quieter, but gaining. Rowan skidded around the corner and threw open a door. Her old room. It smelled of dried roses and mothballs, of old notebooks and pressed linens. The sheets had not been changed. The air was stagnant with memory. She slammed the door behind her and turned the lock.

Outside, Mara's footsteps slowed.

"Rowan," she called through the wood, her voice low. Controlled. "It's time to stop running."

Rowan backed into the room, staring at the door as though it might burst open.

"I'm not running," she said. "I'm hiding."

There was a pause.

"I'm not here to hurt you," Mara said softly.

"You already have."

"I didn't write that note. I didn't take your journal. I didn't kill Charlotte."

Rowan sank to the edge of the bed. Her breathing came in quick, shallow waves.

"I don't know who to believe anymore," she whispered.

"I do," Mara said. "That's the problem."

The lock rattled.

"Mara, please."

"I just want to talk. No one else is going to listen."

"You mean no one else is going to protect you."

Another pause.

Then: "You think I did all this?"

Rowan's eyes filled with tears. "I don't know what I think."

"Then let me in."

"I can't."

Outside, silence.

Then a final murmur:

"You wrote what happened that night. You wrote what Max did. You wrote what I said. That's the truth. But you never meant anyone else to read it."

"No," Rowan said. "I wrote it to forget."

The handle turned again. And this time, it clicked open. The room smelled of old linen, dried lavender, and secrets. The wallpaper, yellowed and peeling near the ceiling, curled at the edges like burned parchment. Dust danced lazily in the strips of light sneaking through the half-drawn curtains, which hung stiff and faded, their floral pattern sun-bleached into oblivion. The carpet beneath Rowan's feet was threadbare, worn down the center from years of pacing. The warped wooden floor beneath it groaned faintly with each step, as if remembering all the feet that had crossed it over the years, some in anger, some in shame.

Rowan stood by the window, her pale hands gripping the wooden sill, knuckles stark against the faded paint. Her nightgown, damp with sweat, clung to her back and legs, and strands of dark hair curled wildly around her cheeks, plastered there by humidity and panic. Her breath came fast, the tips of her shoulders rising and falling in jittery rhythm.

Behind her, the door clicked open with soft finality.

Mara stepped in barefoot, the hem of her black silk dress brushing the tops of her knees. Her cheeks were flushed, not with heat but with adrenaline, and her eyeliner had smudged into a soft crescent beneath her eyes. There was a faint shimmer of sweat on her collarbone, the pulse visible just beneath the skin. She smelled of orange blossom perfume and something chemical, like bleach.

Her posture was relaxed, too relaxed. Arms loose by her sides, fingers slightly curled, as though weighing whether to strike or embrace. She closed the door gently behind her and leaned her back against it, surveying the room with the calm of someone who knew she had nothing left to hide.

"You wrote it all down," Mara said. Her voice was low, husky, almost tender.

Rowan didn't move. The room was still, oppressive with heat and memory.

"I had to," she replied. "I couldn't keep it all inside."

Mara glanced around the room. The vanity mirror across from her was cracked along the lower edge. The bed was unmade, the pillow slightly indented as if someone had just been crying there. The air hung heavy with dust and disuse.

"I read it," Mara continued, stepping forward. Her bare feet made no sound on the rug. "Not all of it. Just enough."

Rowan turned slowly, her face pale and drawn. A bruise darkened her left forearm from where she'd tripped earlier in the hallway. Her lips were dry, slightly cracked. "Are you here to threaten me?"

Mara's head tilted, her expression somewhere between pity and delight. "I think it's too late for threats, don't you?"

She moved toward the dressing table, dragging a finger

across its surface. A trail in the dust. Her gaze lingered on a tarnished silver hairbrush, a forgotten earring, a broken chain.

"Do you remember what he looked like that night?" she asked.

Rowan flinched. "Leo?"

Mara nodded. "Yes. The way his hair was always falling into his eyes. That ridiculous vintage blazer. He thought it made him look 'literary.' It just made him look *small*."

Rowan swallowed hard. Mara turned back to her, eyes gleaming. "He was never meant to be one of us."

The words settled like ash.

"You remember how they laughed at him," Mara went on, stepping closer. Her movements were graceful, predatory. "But you forget who planned the game."

Rowan's legs nearly buckled. She gripped the edge of the vanity.

"It was me," Mara said, her voice flat now. "The wine. The blindfold. The chair. I called it 'Confession Night' like it was a joke. But it wasn't. I wanted to break him." She crossed to the bed and sat, her fingers toying with the frayed bedspread. She looked out the window at the thin slice of blue sky between the curtains.

"Max was easy to push. He wanted to prove something. Soren just smirked and went along with it. And you..." She turned back to Rowan. "You were the glue. I knew you wouldn't talk."

Rowan's face crumpled. "You told me he'd be fine. You said it would be like summer theater."

"It *was*, Rowan. Well, until it wasn't."

Mara stood again.

"He found out that Ben had died. That we'd pushed him over the edge."

Rowan backed away until her spine hit the wall. Her whole body was trembling now, her shoulders caving inward.

"Ben wasn't ever part of it. He was just a kid."

"He thought he could be part of our group. But he never could. And Leo realized what we did to him," Mara said. "That was dangerous for us."

Rowan gasped, hand over her mouth.

"I didn't push him," Mara said. "It wasn't me. But we couldn't have anything like that hanging over us. I realized I'd started something. A purge. And once you start cleaning, you can't stop."

Her smile was hollow.

"You killed Max," Rowan said through clenched teeth.

"In the cellar. He cried. I smiled. And then it was over."

Rowan's legs gave out and she sank to the floor.

"You murdered Charlotte."

"She was going to ruin it. She *found* something, probably in your journal, but maybe not. Doesn't matter now."

"You drowned Noel."

"He thought we might get it on," Mara said, flexing her fingers. "Fool."

Rowan's whole body was shaking. Mara walked toward her and crouched.

"You wanted truth," she whispered. "This is what it looks like."

In a panic, Rowan pushed past her and ran out into the corridor again. Running to escape. Running for her life.

27

FALL

The storm returned like a punishment. Twilight had descended into chaos. The sky boiled in bruised purples and drowned gray, the last light of day devoured by the churning sea. Rain whipped in diagonal sheets, cold and cruel, slapping bare skin with sharp, stinging fingers. Wind tore at the cliffside, tugging at the trees, flattening the tall grass, howling through the gaps in the rocks like it was trying to speak.

Rowan stumbled as she reached the overlook. The world opened before her into blackness. No railing. No safety. Just the craggy edge of the earth, and beyond it, air and ocean. The sea below raged, spitting foam and fury. Waves exploded against the rocks like the earth itself was trying to drown. Mist curled up from the cliffs like ghost-breath.

Her bare feet slipped on the wet stone, but she caught herself on a jagged outcrop, her fingers scraping raw. Her soaked nightgown clung to her legs, the hem torn and trailing like seaweed. Her hair whipped across her face, tangled with rain, eyes red-rimmed with salt and fear.

She turned just as Mara emerged through the trees. She moved with terrifying calm, her dark dress plastered to her skin, now heavy with rain. Her arms hung limp at her sides. The makeup she'd worn had long since washed away. Her eyes, sharp and narrowed, gleamed even in the dimming light. Her face was pale, except for the bright flush of color blooming high on her cheekbones with a fevered intensity.

"You shouldn't have run," Mara said, her voice nearly lost to the wind.

Rowan took a step back. The edge of the cliff crumbled slightly beneath her heel. Pebbles cascaded into the abyss.

"You confessed," Rowan shouted. "You told me what you did. I'll tell them. Matteo, Camille, everyone!"

Mara blinked slowly. Rain streamed down her cheeks. "No. You won't."

And then she lunged. It was like being hit by a wave. The two women collided with a force that knocked the breath from Rowan's lungs. They crashed onto the slick, moss-covered rock, limbs flailing, rain blinding them both. Fingers clawed at skin, at fabric, at wet stone. The wind screamed in their ears, drowning out thought.

Rowan tried to crawl away, but Mara grabbed her ankle, yanking her backward. Rowan kicked out wildly, her heel connecting with Mara's ribs. Mara grunted but didn't let go.

"You'll never tell anyone now," she hissed, dragging Rowan toward the edge. "You'll go over like Leo. Like Ben. It's almost beautiful, really. Full circle."

Rowan's nails scrabbled at the earth, slicing through mud and loose rock. She twisted, catching Mara across the face with the back of her hand. The smack echoed.

They separated for a moment, both panting, bruised, slick with water and blood.

"I trusted you," Rowan said through clenched teeth. "You were my friend."

Mara's lips curled. Her voice dropped to a whisper. "That was your first mistake."

And she charged again. But this time, Rowan pivoted, just enough, and Mara's momentum carried her too far. Rowan shoved her with everything she had left. Mara's foot slipped. She staggered to one knee, then rose, growling like an animal. That's when Camille's voice pierced the storm.

"Rowan!"

High on the path, soaked to the bone, Camille was running full tilt, eyes wide with horror. Behind her, Matteo barreled through the brambles, his shirt torn, arms bleeding from thorns.

Rowan turned her head toward the sound. And Mara struck. A final shove. The cliff vanished beneath Rowan's feet. The drop opened like a throat. She screamed, but before the air could take her, hands caught her wrists.

Matteo. He had launched himself forward just in time, one knee braced on the rock, his entire body straining.

"Hold on!" he roared.

Rain poured down his face, his muscles trembling with effort. Camille dropped beside him, grabbing Rowan's elbow, adding her strength. The world slowed. Rowan dangled above the abyss, legs kicking, her breath tearing from her lungs.

Camille gritted her teeth. "We've got you. We've got you!"

Together, they dragged her upward, inch by agonizing inch. Her knees hit the stone. Her body collapsed. Matteo caught her, pulled her into his arms, wrapping her in his coat, rain pounding down on them all. Behind them, Mara stood stunned, her chest heaving, arms slack.

"I was trying to save her," she whispered, voice trembling. "She slipped."

Camille rose slowly. "No. It wasn't."

Mara took a step back. "She just slipped."

"You're out of moves, Mara," Matteo said, rising to his feet, sweat and rain mixing on his skin.

"No," Mara whispered. "You are."

Rain screamed down in sheets, cold and blinding. The path was nothing now, only a streak of slick stone and torn roots. Somewhere above them, the sky tore open with lightning, casting the entire scene in a wash of blue-white light that made everything appear ghostly, unreal.

None of them saw the rock in her hand until it was rushing up to meet Matteo's head. It struck him square and he reeled backwards, Mara launched herself at Rowan again, tearing at her hair, dragging her back towards the cliff edge. Camille was already moving before the thought had even solidified in her mind.

Her boots slipped on the moss-slick rock as she charged forward, breath burning in her throat. Her world shrank to the three figures at the cliff's edge, a tangle of soaked limbs and desperation teetering too close to the void. Mara was on top of Rowan now, her soaked dress clinging like a shadow to her body, hair plastered across her face, teeth bared in a wordless snarl.

Camille didn't hesitate. She launched herself into the chaos. The collision was bone-rattling. All three women went down in a heap, skidding across the stone with a wet scrape. The momentum sent them sprawling, Rowan toward the edge, Camille twisting her body to keep Mara from rolling on top of her. She felt her shoulder hit the ground hard, heard the crunch of gravel beneath her ribs.

The cliff loomed. The wind roared. Rowan screamed as her leg slid out over the abyss, flailing for purchase. Camille's hand shot out and grabbed her wrist.

"I've got you!" she shouted, but the rain swallowed her voice.

Mara was pulling at Camille's shoulder, trying to pull herself up, not realizing, or not caring, that she was dragging them all closer to the brink. Her nails dug in. Her breath came in heaving gasps.

"You don't get to stop this," she spat.

Camille's grip slipped an inch. Then another. Suddenly Matteo was there again, his eyes wide with fury.

"Rowan!"

He lunged, catching her around the waist and yanking her back in one brutal movement. She gasped, twisting into him, clutching his shirt like a lifeline. Mara tried to hold on. But now she was the one over the edge. Her body dangled above the void, suspended by one trembling hand clutching a crumbling root. Camille turned, rain stinging her eyes. Her arms were raw with scrapes, her side throbbing.

"Mara!" she gasped, crawling forward. "Give me your hand!"

But Mara didn't move. She looked up, eyes strangely clear through the curtain of water. Her lips parted, and in that final instant, she smiled.

"I don't want it to end this way," she said.

The root snapped. Her body fell silently, swallowed by the abyss. Camille lunged forward, catching only air. Wind rushed up from the sea, cold and final. Then, nothing. Just the sound of the ocean, angry and endless.

Rowan curled against Matteo's chest, shaking so hard she could barely breathe. He held her like she might vanish, one hand on the back of her head, the other across her shoulders, steady despite the trembling in his own limbs.

Camille pushed herself back from the edge, her hands red with grit and rain. She sat heavily, her chest heaving, blood running from a scratch along her jawline. They stayed like that for a long moment, the three of them framed by storm and ruin. No one spoke. Finally, Camille found her voice.

"It's over."

Her words were hoarse, barely audible. But Matteo turned to look at her, his expression grave beneath his soaked curls.

"No," he said. "It's only over if we tell the truth this time."

Rowan looked up, her eyes wide and hollow. In that moment, she looked years older. Weathered. Cracked open. The wind eased, just slightly. The sea continued to rage. But above the cliffs, something else broke. A silence long buried. And in that space, truth waited.

28

WHAT WAS BURIED

The rain had passed, but its memory lingered. Villa Limaccia's garden shimmered in the quiet aftermath, like a secret reluctantly resurfacing. Every leaf was heavy with water, every stem bowed as if in mourning. Pools of rain collected in the hollows of broken statues, trickled from cracked urns, and dripped steadily from the torn canvas of the terrace awning. The scent was heavy: bruised rosemary, sodden earth, salt from the nearby cliffs. And beneath it all lay a bitter trace of something older, more human.

The storm had passed, but nothing felt clean. Camille stood at the edge of the overgrown garden, staring at the remnants of what was once manicured and controlled. Now it looked like it had finally surrendered. The hedges, once sculpted into tight domes, had spilled into wildness. Ivy wrapped the marble columns, suffocating the structure it once adorned. The saints lining the walkways were headless, their bodies moss-covered. Villa Limaccia wasn't decaying, it was reimagining itself. And the truth it held had teeth.

Matteo emerged from the side path, water still dripping from his curls. His boots squelched in the softened gravel, each step deliberate. Under his arm he carried something old and frayed: a rolled canvas map, its corners curled, the cloth darkened by decades of use.

Rowan followed behind him. She wore an old linen coat she'd found in one of the wardrobes, the sleeves too long. Her hair was damp, pulled into a low, uneven bun. She looked fragile, but not broken. There was a new steadiness in her silence, as if what had cracked in her the night before had finally hardened into resolve.

Jasper arrived last. His face was drawn, the shadows beneath his eyes deepened by the bruised sky above. He hadn't shaved. His shirt was unbuttoned at the collar, sleeves rolled. There was dried blood on his knuckles and a look in his eyes that made Camille unsure whether he wanted to fight something, or confess everything.

Matteo laid the map on the marble garden table. The metal ring at the table's center was rusted through, and vines curled around the legs, as if trying to drag it down into the earth. He pinned the corners with a pot, a stone, and a broken wine glass.

"This is what you need to see," he said quietly.

The map was hand-drawn, yellowed with age, the ink faded in places but still legible. It showed the villa in a previous life, when the olive grove had been a working farm, the guesthouse a chapel, and the garden paths looped in clean, perfect lines like a labyrinth drawn by someone with something to hide.

Matteo traced the main villa with his finger. "After the war, my great-uncle used this place to move things, wine, silver, paintings. And sometimes people. The tunnels were already here. Older than the house. Older than us."

"Smugglers?" Jasper asked.

Matteo nodded. "And something more. This part..." he pointed toward a shaded corner of the map, near the woods "...

was a chapel. The locals say it was cursed. Used for confessions the Church refused to hear."

Rowan leaned over the table, her breath catching. "You think Alba's down there?"

Matteo looked up. A breeze stirred the trees around them. The branches shifted like hands brushing against one another. The sky above was still heavy, the light slanting gold and gray through the clouds like the last warning before dusk. Rowan spoke, her voice low. "You said there's another entrance?"

Matteo pointed again. "Here. Hidden beneath the grove."

Alba's voice drifted across the garden. "It used to be the original chapel cellar. But after the fire, they buried it. Said it was safer that way."

Camille's heart thudded. "Then that's where we go."

They moved together, pushing through undergrowth and vines that clung like old hands, the path half-swallowed by moss and decades of neglect. A toppled sundial lay on its side, the Roman numerals eaten away by lichen. Rowan paused beside it, brushing a hand across the stone.

"Everything here," she whispered. "Looks like it was meant to stay hidden."

The olive grove was darker than the rest of the grounds, the canopy woven tightly above them. The trees twisted in ancient shapes, roots gnarled like knuckles, leaves silver-edged and whispering with every breeze. As they pushed deeper, the air cooled. Earthier. Heavier.

Matteo stopped at a clearing. To the untrained eye, there was nothing but leaf-strewn soil and stones. But he knelt and began to dig. It didn't take long. The vines came away easily. Beneath the dirt, a ring of iron. The trapdoor was sunken and warped, wood bloated from decades of storms. He pried it open with a crowbar.

A foul breath of air rushed out. Damp. Old. Heavy with rot

and mold and forgotten things. Camille covered her nose with her sleeve.

"Christ."

Rowan took a step back. Matteo pulled a flashlight from his satchel, flicked it on, and aimed it into the black. Steps. Carved stone, narrow and steep, leading down into the unknown. He looked back once, at the others.

"Are you ready?"

No one answered. But one by one, they descended. The dark took them, and the door creaked shut behind them, swallowed by vines once more. The air underground had teeth. It bit at their skin with damp, unseen things, chilling fingertips trailing the back of necks, creeping into sleeves and up spines. It smelled like mildew and ash, like something dead trying to remember itself. It wasn't just old. It was *watching.* The deeper they descended, the more the silence thickened. Not the comfortable hush of a quiet place. This was the oppressive kind. The kind that pressed in on the lungs, coiled behind the ears, begged them not to speak.

Camille led the way, her flashlight cutting a shaky arc through the darkness. The beam landed on stone slick with condensation and age. Roots pushed through the walls like veins, curling and twitching in places, as if the villa itself were listening, waiting to reclaim them. She gripped the light tighter. The thought had come uninvited and wouldn't leave: *this place has held its breath for decades... and now it's exhaling.*

Behind her, Rowan moved in a kind of trance. Her face, pale and tight, was set in concentration, but her eyes darted to every creak, every shadow. Her hands were jammed deep in her coat pockets to keep them from trembling. She had the look of someone who knew the story wasn't over. Who feared she might be the one still holding the last page.

Jasper followed, one hand running along the wall for

balance. The flicker of his lantern made the tunnel dance, twisting the carved stone into cruel shapes. Once, he paused before a stretch of wall where faint markings had been worn nearly smooth, crosses, slashes, some kind of sigil half-erased by time.

"Symbols," he muttered. "Or warnings."

Matteo, at the rear, didn't speak. He didn't need to. His posture said enough. Shoulders squared, jaw tight, flashlight steady. Every movement was deliberate. Protective. But his eyes flicked to Rowan often, and Camille noticed. It wasn't just watchfulness. It was guilt.

The corridor twisted again, then opened abruptly into a chamber. They froze. It was like stepping into a ribcage. Beams arched above them like bones, rotting and half-collapsed. The walls wept with moisture, and the air shifted, no longer moving in currents, but *breathing*, shallow and cold. A long-forgotten room, built beneath the villa, sealed and silenced.

And in its center: the bench.

It looked ordinary. Plain stone. But it sat too perfectly, centered like an altar, untouched by time. Clean, almost reverent.

"This wasn't here by accident," Camille whispered.

She stepped forward. The ground crunched beneath her boots, broken glass, ancient bone fragments, pebbles worn smooth. The beam of her light caught something. It looked like a seam. Almost invisible, carved into the floor beneath the bench.

Jasper moved beside her. "A compartment?"

Together, they heaved the bench. It groaned, resisting at first, then shifted. Dust billowed from beneath. The panel below it was flush with the floor, perfectly square. Camille dropped to her knees, brushed away the debris, and pulled. The lid opened. And there, wrapped in oilcloth, was another recorder.

Matteo took it gently. He didn't speak as he unwrapped the layers, revealing the dull metal, the worn buttons, the cassette still sealed within.

"It's his," Camille said. Her voice had gone small.

Matteo nodded, his mouth a hard line. He wound a crank. Slid the tape in. Pressed play. The recorder clicked. A hiss filled the room. Then... Leo's voice.

"If you find this... I didn't want to die."

Rowan gasped, backing into the wall. Jasper caught her elbow, but she pulled away, her eyes wide with disbelief.

"I thought it was just a game," the voice went on, cracking. "They said it was tradition. Confession Night. Just a dare. But then... the threats started."

Camille stared at the recorder. It didn't feel like a voice from the past. It felt *present*, like Leo was in the room with them, whispering into the wet stone.

"I heard them outside. Laughing. Then shouting. Max told me to tell the truth. I told them I had nothing to confess. That's when I heard Mara."

His voice broke. There was a pause—then, faintly:

"She said I was a problem. She said this was how problems got solved."

The silence that followed stretched too long. Then came the last line.

"If you find this... please tell Matteo. Tell him I tried to reveal the truth."

Click. The tape stopped. Rowan sank to her knees. Her hands covered her face, and she let out a long, low breath that was too controlled to be a sob, but not far from one. Matteo's hand rested on the top of the recorder like it might burn him. His eyes shone, but he didn't blink.

"He knew," he said quietly. "He knew it was coming."

"He thought he could escape," Camille murmured. "And they made sure he didn't."

Before anyone could answer. A scream tore through the air. Sharp. Real. Not recorded.

It pierced the tunnel like a needle, echoing down the passage.

Camille was already moving. "Alba!"

They ran. Boots pounded over stone, over mud, through dust and damp air. The tunnel constricted around them, forcing them into a frantic, single-file sprint. The light from their torches jittered and bounced. No one spoke. When they burst into the garden, the sky had darkened again, clouds sinking low and smothering the light. The trees hissed in the breeze. Vines dragged across the path as if reaching for them.

29

THE SPIRAL

The east wing groaned as if it remembered being opened. Its heavy door resisted Camille's hand, hinges shrieking like something dragged from a grave. As it creaked inward, a wave of cold air breathed from within, unnatural against the thick humidity still lingering in the rest of the villa. The scent hit them instantly, stale air trapped in sunless rooms for decades, heavy with mildew, rotting wood, and old plaster baked and steamed by years of shifting heat and storm.

Camille hesitated in the threshold, flashlight gripped tight in her hand, the rubber damp against her skin from sweat and nerves. Behind her, Rowan hugged her elbows, her breath shallow.

"I thought this wing was sealed," she said.

"It was," Jasper muttered, already stepping through. "But someone wanted it open now."

The corridor beyond swallowed them whole. It was hotter than they expected. A moist, cloying heat, the kind that clings to skin and crawls into lungs. The storm shutters here were bolted closed, casting the space in near-total darkness. Their flashlights cast long, jittering beams across walls streaked with mildew.

Wallpaper peeled in great scabs. Beneath their feet, the wooden floor had softened in places, warping under the moisture that had bled through the foundation for years.

Dust layered everything like snow. But not untouched. A trail had been disturbed.

Camille saw it first. A serpentine line of movement through the dust, as if someone had dragged a foot... or a body. Or walked in slow, measured steps.

"Someone's been here," she said quietly. Her voice felt too loud in the thick, heavy air.

Jasper swept his torch across the hallway. The light caught on a faded portrait of a woman, but her face had been eaten away by black mold. Beneath the painting, a set of footprints overlapped with the dragging trail, leading toward the far corridor.

The air grew worse as they walked. The oppressive summer heat, trapped and fermented, had become sour and still. Even Rowan, who'd grown quiet over the last day, reached up and wiped a bead of sweat from her upper lip with a trembling hand.

They turned a corner and passed under an arch where cobwebs hung like lace, tattered, old, but disturbingly intact, like no one had passed through here in years... until now.

And then the smell changed.

Mildew, still. But layered with something sharper.

"Medicine," Camille said, sniffing. "Like antiseptic."

"The infirmary," Rowan said.

The corridor narrowed. Ahead, a door stood slightly ajar. From within came a soft sound. A scrape. A shift. The kind of movement that didn't belong to a building, but to a body.

Jasper reached the door first. He paused, his hand on the doorknob, listening. Camille moved beside him, breath caught in her throat.

The doorknob turned with a low click.

The door opened into a room lost to time.

It had once been functional, a servants' quarters, perhaps, but now it resembled something forgotten by both the living and the dead. The ceiling was mottled with stains, the plaster above threatening collapse. Two beds stood rusted against opposite walls, their frames orange with corrosion, one mattress collapsed inward, blackened by mold. The walls were streaked with green veins of damp, and the only window was nailed shut from the outside, its glass webbed with cracks.

A chair sat in the center of the room, beneath a single crooked light fixture. And in that chair sat Alba.

Her head slumped forward, braid trailing over her shoulder like a lifeline unraveling. Her wrists were bound with strips of gauze, stained faintly yellow from sweat and time. Her ankles, too. Her breathing was shallow, chest rising and falling in a slow, syrupy rhythm. She looked fragile. Wrong. Like something had drained the spirit from her.

Camille didn't speak. She ran.

"Alba!" she cried, falling to her knees beside her.

The heat was stifling here, the air thick and unmoving. It pressed against Camille's skin as she touched Alba's arm. Her skin was warm and clammy, and her pulse fluttered beneath her jaw like a dying moth.

"She's alive," Camille said, voice tight with relief. "She's breathing. Just... slow."

"She was drugged," Jasper said. His flashlight beam searched the corners of the room. "She didn't walk here."

Camille worked at the bindings. The gauze was wrapped too tightly, digging into Alba's skin, leaving angry impressions. She unwound them carefully, whispering her name between breathless reassurances.

"Alba, it's Camille. We found you. You're safe."

But the older woman didn't stir. Her eyes remained closed.

Her brow twitched once, a faint flutter. Her lips parted, but no sound came.

"She's trying to wake up," Rowan whispered.

"We need to get her out of here," Camille said. "Now."

She and Jasper lifted Alba between them. Her body sagged, light and boneless, as if she'd been asleep for days. Camille gritted her teeth. The air in the room felt tighter now, heavier. Her scalp prickled. She turned her head toward the cracked door and thought, for one second, she saw something shift just beyond it.

A shadow? A breath? Nothing. She shoved it down.

As they stepped back into the hallway, the heat rolled over them again, thick and waiting, like it knew they hadn't found everything.

Halfway down the corridor, Rowan turned. The door they'd left open had swung halfway shut again. Not a gust of wind. Not in this sealed wing. Just movement. As if the house, too, was breathing.

Alba moaned softly as they carried her through the east wing's corridor. Her eyelids twitched, her limbs slack between Camille and Jasper. Rowan kept pace just behind, her breath shallow, darting nervous glances back toward the darkness from which they'd come. The hallway remained silent. As if the villa itself had paused to listen.

They hadn't made it more than ten paces before Rowan whispered, "Stop. Camille... look."

Camille halted and shifted Alba's weight. Her gaze dropped, her torchlight following it, and caught a pale square taped to the front of Alba's blouse. Just beneath the collarbone, flush against the fabric, a piece of paper, no bigger than a postcard. Edges curled. The tape looked old but clean. The writing scrawled in sharp red ink, steady and unhurried. Not messy. Not rushed.

Camille's heart picked up speed. Carefully, Rowan peeled it

away. The tape hissed softly as it came free. She unfolded the paper. The ink shimmered wetly in the flashlight's beam.

She read aloud:

"You were right. But being right won't save you. What you buried is rotting now. Let it all rot."

No one spoke.

A single drop of sweat ran down Camille's back, catching in the waistband of her jeans. The temperature had changed again, the heat hanging heavier than before, more oppressive, as if the corridor had shrunk by degrees and was now pressing in on all sides.

"It's a threat," she said, voice low. "A warning. Maybe both."

Jasper took the note from her, frowning as he read it over again. "This wasn't random," he muttered. "Someone did this while we were searching. They had time to write it, attach it—and knew we'd find it."

Rowan stepped back, her foot crunching on a piece of loose plaster. "What does 'what you buried' mean?"

Camille looked up slowly. "It's not just about Leo. It's about all of it. The lies. The pacts. Every secret we've kept rotting in this place."

And then it happened. A sharp, sudden mechanical *snap* echoed down the corridor behind them, louder than footsteps, louder than breath. It came from the door they'd just exited, the one leading to the old servants' quarters. Then a slam. Not the wind. Not the storm. A deliberate *slam*.

Camille spun. "The door!"

Jasper broke into a run, disappearing back into the gloom.

Camille tried to adjust her grip on Alba.

"We have to get out of here. Now."

But a second later, Jasper's voice rose, sharp with panic. "It's locked."

"What?" Rowan was already moving after him.

Camille staggered forward with Alba, her limbs shaking now under the weight, not just of the woman, but of the moment.

Jasper was at the door, shoulder braced against it, trying the handle again and again.

"It's deadbolted. From the outside."

"Someone's sealed us in?" Rowan asked, breath catching.

Then the lights went out. Not their flashlights, but the overheads. A flicker. Then complete, stifling black.

"Keep the torches on," Camille said quickly, her voice steady despite the pitch-black around them.

And then they heard another sound. A low hiss that didn't belong. It came not from the walls or the door, but from above somewhere in the vents. Camille lifted her head slowly. From the slotted vent in the ceiling, a grey plume drifted down. Light at first. Almost like mist. It curled as it descended, ghostlike. Then it thickened, coiled in slow, deliberate spirals.

Smoke. The smell hit her nose a second later. Burnt plastic. Chemicals. Faintly sweet. Industrial.

"Jesus Christ," Jasper muttered, backing up, hand clamping over his nose.

Rowan froze, staring upward. "It's coming through the vents. Someone's pumping it in."

Camille stepped away from Alba, then turned back and crouched by her side. The woman hadn't stirred again. Her breathing was growing shallower.

"We have to move her. Fast," Camille said.

Jasper was already pacing the perimeter of the corridor, testing every door.

"All locked," he spat. "All of them."

"What about the windows?" Rowan said, half-running down the hall. "There were shutters. Maybe we can force one."

Camille hooked her arms beneath Alba's and dragged her

slowly after them. Sweat was beading across her brow now, stinging her eyes.

The smoke grew thicker, spilling in slow sheets down the corridor. It didn't rise like fire, it clung to the floor, seeping out in heavy fingers, creeping like floodwater.

"It's chemical," Camille said. "It's not from a fire. Someone's using the villa's systems to pump this in."

"Then they planned this," Jasper said, turning with wild eyes. "They waited until we were in the only sealed part of the house and trapped us like rats."

A clang echoed down the corridor. Rowan shrieked and whipped around.

"Up there—" she pointed. "The vent!"

A metal grate had fallen open. For a split second, they all saw it: a figure in black at the far end of the hall, face indistinct, standing just outside the east wing door. Watching and then gone.

The door clicked. Camille dropped to her knees, choking now on the thickening air.

"Matteo!" she screamed. "If you're out there, please open the door!"

No answer. Just smoke. Just silence. Alba coughed once, wet and fragile.

"We're not dying in here," Jasper growled.

He crossed to one of the shuttered windows. With a grunt, he lifted a nearby chair and *slammed* it against the slats. Nothing.

Again. Wood splintered. A crack formed.

"Keep going!" Camille shouted.

Rowan ran to help, grabbing the other side of the chair. The heat was growing unbearable. The smoke was lower now, curling at their knees, wafting up in strange shapes. It smelled artificial. Wrong. Not fire, but something made to feel like fire.

"Tear the shutters off!" Jasper roared.

Another slam. Another crack. Then, finally, air. The chair broke through. Wood flew outward. The smoke shifted, and a rush of fresh air poured in. Camille dragged Alba toward the light. Rowan reached through, unlatching the shutters, flinging them open.

They clambered out one by one, Jasper first, then Rowan. Camille went last, dragging Alba's barely conscious body behind her. Outside, on the terrace, the sea wind rushed to meet them. They all collapsed, coughing and gasping. Camille lay on the stones, her chest heaving, smoke still burning her lungs.

The villa behind them loomed silent. The spiral on the note flashed through her mind again. And its message rang louder than ever. The villa is awake and it wants them all gone.

30

INFERNO

The smoke moved like a creature alive. It pressed through the east wing, slow and thick, a flood of grey curling along the floorboards, licking at the skirting boards, unfurling in corners like coiled snakes waking from hibernation. Not like fire. There were no erratic bursts of flame yet. This was something calculated. Controlled. More sinister than chaos.

From the outside, the villa looked deceptively calm. But anyone close enough could feel the temperature change. The air, once fragrant with thyme, heat, and lemon oil, now carried the acrid tang of plastic and electrical burn. It slid down throats and stung eyes. The shutters of the east wing pulsed like lungs behind the smoke-streaked windows.

On the terrace, Camille dropped to her knees beside Alba, whose eyelids flickered as her body resisted the final pull of the sedatives. Her face was damp with sweat. One hand reached weakly for something. Water? Help? Sense?

"It's okay," Camille murmured, brushing hair from her brow. "You're safe. We've got you now."

"Where's Matteo?" Jasper asked between ragged breaths. He

was hunched over by the balustrade, coughing hard into the crook of his elbow. His eyes streamed from the smoke.

"He went around the front," Rowan said, her voice hoarse, thin with panic. "He said he'd try to break through."

Camille looked up at the east wing again. The glass panes were starting to fog. Her skin prickled. Something was *building* inside. Then came the crash. A thunderous blow, somewhere from within the house. Then another.

Matteo's silhouette appeared through the mist, emerging from around the corner like some mythic figure carved from storm and fury. His sleeves were rolled to the elbows, sweat and soot streaked across his temple. In his hands: a sledgehammer.

Without pausing, he struck again.

The wood groaned.

Smoke gushed from the cracks in the door.

Another swing. Then another.

With the final blow, the heavy oak door split down the middle, and fire *exhaled* through the gap. Not flames, not yet. But orange flickers, greedy and licking like tongues behind bars.

"Move!" Matteo barked.

Jasper was through first, Camille close behind, dragging Alba through the broken terrace window. The heat inside hit them like a slap, thick and angry, wrapping around their skin like cellophane.

The east corridor was lit from below now, flames beginning to snake from the baseboards. Shadows danced across the ceiling. The paintings melted into grotesque smears.

They ran. The smoke chased them like a wave. By the time they reached the central staircase, Alba had started to murmur. Her words were nonsensical, fragmented.

"She knew... she waited... under the stairs..."

Camille didn't have time to ask what it meant. In the drawing room, they laid Alba on the couch, beneath the high fan, which spun weakly, ineffectually, stirring the smoke but doing little to shift it.

Matteo arrived seconds later, coughing, carrying a fire extinguisher he'd retrieved from the cellar. He turned in a slow circle, watching the edges of the smoke. "It's not natural," he said. "This isn't just fire. It's feeding off something."

Alba stirred. Her lips moved. "She... left something."

"Who?" Rowan asked, kneeling.

"Mara," Alba whispered, then fell silent again.

That was when Jasper disappeared down the hallway again. Camille found him moments later, crouched in Mara's room. The sheets were neat. The closet orderly. Something felt terribly wrong. He was already reaching under the bed, fingers sweeping the space like someone blind feeling for a pulse. Then he stopped.

"What?" Camille asked.

He pulled out a small, black burner phone. Taped with white electrical tape, printed in bold black ink:

DO NOT TOUCH UNTIL AFTER.

Camille's chest went tight. "After what?"

Jasper stared at the screen. The battery was low, but it blinked to life in his palm. One number sat at the top of the recent calls. He tapped the screen. The call connected, then another sound buzzed. Close by.

A vibration. Not from his hand, but from the wardrobe. He and Camille locked eyes. Jasper threw the doors open. The scent of lavender sachets and something metallic wafted out. A single duffel bag sat inside. Mara's. The phone inside the lining buzzed once more. Same number. Same tone. Jasper yanked it out.

Camille stepped closer. He handed it to her. She turned the screen on. One app was open.

Timer Paused at 00:03:47.

Camille didn't want to ask what it would've triggered. Instead, she reached into the side pocket. A folded piece of paper, thick and creased like it had been written a long time ago. In Mara's handwriting:

"You never buried the truth. You just covered it in velvet and called it friendship. Let it burn."

Camille's stomach turned.

"She left this to go off *after* she died," she whispered. "She wanted to finish what she started."

"Even from the grave," Jasper muttered. "She's pulling strings."

Outside, a second alarm began to sound. A low, undulating pulse. It wasn't a fire alarm. It was something else. Deeper. More mechanical. Matteo appeared in the doorway.

"You need to see this," he said, voice clipped.

He led them to the hallway junction. From the shadows under the staircase, where Leo had once recorded a whisper of fear, they heard something click. And then a hum. The walls warmed.

Camille backed away.

"What did she do?" Rowan asked, voice cracking.

Matteo's expression was grim. "She's planning on bringing the house down."

And now, the second stage had begun. They gathered in the hallway outside the drawing room, the smoke thinning slightly now that the windows had been opened. The fans were spinning again, sluggishly trying to draw the heat out of the walls, but it was no use. The villa remained a sealed body, sweating, pulsing, alive.

Camille stood with her hands on her knees, trying to catch her breath. Alba had fallen into a deeper, less fitful sleep on the couch, but she'd murmured once more before fading:

"She kept the worst for last."

Now Rowan sat on the bottom step of the grand staircase, her arms wrapped tightly around her knees. Her face was pale, streaked with soot and sweat. The tendons in her neck stood out with tension.

The sound of alarms had stopped. But the silence wasn't one of comfort, it was raw anticipation of something terrible. Matteo had gone to check the cellar and generator controls again. Jasper lingered in the corridor, eyes darting, checking the doors, the vents, the hinges, looking for wires, triggers, anything. He was on edge.

Rowan's voice came quietly, unexpected.

"She never stopped playing with us."

Camille turned to her. "What?"

Rowan looked up slowly, her expression hollow. "Mara. She never stopped. Not really. Not since school."

The heat was thick around them again. The weight of the villa's old bones settled deeper into the walls as if the house was leaning in, listening.

"There was this game," Rowan said. "Back when we were thirteen. Mara used to play it during lunch. 'Who's the Weakest Link.'" Her voice was flat, clinical. Detached in the way only people speaking about trauma could manage.

Camille moved closer, crouching nearby. "What kind of game?"

Rowan stared past her, through the haze that still hung in the air. "Cruel. Quiet. She'd watch us all day. See who stumbled. Who said something stupid in class. Who didn't get invited to a party. Who looked too tired. Too soft. Then, over lunch, she'd announce it. 'This week's Weakest Link is...' And that person? She'd test them."

"Test them how?" Jasper asked, his voice sharp, brittle.

Rowan blinked slowly. "She'd isolate them. See if they cracked. She'd start rumors. Turn friends against them. Dare them to do things they couldn't. She wanted to see how far she could push someone until they broke."

Camille felt a chill crawl down her spine despite the heat.

Rowan swallowed hard. "She did it to me. One term. Because I wouldn't go along with something she said about another girl. Something awful. I stood up to her, just once. And suddenly, I was the target."

Jasper exhaled slowly, kneeling beside Rowan. "And she never stopped."

Rowan nodded. "Not even at university. Confession Night? That was just a grown-up version. A game she wrapped in nostalgia and guilt and pretended it was for fun. But it was always about pressure. About watching people sweat."

"And Leo?" Camille asked.

Rowan's mouth twisted. "He was never supposed to be there. That's what she told me once. He was an outsider. A mistake. So she made him pay for it."

Camille sat down on the step beside her, their shoulders touching. The summer heat beat against the windows again, buzzing through the cracks in the stone. The taste of smoke lingered in her mouth.

"Mara set a trap for all of us," she said.

"She set a series of them," Jasper added. "That burner phone? The timers? It's definitely not over."

Rowan wiped her face on her sleeve. "No. Because one more person hasn't been broken yet."

Camille looked up sharply. "What?"

Rowan nodded slowly. "That's how she worked. One by one. She'd break each person, and then move to the next. She made Leo confess. She made me stay silent. She made Max betray him. Made Charlotte lie. Even tried to destroy Soren and me before the end."

Camille felt the hairs rise on the back of her neck. "So... who's left?"

Rowan's eyes met hers, wide and afraid. "Someone still has something. And Mara knew it."

They fell into silence. Outside, thunder rumbled low along the horizon. Camille stood and walked to the windows, peering out toward the cliffs. The wind had picked up again, and the sea was moving fast, frothing white at the rocks below. The olive trees twisted and leaned, their branches scraping one another in dry whispers.

"She always said secrets don't die," Rowan said behind her. "They just go quiet. Until you stop listening."

Camille turned to Jasper. "You said earlier that you thought someone rewired the villa. Rigged it."

He nodded. "Not just the fire. There's more. Something underground. Something's still ticking."

"Then we need to find it before it goes off," she said.

But even as she said it, a darker truth settled over the group like a shadow. Whatever Mara left behind was designed to destroy them. From the cellar, a sound broke the silence.

It began low, a faint mechanical whine, like the soft click of an old cassette beginning to spool. Then came the hiss. That unmistakable tape hiss, grainy and persistent, like breath over a speaker. They all froze.

Jasper lifted his head. "Did you hear that?"

Another hiss. Followed by a voice. Not shouting. Not urgent. Just calm, clear and familiar.

"...tell Matteo... please. Before it's too late."

Rowan's hand flew to her mouth.

Camille stood slowly from the windowsill, her blood turning to ice in her veins.

It was Leo.

His voice, thin but unmistakable, spilled up through the

floorboards like water from a crack. It carried with it the scent of mold, dust, and something far colder: memory. Guilt.

"...I tried to stop them. I did. But they said if I told anyone... if I said his name..."

Another hiss. Another breath. "...they said they'd make it look like I jumped." The tape clicked. Then rewound. By itself. The noise was too exact, too pointed. This wasn't a relic forgotten and triggered by heat or chance. Someone had *started* the recording, deliberately.

Jasper was already moving. He crossed the room and yanked open the cellar door. A gust of frigid air rose from below, touched with the sharp edge of decay.

Matteo stepped into the doorway behind him. "I didn't press play," he said quietly.

Camille looked at him. "Then who did?"

The question hung in the air like smoke. Then the recording played again. Only this time it didn't stop. Leo's voice returned, more frantic now.

"I wasn't supposed to be in the group. I know that. I heard them say it, Mara and—"

CRACK. A burst of static.

Then: "...she was supposed to *watch*. But she let it happen."

Rowan stumbled back against the banister, her face pale.

"He wasn't talking about me," she whispered. "I never... I never watched anything..."

But Camille was staring at her, her mind racing.

"'She let it happen,'" Camille repeated. "He didn't say 'Mara.' He already named her. He meant someone else. Someone still alive."

A sound behind them made them all turn. Alba, still groggy on the couch, had opened her eyes. Her lips parted. A whisper. Just one word. A name. But they didn't hear it. Because in the next moment the tape clicked once more. And a final line played, heavy and horrifying in its clarity:

"He smiled when I fell."

The room plunged into silence again. But it wasn't empty. Because the echo of that sentence clung to the walls. To their skin. To the space between each of them.

Someone *still* had secrets.

And Mara had made damn sure they couldn't hide anymore.

31

THE FINAL LETTER

The lights flickered again. Just once, an almost imperceptible stammer in the wiring, but enough to make Rowan glance toward the ceiling and pull the blanket tighter around her shoulders. Her damp hair clung to her temples, and her socks, still wet from the earlier sprint across the terrace, squelched slightly each time she moved her foot. The heat hadn't returned since the power cut. Now the villa was too quiet. Too still. And far too cold.

Jasper sat cross-legged on the floor of his room, the tangle of his unpacked duffel bag spilling out like entrails across the floorboards. He wasn't looking for anything in particular. Not at first. Just moving, searching, trying not to think about Leo's voice on the tape, or the final sentence that had burrowed under everyone's skin.

He smiled when I fell.

No one had spoken since. Not out loud. It was as if the house had enforced silence, like the heat once had enforced stillness. Downstairs, in the kitchen, the sound of steel sharpening against stone echoed up faintly through the floorboards. Rhythmic. Relentless. Matteo. Preparing, watching, waiting.

Camille was somewhere in the hallway, pacing like a caged animal. Rowan sat in a wingback chair in the corner, knees drawn up, lost in thought, her eyes flickering every so often toward the door.

And Jasper was here, trying to feel useful. Trying to make sense of anything. But mostly trying not to drown in the rising tide of guilt.

He reached into his bag again, sifting through old shirts, a cracked shaving kit, the charger for a phone he hadn't used in months. Then, something odd. A slim envelope. Unfamiliar. Folded perfectly and slid beneath the lining of the bag.

He froze. His fingers hovered over it, trembling before they even made contact. The hairs on the back of his neck stood up. This wasn't just lost. It had been placed there, like a final card slipped into a player's hand just before the bluff.

He drew it out with slow hands. The envelope was yellowed slightly, thick paper – the expensive kind. No name on the front. Just a wax seal on the back. Cracked. Already opened once, perhaps. Maybe by the sender. Maybe… someone else.

He unfolded it carefully. And nearly dropped it. The handwriting hit him in the gut. Even before he read the words, he *knew*. It was Leo's. That looping tilt. The slightly overlong tails on the y's and g's. It dragged him straight back to university, to passed notes in lectures, to ideas scribbled on paper napkins in the dining hall. It *shouldn't* be possible. And yet.

Jasper's breath stuttered as he read: "You were supposed to tell my story. But you sold yours instead."

His chest went hollow. The words didn't just sting, they sank deep. A hot, thick guilt rose in his throat like bile. He read on.

"You stood next to me and held the camera while they laughed. You said you didn't know, but you knew. You didn't push me, Jasper. But you didn't stop them, either."

The floor beneath him may as well have opened.

His memory scrambled. He hadn't known what Mara planned. Not fully. Not exactly. But he'd seen Leo's face that night. The flush in his cheeks. The way his laugh had cracked, brittle and strained. How he'd kept looking toward the door, as if calculating the distance.

Jasper's fingers curled around the letter as he continued.

"You always said the truth was complicated. That everyone had their version. I only had mine. And you didn't want to share it."

He couldn't breathe.

It was like standing waist-deep in a rising tide, and realizing the shore had vanished.

He stood slowly, the letter shaking in his hand, the room tilting slightly around him.

"Camille," he called hoarsely. "You need to see this."

She appeared by his side seconds later, her skin pale, her hands fisted at her sides.

"What is it?"

He handed her the page. Rowan stood too, silent, wary. Camille read the note carefully, lips moving as her eyes tracked each line. Her expression darkened. Her shoulders slumped slightly, not in defeat, but in understanding. The kind that aged a person in seconds.

"This... this was meant to tip the balance," she murmured. "To shift the weight. Mara wanted to drag you under with the rest of us."

Rowan stepped closer, her voice cold. "You didn't stop them?"

Jasper's head snapped up. "I didn't know. Not fully. I saw things, yes. I saw Leo struggle. But I didn't understand how far it would go. I thought he'd just... brush it off. Like he always did."

"You let him take it alone," Rowan said, her voice a quiet cut.

"I wasn't Mara," Jasper said through gritted teeth.

"No," Camille said softly. "But you weren't Leo, either."

The silence that followed felt heavier than anything the villa's walls had ever held. Jasper looked at them both.

"So what now? Am I next on the spiral?"

Camille folded the letter carefully. "Mara planted this. Or someone working with her. She knew just where to dig."

Rowan's mouth twitched. "Unless she wasn't alone."

A chill passed through the room. Camille said nothing. Because the possibility had taken root in all their minds now that one more person still held a secret. And Mara, dead or not, was still playing her game.

The tension in the room was a living thing. It coiled around their limbs, curled behind their throats. Even the shadows along the walls seemed to hold their breath.

Jasper stood in the middle of the room, letter still loose in his hand, skin waxen, as though the villa itself had leached the color from him. His posture, usually upright and certain, had slumped. He looked deflated. Or exposed. Maybe both.

"You said you didn't know," Camille said, stepping forward, her voice level but tightly controlled. "You said you didn't know how far it would go. But Leo's voice is still echoing through this place. And this letter..." Her eyes flicked down to the page between them. "This wasn't about justice. It was about punishment."

Jasper swallowed but said nothing. His jaw worked like he wanted to speak but couldn't find the words to make it safe enough to say aloud.

Rowan stood in the doorway, arms folded across her chest, her knuckles white where her fingers gripped her elbows. Her silence had weight. Her eyes had judgment.

Camille's voice lowered, sharpened. "You knew this wasn't just a reunion. You were here to finish something too."

Jasper flinched as though struck. "I didn't. Camille, it wasn't..."

"You came here to finish your book," she said, her tone flat now. Accusatory.

He closed his eyes for a moment, and when he opened them, they were red-rimmed. He looked tired. Haunted.

"Yes," he said finally. "Yes, I came here to write. Not about Leo. Or not just Leo. About... all of us. About what it was like then. Who we were. I thought if I could get everyone together again, I could untangle it. Maybe it would help. Maybe it would fix something."

"Or maybe," Rowan said, stepping forward now, her voice cold and clear. "You just wanted the ending."

Silence. Jasper's mouth opened. No words came. Camille took another step toward him. "You lied, Jasper. To all of us. You let us think this was some emotional healing trip. A reconnection. But it was research. You watched us fall apart and took notes."

He dropped the letter onto the table like it had burned his skin. "You think this was easy for me?"

"No," she said. "I think it was convenient."

His face twisted. "I didn't know Mara would twist things the way she did. She found a draft of the manuscript on my laptop. She must've hacked into it. She rewrote it. Inserted details. Changed things. Things I never wrote. She poisoned it."

"You should've told us," Rowan said. "You should've come clean the second you realized."

"I was ashamed," he admitted. "I still am. But by then it had already started. The tension. The clues. The notes. I thought I could manage it. Keep control."

"You're not the author of any of this anymore," Camille said quietly. "She is."

Jasper's lips tightened. "I only realized the extent of it today.

The burner phone. The edits. Mara turned my story into her weapon. Her revenge arc. And I handed her the outline."

Outside, wind slammed against the shutters. The walls groaned slightly, the ancient timbers shifting with the pressure. The villa listened.

Matteo, silent until now, finally moved.

He stepped away from the counter and walked over to the sink. The water had pooled around the blade in a thin, mirrored sheet. He reached down, plucked the knife from the steel, and then, with a sharp motion, tossed it back down into the basin. The clang rang out like a gunshot.

"Then finish it right," Matteo said, turning to face them, eyes hard as stone. "You've spent years hiding behind chapters and memory. Now tell the real story. Or someone else will die."

Jasper's shoulders slumped. "I just... I wasn't there that night. But I saw the video. I saw the fear in Leo's eyes. I saw him look at me like I could stop it. And I didn't. I laughed. I told myself it was all just drama. University antics. But I knew. I *knew*."

"You wrote instead of speaking," Camille said.

He nodded slowly. "Because writing's what I do. It's the only way I've ever been able to understand anything. But now..." He looked at them both. "I don't know if I was ever meant to tell *this* story."

Rowan's voice was barely above a whisper. "Then maybe it's not your story to finish."

A long pause followed. Matteo folded his arms. "Maybe it is now."

The weight of it settled on Jasper's shoulders like an avalanche. His chest heaved once, and he turned, walked to the table, and sat. His fingers hovered above the keyboard of his laptop. He opened a new document. And began to type. Not from memory and not from notes, but from guilt and shame. And truth.

Across the room, Camille leaned against the wall, watching him. Her heart ached, but her hands were steady. They were getting closer now to something painful. Something necessary. And maybe, finally, something honest.

Rowan walked to the door, opened it. Cool air swept in from the hallway.

"We meet in the chapel," she said. "Sunrise. We bring it all."

Camille nodded. Jasper looked up, his eyes wet. "Everything?"

"Everything," Camille said.

32

THE ASHES

The villa no longer shimmered with marble and light. Morning broke gray and cautious, as though the sky itself was wary of looking too closely at what remained. Where once the sun had poured gold over the terraced walls, there was now only the flat glare of daylight diffused through smoke haze. The air was thick with the scent of charred wood and sea salt and something metallic that clung to the back of the throat.

Villa Limaccia stood battered and scorched, its southern wing blackened from within, glass scattered like confetti across the limestone. A window hung crooked in its frame, shutters splintered like snapped ribs. The olive trees around the property had bowed under the wind's assault; their silver leaves were now ash-flecked and limp. And yet, it stood. Somehow, it still stood.

Inside, the survivors had become quiet shadows of themselves. No more shouting. No more accusations. The storm had taken their voices, or perhaps it had only revealed the truth that none of them wanted to speak again. The walls bore the scars. Smoke had stained the ceilings in long black smudges. One chandelier had melted slightly on one side, droplets of glass hardened mid-drip. Photographs on the hallway wall were warped, frames blistered. A picture of the original group, Leo included, had cracked clean down the center, splitting his face in two.

Even the air inside the villa had changed. What had once smelled of rosemary, lemon, and summer wine now stung with the acrid tinge of scorched memories and chemical fire. The scent clung to skin, hair, clothes. No amount of soap could lift it.

In the courtyard, shallow puddles shimmered with oil-slick rainwater. Camille stood at the edge of one, her reflection warped and fragmented by ripples. She barely recognized herself. Her face was older. Her eyes, harder. There was something fractured behind them now, like a splinter of grief that hadn't worked its way out yet.

Rowan stood beside her, silent. Her hands were wrapped in gauze where the glass had cut her palms the night before. The blood had soaked through, faint red halos on white linen. She stared straight ahead, not blinking. Her blouse was stained with soot. Her spine was too straight.

Jasper sat on the crumbled step near the terrace, a notebook clutched loosely in his lap, but his pen hadn't moved in over an hour. The wind had whipped his curls into tangles, and his jaw was peppered with two days of stubble. His eyes were rimmed red, not from tears, he'd cried them all already, but from exhaustion and the weight of shame.

And Matteo, always Matteo, still, strong, but now forever changed. He stood further back in the garden, not moving, watching the horizon like it might bring answers on the next wind. His hands were black with soot, fingernails rimmed with earth from where he'd helped pull smoldering debris from the east wing before sunrise. Beneath his shirt, his chest rose and fell in slow, measured breaths. Controlled. Contained. Until he no longer needed to be.

Just after nine that morning, the low thrum of helicopter

blades echoed off the cliffs. The coastal road had finally reopened, landslide cleared, debris pushed back, cell signal partially restored. The first team arrived in a sleek white chopper that hovered briefly above the chapel ruins before descending in a gust of gravel and broken leaves.

Two paramedics rushed out, cutting through the silence like a scalpel through tissue.

They carried Alba out on a stretcher. Her face was pale and slack, oxygen tubes looped under her nose, her body still. But she was alive. Camille watched them strap her in, wordless. Rowan didn't move. She stood with her arms tightly wrapped around herself, and in the silence of the morning, Camille could hear her breathing: shallow, rhythmic, like someone holding back a scream with every inhale. No one spoke.

Jasper turned away, unable to watch the stretcher leave. Not because he didn't care. Because he did. Too much. A second team arrived minutes later. This one the local police. Two plainclothes officers walked in, their faces grim. They took one look at the villa, exchanged a glance, and adjusted the notepads in their hands. No one greeted them with ceremony.

Matteo approached first, wordlessly handing over a sealed canvas bag. Inside: Leo Marinetti's journal, the USB drives, and the half-melted recorder that had played his last words.

"There's more," Matteo said. "Interviews. Footage. And one survivor who's ready to speak."

The officers looked toward Rowan. She nodded once, then turned and led them inside. They sat her in the drawing room, the furniture still smoke-stained and crooked. Rowan didn't ask for water. Didn't flinch when they began recording. She told them everything. About the summer it happened. About the dare. About Leo's terror, hidden beneath his careful smile. She named them: Max, Mara, Soren. And herself.

"I knew," she said, voice calm. "I didn't push him. But I knew.

And I said nothing. Because I wanted to believe it wasn't my responsibility. That if I didn't look directly at the guilt, it wouldn't become mine."

Her hands trembled for the first time.

"It was easier to pretend we were just kids," she said. "But it was worse than that. We were cruel. And we let it happen."

Her voice cracked at the end, just a hairline fracture, but enough to split open everything she'd been holding back. When the statement was over, Rowan signed it. No hesitation. Her fingers smudged the ink slightly. A perfect mark of imperfection. Meanwhile, Camille stepped outside. Another car had arrived, this time, it was the press.

Only one journalist, but still, a public voice. She was young, her notebook shaking in her hand. Camille asked her name. Then she sat beside her on the stone wall, legs crossed, hands resting in her lap.

"I won't give you the villa," she said. "I won't give you a headline. But I will give you a name."

The reporter blinked. "A name?"

Camille nodded.

"Leo Marinetti," she said softly. "He died here ten years ago. And we buried more than just his body."

She paused.

"We buried who we were. And now we have to live with what's left."

The journalist didn't speak for a moment. Then she simply nodded, and began to write.

The chapel was little more than a skeleton now. Stones half-sunk into the earth, ivy curling over broken pillars, the altar fractured by time and neglect. In another life, perhaps it had been a place of sanctuary. Now it was a ruin. A graveyard. A confessional box shattered by truth.

Camille stood just inside the broken archway, staring at the altar. A jagged piece of the marble slab still bore a smear of soot from the fire that had raged only days before. Beneath the floor, Matteo had said, the foundations ran deep. Older than the villa itself. This ground had always known suffering.

She wasn't alone. Rowan, Jasper, Matteo, and Alba were gathered in the ruined nave. No one spoke at first. The wind was back, softer now, but insistent, carrying with it the scent of salt and ash. It whistled through the broken windows like a voice too tired to scream.

The police had finished their interviews. The press had taken their footage. Emergency responders had done their work and moved on. This was their last moment at Villa Limaccia. Their last choice.

Rowan stood slightly apart from the others, her hands tucked into the sleeves of her cardigan, her face drawn. The bruises beneath her eyes had settled into deep shadows, but she hadn't cried again. She simply stood still, watching the altar, as though expecting it to speak. Jasper cleared his throat.

"I finished the manuscript," he said softly.

Camille turned to him. "What did you call it?"

He hesitated. "*The Truth We Buried.*"

Rowan let out a breath like a laugh, but it wasn't humor. "That's a lie too, isn't it? We didn't bury it. We poured cement over it and built a palace."

"And it cracked," Matteo said. "As everything buried does."

Camille looked down at the small object in her palm. Leo's broken cassette. What remained of it, anyway. Matteo had offered to take it. But she'd refused. There was something right about her holding it. She'd been the outsider once. The observer. Now, she felt like the keeper of ghosts.

Alba stood beside her, eyes closed, face lifted to the wind.

"I stayed here after everyone left," Alba said quietly. "The years passed, but the stories didn't. They settled in the walls. I tried not to listen. But the house..."

"Remembers," Rowan finished.

Alba nodded. "Yes. And now it has spoken."

Jasper stepped forward. "I've arranged for Leo's remains to be reburied. Properly. With a marker. With his name."

No one responded at first. Then Camille said, "It's the least we can do."

Silence wrapped around them again. Not uncomfortable, just full. The kind of silence that follows war. And then Rowan turned toward the balcony that jutted over the sea. Camille watched her go. She didn't ask where she was going. She already knew.

~

The wind was stronger on the cliffside. Rowan stood alone, the last remnants of her old university diary in her hands. Pages she had once filled with laughter and longing, late-night games and inside jokes that now tasted like ash on her tongue. It had survived the fire, barely. But not this moment.

She struck the match with practiced fingers and held it beneath the first corner. The paper curled, blackened and crumbled. She fed one page after another to the flame, watching them disintegrate, one memory at a time. Soren's scribbled notes in the margins. Mara's cruel drawings. A doodle Leo had once added on a dare. And in between, her own guilt were paragraphs of silence, page after page of I saw but said nothing.

The ashes fluttered out over the cliffs, dancing briefly before vanishing into the wind. Matteo stepped up beside her. He didn't say anything at first. Just stood there, watching the smoke coil into the sky.

"You did the right thing," he said eventually.

Rowan didn't turn to him. Her eyes remained fixed on the horizon, the sea rising and falling with a slow, exhausted rhythm.

"No," she replied. "I did the final thing."

Behind them, Camille walked back into the villa one last time. She ran her fingers along the scorched wall, tracing the lines where photographs had once hung. Her reflection stared back faintly from a cracked mirror in the hallway. She was different now. Older. And more honest.

She found her bag in the main foyer, where responders had stacked their things. Her phone buzzed weakly with signal. Dozens of messages. Emails. Calls. She didn't open any of them. Not yet.

Outside, Jasper stood next to the car that would take them away. The engine was already humming. He didn't get in. Instead, he looked toward the chapel. Toward where it had all started.

Alba stayed in the garden. She said she wanted to walk the grounds one last time. To say goodbye. Not to them. To the house. Camille understood. The villa had been part of Alba's life for longer than any of them. She had buried secrets in its corners. Cleaned up its messes. Heard the confessions it stole in the dark.

And now she would finally be free of it. But freedom came with a cost. They were all changed now. Wounded and marked. Not one of them would go home the same. Some of them wouldn't go home at all.

By late afternoon, the vehicles pulled away from Villa Limaccia. From the cliffs, it looked like the house was exhaling. As though it, too, had finally released what it had held for so long.

Inside the chapel ruins, the last gust of wind stirred the dust. A single scorched page from Rowan's diary caught on the stone altar, edges curled and blackened. Just one sentence remained visible:

We thought we were untouchable.

Then it, too, lifted into the sky. The smoke swirled upward, caught in the columns of wind rising from the cliffs, twisting with the smell of salt and something older. As if the land itself was absorbing what had finally been confessed. As if the villa had grown tired of keeping its secrets.

The villa stood alone once more, quiet but never truly still. Because in the walls, in the chapel stones, in the olive trees lining the path to the cliffs something still pulsed. A memory. A weight. A name. And above all, a truth that could never be fully buried. Because no one ever leaves Villa Limaccia the same.

Some don't leave at all.

EPILOGUE

THE ROSE

Six months later.

The sun rose soft and slow over the hills outside Florence, casting pale gold across the olive groves. The trees bowed lightly in the morning breeze, their silver leaves flickering like whispers. Beneath them, in a small cemetery bordered by cypress, the light filtered through so gently it looked painted, watercolor light, Camille thought. The kind that couldn't exist anywhere else but here, where memory and myth blurred at the edges.

She stood at the end of a gravel path lined with weathered stones, the toe of her boot nudging a sprig of rosemary. Behind her, the car ticked faintly as it cooled in the shade. In her hands, she held two things: a single white rose and a leather-bound copy of Jasper's memoir.

The Last Invitation.

She walked forward, her footsteps soft, hesitant.

Leo's grave was set beneath a twisted olive tree. Its branches reached out like an old man's fingers, crooked and steady. The headstone was simple. Pale limestone, smoothed by rain and sun. The name had been carved cleanly, no embellishments.

LEO MARINETTI

1990 – 2014

Beloved. Missed. Remembered.

Camille knelt slowly, brushing a few dry leaves from the base of the stone. The soil was freshly turned, the grave reinterred with care. Matteo had arranged it himself, quietly, precisely. No ceremony. Just a promise kept.

She laid the white rose against the headstone, then placed the book beside it. The title gleamed faintly in the light.

The Last Invitation had not been a bestseller. Jasper hadn't done a book tour. There were no interviews, no press junkets. He had released it into the world quietly, like an apology whispered through pages. The cover was stark: a photograph of Villa Limaccia at dusk, a figure silhouetted against the chapel ruins.

The final chapter was titled simply: Leo. Camille ran her fingers across the top of the stone.

"I'm sorry," she whispered.

The words were useless, of course. They always were. But saying them mattered, even if they dissolved into dust the moment they left her lips.

"I think about you more than I expected," she continued. "Not because I knew you best. I didn't. I was barely part of the group. You always looked past me."

She smiled, softly. "Maybe that was your kindness."

The wind shifted, stirring the trees.

"They know now," she said. "Everyone. What happened. What it cost. You gave them the truth, Leo. You asked us to. Eventually, we listened."

She paused. Then her hand moved gently to the small brass plaque set into the earth beside the grave.

"I wanted to belong. I didn't know belonging meant vanishing."

Camille remembered the moment she had read those words in his journal. They had undone her. Not for their elegance, but their honesty. Leo had been smart, sharp, guarded. But that line... that had been the beating heart of everything they'd tried to forget.

She sat there for a while, knees damp from the grass, until the sound of approaching footsteps stirred the quiet.

Matteo.

He said nothing as he arrived, just knelt beside her. He wore a clean white shirt and dark jeans. His beard had grown out slightly, peppered with silver, and there were new lines around his eyes. But his presence was stillness itself. Grounded. They didn't speak. They didn't need to. Together, they stayed like that for long minutes. Not praying. Not mourning. Just being.

Eventually, Camille rose. Matteo followed. They walked back to the path, step by slow step. Before climbing into the car, Camille turned one final time. Her eyes fell on the headstone, and then just to the left. She froze.

Nestled beneath the roots of the olive tree, almost camouflaged by vines and stone, was a second marker. Small. Unadorned.

Just two letters, carved into the moss-flecked face.

M.B.

Camille didn't move closer. She didn't need to. The initials were enough. She stared at it for a long time, until Matteo touched her shoulder gently.

"She's gone."

"Yes," Camille said. "But she wanted to be part of this. Even at the end. Especially then."

Matteo nodded.

"She left her mark."

Camille exhaled, her breath shaky. "She always does."

They climbed into the car. Neither spoke as they pulled away, the gravel crunching beneath the tires. The olive grove blurred in the rearview mirror, the twin headstones shrinking, shrinking, until they were nothing but shadows among the trees.

And yet, they stayed. Rooted. Enduring.

The wind stirred once more through the cemetery, rustling the rosemary and lilies, curling around the stones like a breath. The two markers sat side by side. One born of truth. The other, of the cost to reach it. No birds sang. No bells tolled.

But still, something moved beneath the soil. Something unseen, but felt. And if one stood there long enough, quiet enough, they might feel it too. The hum of regret. The ache of unfinished sentences. The pulse of memory, warm and terrible, blooming even now. Because the past doesn't stay buried in Villa Limaccia.

It flowers.

Printed in Dunstable, United Kingdom

64865219R00150